MUFFIN TO HIDE

MUFFIN TO HIDE

AUNTIE CLEM'S BAKERY
BOOK TWENTY-THREE

P.D. WORKMAN

PD WORKMAN

ISBN: 9781774686836 (KDP Paperback)
ISBN: 9781774686850 (KDP Hardcover)
ISBN: 9781774686867 (Large Print)
ISBN: 9781774686874 (Lulu Paperback)
ISBN: 9781774686843 (ePub)
ISBN: 9781774686881 (Accessible Audio)

ALSO BY P.D. WORKMAN

FIND MORE BOOKS AT PDWORKMAN.COM

MYSTERY/SUSPENSE:

Auntie Clem's Bakery

Culinary & Pet Cozy Mysteries

Gluten-Free Murder

Dairy-Free Death

Allergen-Free Assignation

Witch-Free Halloween (Halloween Short)

Canine-Free Christmas Caper (Christmas Short)

Stirring Up Murder

Brewing Death

Coup de Glace

Sour Cherry Turnover

Apple-achian Treasure

Vegan Baked Alaska

Muffins Masks Murder

Tai Chi and Chai Tea

Santa Shortbread

Cold as Ice Cream

Changing Fortune Cookies

Hot on the Trail Mix

Fateful Plateful

Cut Out Cookie

On the Slab Pie

Wedding Cake Crush

A Waffle Death

Murder Meringue Pie

A Fowl Play on Christmas Day (Christmas crossover story)

Cinn-Full Secrets (Coming Soon)

Muffin to Lose (Coming Soon)

Custard Cream Conspiracy (Coming Soon)

Recipes from Auntie Clem's Bakery

Parks Pat Mysteries

Police Procedural Set in Canada

Out with the Sunset

Long Climb to the Top

Dark Water Under the Bridge

Immersed in the View

Skimming Over the Lake

Hazard of the Hills

Knows the Hills

Spanning the Creek

Sanctuary in the Stream

Echoes of the Engine

Bench with a View

Beneath the Icy Depths

High-Tech Crime Solvers Series

Virtually Harmless

AND MORE AT PDWORKMAN.COM

For those at the center of controversy
they never sought

CHAPTER 1

"*D*o you really think there is a possibility that Gerald Montgomery would come all the way to Bald Eagle Falls?" Vic asked. Her tone was doubtful, but her eyes were bright. She was, Erin thought, trying to tamp down her excitement over the idea, not wanting to get her hopes up for something she considered to be unlikely.

"I didn't think it was possible," Erin admitted. She and Vic sat at the table in Erin's kitchen with their heads together, going over their plans for the next week. "It seems like a stretch that anyone would want to come way out to rural Tennessee to a little bakery like Auntie Clem's. But my sources say we are on *Montgomery's Muffin Mania* tour route." She shrugged, holding her hands palms up. "If he's going to be in the area, then he's coming to Auntie Clem's. It's the only bakery around that makes gluten-free muffins. Even in the city, only one place makes its own gluten-free cupcakes and muffins. Everyone else either orders from them or gets commercial stuff shipped from Nashville."

And that meant that they weren't fresh. Gerald Montgomery wasn't interested in something pulled from the freezer or sitting on the shelf for a couple of days. He had criticized restaurants or bakeries in the past for trying to pass something off as fresh when it was a day or two old. It wasn't worth his attention if it hadn't just come off the stove or been baked in the last few hours.

"Your sources?" Vic swept her long blond hair back, tucking it behind one ear. "How reliable are these *sources?*"

Erin Price couldn't blame her young assistant for being skeptical. Rumors that came over the grapevine in Bald Eagle Falls were plentiful but not necessarily accurate. The women of the town—and many of the men, too, Erin suspected—enjoyed gossiping about their neighbors. If there wasn't anything legitimate to discuss, they didn't seem to have any scruples against speculating or flat-out making something up. Some of the rumors that got back to Erin about herself or Vic or another friend or employee of Auntie Clem's Bakery were so far from the truth that Erin wondered whether the person who had started them was testing to see just how bizarre a rumor had to be before people would begin to question what they were hearing.

"Well, you know Cherise, the woman who runs the restaurant supply store in the city?"

Vic nodded, leaning forward with interest.

"Well, her nephew works in Gerald Montgomery's office. He saw Montgomery's travel itinerary for this tour and Bald Eagle Falls was on it. He figured she probably knew the bakery he would visit, so he called to share the news."

"And Cherise called you."

Erin nodded. "She knows I run the only bakery operating in Bald Eagle Falls and that everything here is gluten-free, so it was a no-brainer that if Montgomery is coming to Bald Eagle Falls, he is coming to Auntie Clem's Bakery."

"How did her nephew know he was coming through Bald Eagle Falls rather than just staying in the city? His itinerary is that detailed?"

"He's staying at the B&B."

"Which one? Mrs. McClung?"

Erin nodded. She had already confirmed the booking with Mrs. McClung. There wouldn't be any reason for Montgomery to stay at the B&B in Bald Eagle Falls unless he was planning to go to Auntie

Clem's Bakery. If he wanted to go to the bakery in the city that made gluten-free muffins, he would have stayed in the city. The accommodations would be more convenient than staying in Bald Eagle Falls.

"Well…" Vic drew the word out long in a drawl. "Don't that beat all. He's coming to Auntie Clem's Bakery!"

"Who's coming to Auntie Clem's Bakery?" a male voice asked.

Erin didn't need to look up to know it was Officer Terry Piper, her… significant other. She really hated the word boyfriend. Partner sounded too much like business. Spouse wasn't right since they were not married, much to the dismay of the church ladies who patronized Auntie Clem's Bakery.

Erin sat back in her chair and stretched her back and shoulder muscles. Terry entered the kitchen to fetch a bottle of beer to drink while he watched the game on TV. Erin wasn't sure what game he was watching or even what sport. He had told her, she was sure, but she had been too distracted by the news of Gerald Montgomery's tour to retain any details.

"Just Gerald Montgomery," Vic said, her voice high and dramatic. "Just one of the most famous food critics in the country, coming to taste muffins at Auntie Clem's Bakery."

Terry looked at Erin. "Really? That sounds pretty prestigious."

"If he likes it, yes. If he doesn't like what he tastes… a review from a guy like Montgomery is enough to make or break a bakery. And he's very tough."

"Sounds like the plot of a Hallmark movie," Terry said. "If you can just find the right recipe to impress him, he'll give you your five gold stars and you can save the bakery from certain ruin and pay off the mortgage and fix all of the appliances in need of repair…"

"Well, there's no mortgage to pay off or appliances needing repair, but we *do* need to figure out what to serve him when he gets here. We can't just serve him an everyday rice bran or blueberry muffin and expect him to be impressed."

"Why not?" Terry challenged, "Your baking is the best. You shouldn't need to do anything special to impress him."

He removed the cap from the beer and had a swig.

3

"He'll be expecting something special," Erin said. "The everyday fare at Auntie Clem's is just fine—"

"Outstanding, even," Vic inserted.

"—But this guy is testing gluten-free muffins all across the country. You think he will be impressed with just any old muffin?"

"I don't think you sell 'any old muffin.'" Terry said generously. "You can't even tell them apart from a muffin made with regular wheat flour. And when you dress them all up with icing and other little bits…"

"Decorate them," Erin advised.

"When you do that, it takes them to a whole new level."

"Those prepackaged gluten-free blueberry muffins you can get at the store," Vic said slowly, "they don't even have real blueberries in them. They have *simulated blueberry nuggets…*"

Erin shuddered. "Well, anyone can make a muffin better than that. But we have to make a muffin that's better than them all."

Terry and Vic both looked at her. "That's a pretty tall order," Terry said. "You're not baking these muffins in the fires of Mount Doom."

It was Erin's turn to stare. "What?"

"Lord of the Rings," Terry advised. "The one ring to rule them all…"

"Oh." Erin gave a nod. "Yes, you're right. I won't be baking them in the fires of Mount Doom." she paused for dramatic effect, "but it *will* be the one muffin to rule them all."

CHAPTER 2

*W*hat kind of muffin are you going to make?" Terry
asked.

"I don't know, that's what we need to work out. We need to
create something truly special. He'll take some of the other varieties, too; he always explores your range, but we need something
that is… new, different, and special." Erin looked at Vic. "What do
you think?"

Vic nodded, pursing her lips. "We should probably look over
what he has liked at other restaurants and bakeries. Get a feel for
what he likes or dislikes. Some people like a lot of rich sauces or
rare ingredients, and some really like simplicity and making sure
you have a solid grasp of the basics."

"Good," Erin nodded. "That will give us a good place to start.
I've heard he also has allergies, so we'll need to get a list of what he
can't eat. We want to have lots of options available to him. It
wouldn't do to have a specialty bakery where he can't eat anything."

"It must be hard for him to be a food critic if he has multiple
allergies. It can be really hard for some people to find anything they
can safely eat."

Vic had learned all about how complicated it could be working
with Erin at Auntie Clem's Bakery. People who needed to eat a

gluten-free diet due to celiac disease often had other food allergies as well, and Vic knew of a few customers who came to Auntie Clem's—some from quite a distance—because they knew that Erin would work with them to find or create something they would be able to eat.

The Fosters were among their favorite customers in town. The oldest child had celiac disease and was very sensitive to any traces of gluten, and they were still trying to sort out all of the sensitivities of the youngest Foster child, Allan, to figure out what he could eat without digestive distress.

"I guess it would give him a chance to test out the service level of the restaurant, too," Erin suggested. "He can get a feeling for how they treat people with allergies or special needs, whether they have the right protocols in place to protect people who have allergies. Or else if they are sloppy and act like they don't want to deal with a customer who is particularly demanding."

Vic nodded. "I'll do some internet research and start pulling together a dossier. We'll get it all pinned down so we have plenty of safe choices for him."

Terry nodded at the two women and headed back to the living room as the commercial break ended and his game started up again.

"He *shore* likes his football," Vic drawled, drawing the word out.

"Is that what he's watching? I wasn't even paying any attention."

Vic laughed. "Growing up with so many boys, there was no escaping the almighty pigskin in the Jackson family. And I was right in there with the rest of them. My poor ma!"

Vic was transgender and had grown up as one of the brothers in the Jackson family before running away at seventeen to live as Victoria instead of James. Even knowing Vic as well as she did, Erin had a hard time remembering that the pretty young blond had once been a rough-and-tumble, shotgun-toting farm boy in the Jackson clan, one of the notorious organized crime organizations in the area. Vic had certainly transformed her life in the short time she had been living in Bald Eagle Falls.

"Did you want to go check the score?" Erin offered.

"I'm fine!" Vic assured her. "I'll watch the highlights with Willie later."

Erin nodded and glanced across the backyard toward the loft apartment over her garage, where she assumed Willie was sleeping or doing computer work. Willie still had his own house but hadn't been there much lately. Since he had started chelation protocol to reverse heavy metal poisoning, he had been in Vic's apartment most of the time, too tired and ornery to see to his own meals and other needs. Willie had always been totally independent, and none of them had expected the chelation to affect him as much as it had.

The doctors had suggested he would be dealing with "flu-like symptoms." But Erin felt like it was more like going through chemotherapy. He was constantly exhausted and nauseated, along with a whole host of other symptoms, not the least of which was "irritability." Vic was a saint for putting up with his whining, demands, and moodiness.

"How is he doing?"

"Well, William Andrews ain't the best patient in the world. But he *does* try my patience."

Erin chuckled. "I'm sure he does."

Vic looked at the clock on the wall. "He should be good for a while yet. Let's spend a few more minutes on the muffins and Mr. Montgomery before he wakes up from his nap."

"Have they said how long it will be before Willie is done with the chelation and can return to normal?"

"They just say he's progressing, still clearing heavy metals from his system, and sooner or later…" Vic sighed and held her hands up in a gesture of surrender. "Sometime…"

Erin grunted. Wasn't that the way it always worked? The doctors had a prescribed protocol, but how long it would take and what the side effects would be were far less predictable than they would have liked.

"So this Montgomery," Vic insisted on turning the conversation back to the critic, "I've seen the guy on TV. He's tough. You sure you want him coming to Auntie Clem's?"

"Well, it isn't like I can tell him not to! I didn't arrange for him to come and can't exactly turn customers away. If I told him I wasn't interested in a review, he'd just give me a bad one."

"You have the right to decide who to serve."

"And he has the right to say whatever he wants to in his show."

Vic grunted and nodded. "Do we at least know when he's coming?"

"We know *Montgomery's Muffin Mania* has already started, though they're not revealing where he has been or where he is going next. I have the dates that he has reserved a room at the B&B, but I'm sure he doesn't plan to be here more than one night, so he must not be sure exactly when he will arrive."

"So we need to be prepared that whole time."

Erin nodded. "And it's not so bad. We can make a special muffin several days in a row and just not roll it out until he gets there. I want it to be a surprise, for him to be the first person to try it out. If we make a batch each day and those just go into the freezer if he doesn't show up, that's fine. Then when he comes, we roll them out and he gets to tell the world what he thinks of them."

Even though Erin said it casually, breezily, her stomach tightened at the thought of it. What if Montgomery didn't like them? What if he *really* didn't like them and gave them one of his trademark horrible reviews and everybody thought that Auntie Clem's Bakery was sub-par?

"Everybody here knows Auntie Clem's is a great bakery," Vic assured Erin, reading her expression. "They love your baking. If moody Montgomery doesn't like the baking, that won't change."

Erin knew that was true. Her customers already knew her product. But it would cut down on the number of people out of town who made the trip to see what she had to offer. If Montgomery gave her a rave review, the traffic from the surrounding areas would increase. Maybe by quite a bit.

"We'll get a good review," Erin declared, making a positive statement like all of those build-your-success books said to. She didn't know if she believed in all of the positive-affirmations-lead-to-success stuff. But it couldn't hurt. "He'll give us a great review, and it will be great for the business."

CHAPTER 3

The next few days were a blur as they learned everything they could about food critic Gerald Montgomery. They read about him, stalked his online profiles, and watched his shows, making copious notes about everything he ate and what he liked and disliked.

On the one hand, Erin liked how the man forced the restaurants and bakeries he visited to 'up their game,' putting out new offerings, pumping up what they had, and changing ingredients based on whatever demands Montgomery might make. She and Vic quickly discovered that Montgomery never informed the restaurants and bakeries in advance about his allergies, instead expecting them to adapt on the fly. Which was really difficult when he came for muffins that had already been baked as opposed to table service at a restaurant. But Montgomery was adamant that the restaurants he visited not share what his allergies or requests were so that it was a level playing field. It was apparent what special requests he had made in some episodes, especially if the restaurant did not follow them correctly. But they never specified on TV which foods were allergens and which requests were just show challenges. Auntie Clem's Bakery would not be given the list of Montgomery's allergens until he arrived.

"But we know some of the restrictions," Vic said, looking down at her latest list as they sat on stools at the counter in the kitchen of Auntie Clem's during their early lunch break. The room was redolent with the aroma of baking cinnamon rolls. "We know that this particular tour is for gluten-free muffins. That's not hard since everything we make is gluten-free, and we always have at least three varieties of muffins available each morning. He's not vegan, so the maple bacon muffins should be okay. Sometimes, he demands dairy-free but, sometimes, he allows it. He usually allows eggs in baking but not cooked egg dishes."

"We always have at least one egg-free, dairy-free muffin."

"I think this special muffin you develop should be egg and dairy-free. Just in case Montgomery decides not to allow either."

"Baking that is egg, dairy, and gluten-free can be pretty challenging," Erin said, thinking over her favorites and trying to decide what seemed to match Montgomery's tastes the best. "At least muffins are pretty forgiving, and he's not going to ask for the near-impossible, like egg-free angel food cake or meringue."

"You've made that aquafaba meringue," Vic pointed out.

"I know... but some people just can't tolerate it, so I don't use it too much. Muffins are a lot easier to adjust for multiple allergens."

Vic nodded. "Yeah. I'm glad it isn't going to be anything fussy. Because... he's fussy enough without adding another challenge."

"I like his show," Erin offered. "I like watching him work and learning about the foods he is exploring and the different ways to prepare them. But all of the stuff I've read about him that talks about how disagreeable he is... above and beyond being harsh with his criticisms... I'm terrified to meet him. I'm sure he's just a normal guy like anyone else, but the image I have of him from TV, with the addition of all of the other criticisms and accusations that fly around about him online... he's kind of like a supervillain in my mind. And I don't think I want to meet a supervillain in real life."

"You've got the baking superpowers," Vic assured her, grinning. "You'll come out okay. I'm sure he won't shoot lasers at you or anything."

"I hope not. I don't think I'm laser-proof."

"Just remember, in a few days, it will all be over."

Erin wasn't sure she found that any more comforting than the thought of meeting Montgomery face-to-face.

CHAPTER 4

$\mathcal{E}$rin didn't have long to wait.

The day Gerald Montgomery showed up, she was glad Vic was there to back her up. The other employees were wonderful, but Vic was the one that Erin really depended on and who put in almost as much time at the bakery as Erin did. Even though Charley was part-owner of the bakery, she didn't put in a lot of hours.

Bella was also on duty. She was a high school student, a few years younger than Vic, a curvy girl with wavy blond hair and a good nose for business. She hoped to get a degree and start her own business after graduating. Erin suspected that most of the money Bella made at the bakery went directly to her college fund. Would she want to open a business in Bald Eagle Falls or another small town? Or did she dream of opening something in the city with its noise, bustle, and plenty of walk-by traffic? Erin wasn't sure what kind of a business Bella hoped to open. Whatever she chose, Erin was sure it would be a success.

Bella was on the heavy side and, when people saw her round face and youthful appearance, they tended to underestimate her intelligence, experience, and people skills.

Erin didn't see Montgomery enter the bakery. It was the lunch rush; so many people were hurrying in during their breaks from work or school to grab something to go along with their lunch or maybe buy a muffin or trail mix bar that would serve as a meal replacement.

But as Erin finished serving Lottie Sturm and looked up to see who the next customer was, she was startled first to see an unfamiliar face, but then realized that she did, in fact, know who he was even if he hadn't ever been in her bakery before.

Montgomery wore a suit and tie and had a short beard and permanent frown lines between his eyes. He looked a little too thin to be a food critic, making Erin worry that he was even more critical than she had seen on TV. The camera really did add ten pounds. Which didn't make Erin feel good about how *she* would look on the show. But it was too late to worry about losing weight now.

"Oh!" Erin's mouth went dry, and she couldn't think of anything to say at first. After a few seconds of awkwardness, habit kicked in. "Welcome to Auntie Clem's Bakery. How can I help you?"

Montgomery's crew tried to be as unobtrusive as possible. Still, they carried extra lights, microphones, and handheld cameras, spreading out to get the different angles they wanted for the show. Erin licked her lips, wishing she had a water bottle handy. She kept a smile pasted on her face.

"I am Gerald Montgomery, food critic," Montgomery announced self-confidently. "You may recognize me from Montgomery Meals and Reels online or on network TV. I am on the *Montgomery Muffin Mania* tour, looking for innovative twists on this delicious staple that are available for the gluten-intolerant or sensitive. Or even people who are just trying out a gluten-free diet."

He paused. Erin wasn't sure whether he was expecting her to answer or whether it was just a dramatic pause or where they would make a cut when they were producing the show.

Montgomery looked down at the display case. "I understand that everything at Auntie Clem's Bakery here in Bald Eagle Falls, Tennessee is gluten-free. Is that really true?"

Erin nodded. "It was my dream to offer a wide variety of gluten-free products to those who are unable to eat conventional baking and always end up with few, if any, choices at a regular bakery. Instead of being given the option of one kind of gluten-free cookie sitting on the shelf at the grocery store going stale and having to go into the city to special order things like birthday cake, my gluten-free customers can come in here and choose anything they see. Unless they have other allergies, of course. But everything that is made strictly follows a recipe and avoids cross-contamination, so we know the exact ingredients in everything we sell."

She took a deep breath and considered what else the at-home audience would need to know about the bakery.

"By only using gluten-free ingredients and offering gluten-free products to our customers, we avoid the problem of pans or other tools being contaminated with gluten, even in microscopic amounts."

"I'm sure your customers who must follow gluten-free diets appreciate that."

Erin nodded.

"I understand you run the only bakery in town. Do you get many complaints from those who don't want to be forced to eat gluten-free and would prefer that you offered both?"

"New customers are sometimes surprised but, after they've tasted the baking, I usually win them over."

Montgomery gave her a sardonic smile that made Erin feel guilty for bragging about her baking. But she wasn't about to be cowed by this food critic before he even tasted the goods. What Erin said was perfectly true. It didn't matter if she was blowing her own horn.

"So, what muffins do you have on offer today?" Montgomery asked.

Erin indicated the varieties in the display case. "In addition to these, I actually have a new muffin variety that I am just debuting today," Erin informed him. "If you choose, you can be the first person other than me to taste it."

Montgomery raised an eyebrow. "Are you telling me that purely by coincidence, you have a new variety of muffin for me to test today?" He looked around at his crew. "Do I have a leak inside my organization? Did someone tell you I would be here today?"

"I heard a rumor you might be going through this part of Tennessee," Erin said, "But I couldn't get any information from your office as to when that would be."

Montgomery nodded. "Good. Well, what is this new variety of muffin, then?" He turned his gaze away from Erin to Bella. "If you could please package up one of each of these." He gestured to the display case.

"Sure," Bella agreed. "Of course." She was flushed around her neck but kept her composure. Hopefully, she wouldn't drop anything on the floor.

Hopefully, Erin would not drop anything on the floor either. She could just picture herself tripping as she retrieved the special muffins, sending muffins flying off of the tray and rolling across the floor in all directions.

She hoped she hadn't jinxed herself by thinking of it. She gave Montgomery and the cameras a nod that was not as confident as it looked. She gulped as she turned around and went into the kitchen. She went to the sink first and got herself a glass of water. She drank a few swallows, taking it slowly so she wouldn't inadvertently choke and end up coughing uncontrollably.

Calmer after the drink, she retrieved the fresh muffins, centered the little card at the front of the tray, and walked them slowly out to the front of the bakery. She took a deep breath, savoring the sweet vanilla smell of the fresh muffins. They were still warm from the oven.

Vic had the ingredient Bible out and was comparing the ingredients for each muffin she had packaged up for Montgomery to the card she now held in her hand.

Erin set the new muffins on top of the display case and looked around Vic at the small print on the wallet card. It was headed *Food must not contain*, followed by a list of ingredients. Most of them were gluten-containing ingredients. A few nuts. She didn't have to worry about gluten or nuts since they didn't use either at the bakery. A few other random fruits, additives, and shrimp.

Erin nodded. "Yes, these are all safe."

"And what do you have here?" Montgomery looked at the new muffins. "Morning Sunshine Muffins." He looked over the golden-brown tops.

"They're a—" Erin started, but Montgomery held up his hand to stop her.

"Since you have not named them descriptively, the flavor is intended to be a surprise. Please check the list of prohibited ingredients to ensure they comply; if they do, don't tell me anything more about them. I will taste-test them without any preconceptions."

Erin dutifully took the wallet card from Vic and read through it again. As she already knew, they were completely safe for Gerald Montgomery. He could taste-test them at his leisure, knowing that she had checked and double-checked the ingredients.

"Yes, you're good to go," she told him, smiling. "I hope you really enjoy them!"

He nodded. "Yes, we will see. Please ring those up," he told Bella. He looked down at the wallet he still held in his hand, fingers poised over the credit cards, then shook his head. "I forgot. Michael, would you...?" He flicked a hand at one of his crew to direct him to pay for the muffins.

CHAPTER 5

*I*n a few minutes, they were all gone again. Montgomery and his crew cleared out of the bakery, leaving it feeling suddenly empty and quiet despite the customers who were still gaping at what had just happened and whispering to each other.

"I can't believe you had Gerald Montgomery here!" Lottie exclaimed. "In Bald Eagle Falls—in our bakery!"

It was probably the first time Erin had ever heard Lottie say *our* bakery. She had never been complimentary about Auntie Clem's. She often complained about it being the only bakery in town. Despite what Erin had told Montgomery, the bakery did have its detractors. Those who, even after tasting her baking, still felt like there should be another bakery operating in Bald Eagle Falls or that it was Erin's duty to offer both gluten and gluten-free options rather than subjecting all of the townsfolk to her gluten-free creations.

Lottie was not someone who had ever been thrilled with the idea of a gluten-free bakery or supportive of Erin and her business —even though, voting with her dollar, she continued to shop at Auntie Clem's rather than going into the city to a conventional bakery.

Erin suppressed a smile at Lottie's sudden turnabout in now referring to Auntie Clem's Bakery in the possessive.

"It's quite something, isn't it?" she agreed. "I was excited when I heard he would be coming here."

Lottie fanned herself with her hand. "Lordy, I thought I would faint when I saw him. And all of those cameras and lights. You don't realize when you see him on TV all of the equipment they use to film those scenes. I always thought of him as being incognito, but you really can't hide all of the equipment, can you?"

"It's all part of the fantasy," Vic said knowingly. "It's the same thing when you watch *Survivor* or *Manhunt* or any of those shows. You feel like you're the only one watching, that you just have this little window into what's going on on the island, and the participants have completely forgotten that anyone is watching them. But they've got a whole camera crew and production team following everyone around, as well as whatever surveillance or hidden cameras they have around the place. The participants can't forget that everything they do and say is on tape."

Lottie shook her head. "I never even thought about it. I guess I thought there was just one person with a camera on their shirt button that everyone could forget was even there. Isn't it amazing?"

She looked over the items in the display case, but it seemed like she was still dazzled by having witnessed Montgomery's appearance, and she didn't focus on any of the items she usually bought.

"I think—why don't I try those Morning Sunshine Muffins? They look really good."

In other words, she wanted to share the experience that Montgomery was having. To be the first to say she had tasted the muffins right after Montgomery. Or even before. She could get a review and comments on social media before Gerald Montgomery and show off to her friends.

"Actually, the Morning Sunshine Muffins will not be on sale until after Gerald Montgomery's tasting airs," Erin advised. "Then they'll go on sale and everyone else can see what they think."

Lottie stared at her. "What do you mean they're not on sale yet? Didn't you just say they are debuting today?"

"They are. But only to a limited audience. After Mr. Montgomery gets his review up, everyone can try them out."

"But that's not fair."

Erin could feel Bella laughing beside her and didn't turn to look at her, keeping her focus on Lottie, but also making the announcement to the rest of the customers as well.

"I'm sorry you feel that way, but this is a special event, and we're making the most of it. The Morning Sunshine Muffins will not be on sale until after Montgomery Meals and Reels airs the tasting."

"Well," Lottie huffed. "You're getting a mite big for your britches. If there was anywhere else in town to go for my bakery needs... you can bet I wouldn't be spending my money here."

But there wasn't. So Erin just smiled pleasantly and waited to see if Lottie would place an order or walk out in a snit. Lottie eventually picked out the bread and other items that she wanted.

"And you can bet I won't be coming back here tomorrow to buy any of your precious Morning Sunshine Muffins," she declared.

But Erin figured she would be, just like everyone else.

After Lottie was gone, Erin served the next couple of customers. Lottie had drawn enough attention to herself that everyone understood that the new muffins would not be available until after Montgomery's tasting aired and, though they cast interested and longing glances in the direction of the tray holding the remaining muffins in the batch Erin had made that day, they did not demand the right to purchase them.

Erin had seen Peter Foster enter the bakery, opening and closing the door quietly with the bare whisper of bells, and moving in behind the adults. She was surprised at the lack of his usual exuberance and his solemn expression when it was his turn to approach the counter.

Erin raised her brows and gave him a tentative smile.

"What's up, Peter?"

He looked listlessly over the goods in the display case. Usually, he was excited to be able to choose from all of the gluten-free wonders Erin baked. He was a celiac, and it was for people like him that Erin had opened Auntie Clem's Bakery. People who couldn't have gluten-containing baking. People who had no choices at a conventional bakery and just a few prepackaged goods on the shelf at the grocery store.

"I don't know. I just wish…" He looked at the baked delights before him and sighed.

Erin waited for him to finish his thought, but he didn't. "What's wrong?" she asked after a moment. "Are you not feeling well today? Or…" A thought occurred to her. Maybe he didn't have any money for a treat today. His family had gone through some rough patches with work lately, and they had a lot of children to support. Maybe he didn't have the pocket money that he'd had other days when he had come to Auntie Clem's after school. "Did you want your Kid's Club cookie early this week? I could sneak in an extra one for my very favorite customer."

He looked surprised. "No, that's okay. I'll come with the girls for Kid's Club. I have money today." He jingled coins in his pocket. Erin suspected he did chores for neighbors to earn a little spending money.

"Okay…?"

"I just wish… that I could eat normal stuff."

Erin couldn't help feeling a little hurt that he would say such a thing when she had dedicated her life to opening Auntie Clem's and serving people who couldn't eat gluten a wide variety of "normal" baked goods. With no other bakery in Bald Eagle Falls, Peter had precisely the same choices as anyone else.

"Is there something specific I could make you that you wish you could have?" she suggested.

"No. You make all of the gluten-free stuff I need."

"But you still wish you didn't have celiac disease."

He nodded. He looked at the customers behind him and moved closer to Erin, speaking quietly so that she could hear him, but the others wouldn't.

"Kids at school say that the reason Auntie Clem's is gluten-free and they have to eat all gluten-free baking is because of me. If it wasn't for me, you would just have a normal bakery and they could eat normal food with wheat flour in it because you wouldn't have to worry about making anyone sick."

Erin's anger rose at the cruelty of the other children. There was just enough of the truth in what they said to hurt Peter and make him feel guilty and bad about himself and his condition. What did it hurt them to eat gluten-free baking? It was just as good as what they would find at a conventional bakery. Most people couldn't tell the difference. It didn't hurt them to have the tables turned so that they were the ones who had to make a special trip to find a conventional bakery, if it made that much of a difference to them. That was what celiacs and others with food sensitivities had to do all the time. The rest of the townspeople had choice. They could eat the gluten-free goods if they wanted to. A celiac couldn't choose to eat conventional baking if they planned to stay healthy.

"Peter… you aren't the only one in town who has to eat gluten-free. Other people need this kind of baking, too. And baby Allan probably has celiac disease. You know how much trouble he's been having with his digestion and being unhappy all the time."

"He's a lot better now."

Erin nodded. "It makes a difference when you eat stuff that doesn't hurt your tummy. You know you aren't very happy when you're sick."

"I know it's not just me," Peter admitted. "But wouldn't it be good if no one was celiac and had to eat gluten-free? If we could all just eat the same things?"

Erin shrugged. "I guess so. But that's not the way it works. Did I ever tell you about my foster sister Carolyn? The one who was celiac?"

He shrugged with one shoulder. "You've mentioned her, I guess."

Erin considered what to tell him about Carolyn. He was just a kid, and his mother would not appreciate Erin telling him that she had died because she had refused to follow her special diet. That was a pretty harsh reality for a child.

"It was because of my sister Carolyn that I wanted to open a gluten-free bakery," she said. "Because when we were growing up, she didn't have any good choices for gluten-free baking, and it made her really sad. Sometimes, she snuck gluten foods so that she could eat with her friends. It made her sick, but she was so sad about not having any good food to choose from and not being able to eat with her friends that she didn't care."

Erin was aware that other customers were waiting behind Peter. She reached into the display case and grabbed him a chocolate chip cookie, which she put in a wrapper and handed it to him.

"The name of the bakery might be Auntie Clem's Bakery after my aunt Clementine, but it could just as easily be called Carolyn's, because she's the reason I opened it."

"Does she ever come here?"

"No, she passed away a long time ago. But I still remember how hard it was for her, and I wanted to make it easier for people like her. And you."

Peter took the cookie and dug in his pocket for his money.

"This is a special occasion," Erin said. "No charge. I just want you to know that there are a lot more people than you think who need Auntie Clem's Bakery. People with celiac disease, gluten intolerance, and other food allergies. And people who want to share with you and their other friends. People who only want to eat gluten-containing baking can eat wherever else they want to."

Peter nodded. "I guess."

"Bella," Erin motioned to the next customer. "Can you take over here for a minute? I'm just going to walk Peter over to the Book Nook. Is that where you're going, Peter?"

His father worked at the Book Nook now, so Peter was usually on his way there when he stopped in at Auntie Clem's after school.

He nodded. "I can go by myself," he pointed out.

"I know. I just wanted to talk for a minute longer."

Bella took Erin's place at the counter and invited the next customer forward. Erin walked around to Peter and they exited the bakery together.

"The people saying those things are just being mean," Erin told Peter. "Or they don't understand about celiac disease and other sensitivities. We have to educate them."

"We do?"

"Just like your mom taught you to look after your own health and find out what is in the food you eat to make sure that it is safe. She taught you really well, didn't she? So that you know all of the questions to ask about the ingredients."

"Yeah."

"You're really smart, and you learned that stuff pretty quickly. But these friends of yours who are teasing or bullying you… they need to be taught about what celiac disease is and how many people have celiac disease or gluten intolerance or other allergies or sensitivities like Allan. It isn't their fault that they don't understand. Their parents didn't teach them because they didn't need to know, like you did, or because their parents don't know it themselves."

Peter pondered this as they walked into the Book Nook and looked around for Mr. Foster.

"Do you think it would help?"

Erin sighed, thinking about Lottie in the bakery. If adults didn't know how to behave themselves, how could they expect the children to? There were still too many people who thought that allergies and intolerances were just over-dramatization. People looking for attention.

"Maybe one day they'll see," she told Peter. "I hope so."

CHAPTER 6

*H*aving watched several episodes of Montgomery's show online, Erin knew that he did not use a crew to film the actual tasting. He was very particular about being alone and undistracted when he tasted the products. He had a tripod stand for his lights and cameras and operated them himself.

Erin didn't know if this was some kind of OCD or sensory issue, or if it was just his own little dramatic twist to make his show unique. It was very interesting to watch him take a bite or two of a dish or baked good, chew or roll it around in his mouth, staring off into space or closing his eyes as he considered the taste and texture. At times, his reactions were intense, spitting and wiping his mouth in disgust, even though the dish seemed perfectly edible and likely received praise from other customers.

And sometimes he was more thoughtful, making notes to himself as his face moved through several different expressions, considering what he had just consumed.

His video would not be shown to Erin until his crew and producer had viewed it and discussed how it would be presented to the public. It wasn't like she had seen in movies about food critics, where the owners were peeking out the kitchen door to watch the critic take his first few bites of the meal, or the staff was lined up in front of the critic's table, watching his expression as he tasted it for the first time.

No, she would have to wait. Not just a few minutes or hours, but overnight, and then as long as it took in the morning for everyone involved to view the video and have an opportunity to pass on their comments on how it should be showcased for the best dramatic effect.

Until then, Erin and her employees would have to wait and wonder.

CHAPTER 7

From the time she woke up, Erin was on pins and needles waiting for word of the results of Montgomery's tasting. She knew it would be hours before she knew what he'd had to say about the muffins, particularly the new recipe. He would send the recording to his people, and they would take time to look at it, review it, and discuss the treatments and approaches they would use. Eventually, someone would get back to her.

At least they didn't make her wait until it aired for her to find out what Montgomery thought. They didn't film her reaction live on the air, letting her find out in front of millions that he'd found them too dry or too moist, that they didn't have a perfect crumb, or that he thought them cloyingly sweet.

Instead, she would find out today, in the privacy of her own bakery, whether Montgomery's review would have a chilling effect on her business or bring a rush of new customers from the surrounding areas.

She supposed that either way, there would be new people coming around to check out Auntie Clem's Bakery, the bakery that had been on Gerald Montgomery's show on TV and the internet. He had millions of followers. Some of them would check out any restaurant or bakery in the state that had appeared on Montgomery's show. Maybe any bakery in all of Appalachia. Or the country.

Were there groupies who traveled the country to visit every restaurant he had reviewed? He had enough followers. There probably were. If it were a negative review, would they actually order the Morning Sunshine Muffins to see if they were as bad as Montgomery said they were and render their own opinion? Or would they laugh and refuse to buy anything from Auntie Clem's, just coming to gawk at her and the little backwoods bakery that had attracted so much attention?

"You'll find out soon," Vic said.

Erin looked up from the pan of apple crumble dessert bars she was cutting to look at Vic, who was watching her from the sink, where she was washing out several mixing bowls as they prepared to open.

Vic raised a brow, smiling. "You're off in your own little world, boss," she observed, "but I know what you're thinking."

Erin rolled her eyes and didn't deny it. "I'm sure it's pretty obvious."

Vic chuckled. "I want to know just as much as you do. It feels like everyone in town is holding their breaths, waiting. I'm as anxious as a cat in a room full of rockers."

"I just can't help wondering if it will be great for business… or devastating. What if it's a bad review and I end up having to shut down?"

"That's not going to happen. Even if it was a bad review—and that's not going to happen—everyone in Bald Eagle Falls already knows how great your baking is. They won't stop coming here because some internet celebrity decides he doesn't like a muffin. And you'd probably get a bunch of lookie-loos who just want to see the place just because it was on TV. Or to try out the awful muffins for themselves. Either way, you're golden. You won't have to shut down the bakery because he gives you a bad review. And he's not going to give you a bad review."

"He could. He's ruined plenty of other people who were really popular and had lots of great reviews saying how wonderful their food was. Then Montgomery comes along and says how crappy it is, and they lose too much of their customer base and have to close their doors."

"That's not going to happen to you. For one thing, you're the only bakery in town. Where is everyone going to go? You think they're going to drive into the city to go to a bakery there? Or start buying their bread and muffins off the shelf at the grocery store?"

"People do eat grocery store bread," Erin pointed out. "Lots of it."

"Well, people who are used to your baking will not want to go back to grocery store bread. They will keep coming here, whether some ninny has said that your baking is good or not."

Erin smiled and went back to cutting the apple crumble bars.

Mary Lou was one of the early-morning customers. She liked to hit the bakery before she opened up The General Store and started her own workday. On occasion, she would join the before-dinner crowd after closing The General Store, but she was tired after work. No one liked to shop when she was exhausted.

Mary Lou touched her gray bob to ensure there wasn't a hair out of place—there never was—and smoothed her pantsuit over her hips.

"Have you heard anything from your critic yet?" she asked Erin. All of her regular customers, and the church ladies in particular, knew about Montgomery; that he had been coming, what kind of a personality he was, and that he had been there the afternoon before. News spread fast in Bald Eagle Falls. It was not an easy place to keep secrets. Even things that had happened years ago tended to pop up again sooner or later.

"No, no word yet," Erin told her, as she had told everyone else.

"I'm sure he'll give your muffins a good review," Mary Lou assured her. "They're perfectly normal muffins." She decided she might have come across the wrong way and amended it. "What I mean is, they are no different than normal, non-gluten-free muffins. There's no difference. So when he tastes them, he'll say the same. And they're good. You always have a nice variety on hand, and you even developed a new recipe just for him."

Erin nodded. "I'm having second thoughts about that," she admitted. "Why would I try something new instead of sticking to the old favorites? A recipe needs to stand the test of time; you need to know that it works for everyone and to make little adjustments here and there until everything is perfect. But I didn't go through that process. No one else has tasted them other than me."

Mary Lou looked at Vic. "And Victoria, I'm sure."

Vic shook her head. "Not even me. Erin wanted Mr. Montgomery to be the first person to taste them. I'm as eager as everyone else to get my chance at a Morning Sunshine Muffin."

There were, in fact, a couple of batches baking in the ovens as they spoke. Erin figured she would sell out in short order. People would be eager to try the new muffin that Montgomery had reviewed, whether his review were good or bad. She had been counting on it being good for the publicity. But what if she had been wrong and it didn't move the needle? What if nobody cared and Montgomery's audience of millions didn't make any difference to a tiny bakery in the Tennessee backwoods?

"Do you have them on sale yet?" Mary Lou asked, looking over the offerings in the display case. "I don't see them."

"Not yet. Not until I see Montgomery's review," Erin said.

She had a whole marketing plan surrounding the Morning Sunshine Muffins and Gerald Montgomery's review. She had read everything she could get her hands on about marketing after a celebrity endorsement. She was doing everything she could to build the excitement and anticipation.

"It's all very exciting," Mary Lou said. "I suppose I must come over after work to snag one. Though you'll probably have sold out by that time. Would you set one aside for me? I'll pay now."

Mary Lou's request was a testament to the success of Erin's marketing. Mary Lou rarely bought anything sweet for herself, very careful of what she ate in order to maintain her slim figure. If she was going to eat one of the muffins, or even just have a few bites of one, it was a special occasion.

Erin shook her head, feeling bad about the decision. "I've already said there are no reservations," she explained regretfully. "I'd like to make an exception for you, but I really can't."

"You're very clever," Mary Lou said with a smile. "You'll get a lot of people in when you finally release them. I'm sure everyone is just as excited to try them out as I am."

"I'll try to keep up with the demand. So you might luck out and still be able to get one after you finish at The General Store."

"If not, then maybe tomorrow."

Erin was glad that Mary Lou didn't resent or take the policy personally.

"We'll have some in the oven first thing tomorrow," she promised.

"I look forward to it."

CHAPTER 8

*I*t wasn't until Mary Lou had picked out her week's baking and was counting out her change for Vic that she mentioned offhandedly, "There's something going on down the street. Did you see the police cars?"

Erin looked at her. "No, what police cars?"

Even though other customers were waiting, Erin went around the counter and to the front door. She couldn't see the police cars until she opened the door and leaned out, and then she could see them a couple of blocks down the street.

"Are they at a house? What's going on?"

She resumed her place behind the counter and continued the conversation with Mary Lou even though she was finished. It was time for Erin to serve the next customers waiting there patiently, Betty Thompson and her husband.

"Yes, one of the houses just past the commercial district," Mary Lou confirmed. "Maybe something at the B&B?"

Erin froze. "At the B&B? Where Gerald Montgomery is staying?"

Mary Lou shrugged. "That doesn't mean it has something to do with him. Though, of course, being an outsider, he is probably behind any disruption. He's a celebrity; maybe someone was harassing him. Tried to get into his room to get a picture of him."

That could be it. Erin didn't have to assume the worst every time something happened in Bald Eagle Falls. It might be a slow, sleepy little town, but it still needed a police presence. People still broke the law; it didn't have to have anything to do with her or anyone she was associated with. Erin let out her breath slowly.

That was it. Just someone who was stalking Montgomery, wanted an autograph, or had been getting in the way of his crew while they were trying to get things set up. Undoubtedly, his presence in Bald Eagle Falls had attracted some outsiders who didn't necessarily know how things worked in a small town. They thought they could get away with things, that there wouldn't be any scrutiny because they were such a small place. There wasn't even 9-1-1 service. People might think that there were no police.

Erin pulled out her phone to look at it and ensure that Terry hadn't messaged her. Officer Terry Piper, also known by Vic and some of the other ladies as Officer Handsome, might have some insight for her into what was going on. But if an active crime investigation were underway, he wouldn't be calling or telling her anything about it until the crisis was over. Then, she might hear some inside information about it if she approached it correctly.

"Tell me if you can see anything when you go to The General Store," Erin told Mary Lou. She wouldn't be walking as far as the B&B, but she might be close enough to see what was happening there.

Mary Lou smiled at Erin and raised her brows. "Oh, now you want a favor from me. Maybe we could trade."

"Trade?" Erin echoed, not following her train of thought.

"Barter," Mary Lou said, leaning closer and speaking softly. "A favor for a favor."

It took Erin a moment too long to connect the two conversations. Mary Lou wanted a Morning Sunshine Muffin put aside for her. Erin wanted information on what was going on at the B&B. They were both in a position to offer the other person something if they wished.

Erin looked at Vic to see what she thought about this. Vic had been on board with Erin not letting anyone have a Morning Sunshine Muffin until after the results of the critic's tasting were known. Should Erin stick to her guns or bargain with Mary Lou?

Vic shrugged. "It's up to you," she murmured. "They're your muffins and it's your plan."

"Well…" Erin considered, then finally nodded. "All right. I will put a you-know-what aside for you. You don't get one before they go on sale, but I'll make sure there is still one here for you when you can get back. And…" Erin made a twisting-key movement at her lips.

If others of the church ladies found out that Mary Lou had been given special treatment over them, there might be a mutiny. She couldn't give away that she had given Mary Lou a special favor over everyone else.

"Deal," Mary Lou agreed, giving a firm nod. She walked to the front door and put her hand on the handle. "I'll let you know."

She pushed open the door and left. Erin turned back to Vic before serving Betty Thompson. "Have I just sold my soul to the devil?"

Vic snickered. "Well, I couldn't say no for sure. But I think your soul is safe for now."

Erin blew out her breath dramatically and turned to Betty. "And what can I get for you today, Mrs. Thompson?"

"How about one of those lovely muffins I keep hearing about? You know, the…"

"The ones that aren't available yet?" Erin challenged.

Betty smiled. "Well… I'm not sure about that. You must have sold one or two, Or I wouldn't be hearing about them."

"No, they're not available yet. But I'll be sure to let you know when they are. From what I have in the case today… is there anything I can get you?"

"Oh, dear. I was hoping for a muffin today…"

"Today, you have the options of a blueberry muffin, raisin bran, or chocolate chip duo." Erin indicated each in the case as she spoke. She hoped Betty could be distracted from the

Morning Sunshine Muffin, much like a toddler from his favorite toy.

"Chocolate chip duo?" Betty asked, leaning closer to get a good look at it. She was a retired lady, older like Mrs. Peach, still vigorous and in good shape. Erin hoped that she would be doing as well at seventy or eighty.

"It has milk chocolate and white chocolate chips," Erin told her.

"Ooh. That sounds very good."

"Shall I get you half a dozen of those?"

Betty looked back at her husband, resting with his hands on the bars of his walker.

"Those sound great," Mr. Thompson encouraged. "If that's what you want."

"The doctor said I should be watching my chocolate intake."

"They don't have a lot in them," Erin pointed out. "The muffin itself is vanilla, so there is no cocoa in them. And just a few chips to make it more decadent. It couldn't be more than… a tablespoon of chocolate chips per muffin. Maybe two."

"That doesn't seem like very much," Betty agreed. "I'm sure the doctor would say that a tablespoon of chocolate chips every now and then would be fine."

Erin didn't want to put words in the doctor's mouth or to give Mrs. Thompson medical advice. For all she knew, Betty's doctor had told her not to have *any* chocolate.

"Well, let's go with that," Betty said finally. "And six of the blueberry muffins. Blueberries are very high in antioxidants."

"So is chocolate," Erin laughed. She packaged the chocolate chip and blueberry muffins for Betty and passed them over to Vic to ring them up.

Erin's phone vibrated in her apron pocket and then, the next time she went into the kitchen to take a batch of the Morning Sunshine Muffins out of the oven, she took the opportunity to check the screen. Mary Lou had texted her as promised.

They are at the B&B. Can't tell what's going on. Several police cars.

Several police cars likely meant all of the Bald Eagle Falls police department. So it was something big. They had even called in the off-duty officers.

It seemed sort of a waste to have promised Mary Lou one of the muffins when all she had provided was the information that there were police at the site, which they already knew. But Erin put one of the hot muffins to the side for her anyway. If she physically separated it from the rest of the products, then none of them would accidentally put it out for sale when Erin had promised to hold it.

She sent Terry a quick text asking him what was happening at the B&B, then returned to the front of the store where Vic was manning both the counter and the till. On Erin's return, Vic moved back over to the till.

Even not knowing the results of Montgomery's taste test yet, people's curiosity brought them to Auntie Clem's Bakery in a steady stream all day long.

CHAPTER 9

It was late afternoon when Erin glanced over the customers waiting for service and saw that, with the last jingle of bells, Terry had entered with K9. She smiled at him and kept serving the customers ahead of him. He waited patiently to get to the front of the line, and Erin handed him a biscuit for K9 and offered to refill his water bottle.

Terry shook his head. "I need to talk to you."

"You need to talk to me?" Erin shrugged. "Okay."

"It would probably be best if this was done in private."

Erin looked at the other customers who were still waiting to be served. "Can it wait until closing? It's been busy all day and we don't have much longer."

He stood there unmoving, considering it. "You asked about what happened at the B&B. Why everyone was there."

"Yeah, what was going on over there?"

"I'd like to talk to you about it. In private."

"Oh. Okay." Erin's stomach knotted. It obviously wasn't good news, but she didn't know what to expect. Maybe it wasn't just a fan crowding Montgomery. Or breaking in. Maybe they had made threats.

She tilted her head to indicate she was going to the back. The door opened with another jangle of bells, ringing wildly this time.

Erin thought she recognized this dramatic entrance. People were usually pretty quiet coming into Auntie Clem's. People who came to pick up a loaf of bread or pizza shell for supper were usually not dealing with emergencies. A few last-minute shoppers would always be rushing against the clock at closing, but it wasn't quite six o'clock.

Erin looked at the new arrival and saw exactly who she had expected. Melissa Lee, her spiraling dark hair in disarray, red-faced from her excitement and rush to get there. She stepped around the waiting customers to address Erin directly, then saw Terry. She froze.

"Miss Lee," Terry greeted gravely. "Or should I say Missus Plaint."

"Oh," Melissa flushed further. "You know I don't usually go by that. Just… for special occasions."

She had recently married Davis Plaint, a resident of the nearby penitentiary, and preferred not to attract too much attention to the fact in the course of normal conversation.

Terry and Erin waited for Melissa to say something. She closed her mouth and stood there awkwardly, pretending to be studying the contents of the display case.

Melissa was a member of the administrative staff of the police department and their biggest leak, and both Terry and Erin knew very well why she was there. She was there to tell Erin whatever it was Terry had come to tell her, hoping to be the one to break the news to her. But she had been foiled by Terry's arriving before her, and would now have to buy something chocolate to soothe her injured spirit and justify her presence in Auntie Clem's. She couldn't very well say that she had come only to fill Erin in on the latest gossip.

Erin looked at Vic, raising her brows, then turned and entered the kitchen. Terry walked around the counter and followed her in. They moved away from the doorway but didn't go into Erin's office, which was closet-sized and claustrophobic.

"Well?" Erin asked, looking around the kitchen for something to keep her hands busy while they talked, and settling on filling a sink with water to start soaking pans. Maybe turning on the water wasn't the best choice of activities, since it was loud and Terry waited until she turned it off again before attempting to speak to her.

"I'm sure you know that Gerald Montgomery was staying at the B&B."

Erin nodded. "Sure. I thought he must be involved in whatever all of the police were there for. Maybe he was being harassed? A stalker or threat?"

Terry nodded. "That would be a good guess—"

"I figured as much."

"—But not correct," Terry finished.

Erin looked at him, startled. "Oh. What was it then?"

"Montgomery died last night."

"He died?" Erin gaped. She couldn't remember how to breathe. "What?"

Terry nodded. He walked over to the other sink and filled a glass with cold water. He handed it to Erin. She took it carefully, unable to feel it in her hand, and took a long drink of the cold water before looking at him again.

"How could Montgomery be dead? Was he sick? He looked okay yesterday. He wasn't... sweating or coughing. He didn't look sick."

She had held a number of elder care jobs. She might not be a doctor, but she recognized more quickly than others when someone was sick.

"No, I don't think he was sick when he saw you."

"Oh, well. An accident, then? Or..." Erin hated to suggest it, "It wasn't homicide, was it? I mean, celebrities... they can be vulnerable to stalkers when they spend so much time in the public eye." Erin swallowed. "How horrible..."

"Why don't you sit down?" Terry suggested, motioning to one of the stools Erin used when she had work to do but couldn't be on her feet any longer.

Erin didn't have a good feeling about this. She grabbed the nearest one and sat, looking at Terry for his revelation of the bad news.

K9 was tired of waiting for Terry to give him his biscuit and gave a little whine. Terry looked down at him and offered him the treat. "I'm sorry, boy. Here you go. Chew on that for a minute."

K9 took the biscuit from his fingers and lay down on the floor with it between his front paws. Off duty for a few minutes. *Code seven*, in cop talk.

"Erin, it looks like Montgomery died from an allergic reaction."

"Oh, dear."

"Did you know that he had allergies?"

"Yes. It was known, and he gave us a card with his allergies on it when he was here."

"Do you have that handy?"

Erin looked around, trying to remember where she had put the card after Montgomery had left. Of course, she didn't have any paperwork out in the kitchen. The only thing they used in the food preparation area were her recipe and procedure books.

"Uh… probably in my office. I don't remember putting it down."

"Do you remember what his allergies were?"

Erin tried to picture the card and remember her thought processes as she had looked over the ingredients in the Morning Sunshine Muffins. She recited the ones she could remember to Terry and he wrote them down in his notebook.

"Was it something he was served at the bed and breakfast?" Erin asked, thinking of how Mrs. McClung must be feeling if something she had fed Montgomery had killed him. "Or did he order something from one of the restaurants?"

There was a delay of several seconds before Terry answered her.

"Erin… we think it was your muffins."

"What?" Erin's eyes went wide with shock and she felt the blood drain from her face. She held on to the counter to steady herself. This was why Terry had told her to sit down. He hadn't wanted her to collapse when he told her the news. She fought back against the black spots and flashes of light that obscured her vision. She knew Terry was looking at her with concern, but couldn't see him clearly through the visual disturbances.

"Have another sip of water," Terry suggested.

Erin shook her head. She didn't know where she had put the cup of water down and couldn't find it now.

"How could it be...?" Erin fumbled for words. "It couldn't be the muffins. I checked the ingredients against his list. There's no way it could have been something on his list."

But she knew there were other possibilities. A new allergy that he hadn't had to deal with before. Cross-contamination of an ingredient in the field or factory before it had made its way into her kitchen. Something that Montgomery had added when he sat down to eat. Maybe a snack he had gotten out of the mini-fridge in his bedroom. There were many possibilities, none of which were Erin's fault. She had followed proper procedure when she had made the muffins. And she had checked the ingredients against his card. There was no way it had just slipped by her.

"We won't know all the details for a few days," Terry told her.

Erin knew from past cases that Montgomery's body would have to be sent to the city for autopsy and testing. Those things took time. Sometimes weeks or months, not just a few days. It wasn't like on TV, where everything was wrapped up in a few hours.

"No, of course not," Erin said faintly. "But... you think it was the muffins... that was the last thing he ate?"

It wasn't enough that someone had poisoned one of Erin's cinnamon rolls? Now someone had to tamper with her muffins too?

But poisoning was different from an allergic reaction. People could react to totally innocuous ingredients. Things that you thought no one could be allergic to.

"Yes," Terry confirmed. "He went back to the B&B, and then I guess he does a private tasting. No one else is allowed to be around."

Erin nodded numbly. "Yes. That's his usual procedure. Always alone."

Terry shook his head. "It seems counterintuitive that someone with serious, possibly life-threatening allergies would put himself in a situation where he was eating something potentially dangerous all alone, with no one to help out if he had a reaction."

"Well, you can't be with other people all the time. I don't know; it was just one of his quirks. Or one of the things his show had set up to catch people's interest."

"Doesn't seem like a good idea."

"In retrospect… no," Erin admitted. "And I did watch some of the shows where he had an allergic reaction to something he had been fed. He handed out these allergy cards to ensure the chefs or bakers didn't include any of his allergens. But sometimes people did anyway, and he always failed them if they did…"

"I would guess so," Terry said dryly.

"But the shows I watched… He would recognize that a dish contained one of his allergens, and he would take an antihistamine. Or epinephrine if it was one of the bad ones."

"This had happened before? So why didn't he change his protocol? Make sure someone was in the adjoining room with the door open?"

"I guess he figured he'd always been able to handle it by himself before."

Terry shook his head. But he didn't argue the point. It wasn't Erin's opinion; she wasn't the one who had set up Montgomery's protocols. She was just suggesting what his thought process might have been.

"I suppose. But it seems so stupid. Like playing Russian roulette. Just because you've never killed yourself before, that doesn't mean it isn't going to happen eventually."

Erin nodded. She was glad not to have to deal with any life-threatening allergies herself. She had seen what had happened to Angela Plaint when she had been poisoned with wheat flour. And her son, when he had been exposed to dairy. It was not something Erin treated casually.

And she *knew* she had checked Montgomery's allergens against the ingredients for the Morning Sunshine Muffins. And Vic had checked them against the ingredients for the other muffins Montgomery had bought. And there hadn't been anything unusual in his allergen list. Not anything that Erin could see being cross-contaminated in the kitchen.

"Do you know what he was allergic to? What did he react to?"

"Our best information at this point is strawberries."

"Strawberries?" Erin repeated in horror.

The Morning Sunshine Muffins were filled with a strawberry compote.

CHAPTER 10

*T*erry read Erin's expression easily. He put a steadying hand on her shoulder.

"It's okay. Just stay calm."

"He was allergic to strawberries?" Erin demanded. "Why weren't they listed on his allergy card? What's the point in handing out an allergy card if you don't list everything you are allergic to?"

"They are listed on his card."

"No," Erin shook her head adamantly. "I read the card. Vic read the card. It didn't include strawberries. We would never have let him have those muffins if it had said that he was allergic to strawberries."

Terry knew how careful she was about customers' allergens. Sometimes, it seemed like she knew them better than the customers themselves, who sometimes forgot to check for a particular allergen when making a purchase, and Erin had to stop them. She would never let anyone purchase anything that contained one of their known allergens. Unless, of course, they told her it was for someone else. But that was how Trenton Plaint had been killed. With a cupcake purchased from Auntie Clem's Bakery.

She tried to wipe the memories of those events out of her mind. That had been beyond her control. Joelle had known exactly

43

what she had bought. It had all been planned out. It hadn't been Erin's fault. No more than it was the shopping mart's fault if someone poisoned their spouse with antifreeze or eyedrops purchased there.

But people in Bald Eagle Falls had still blamed Erin.

And now they would blame her for Gerald Montgomery's death.

And he wasn't just some backwoods hick. He was a national celebrity. Internationally known. He had followers all over the world, and they would all know soon that Erin had given him the food that had ended his life.

She covered her face, trying to compose herself.

"I can't believe this. How could something like this happen? Why didn't he list strawberries on his wallet cards? That doesn't make any sense."

"Do you still have it?"

Erin looked around her again. Of course, it wasn't there in the kitchen. They would not have left it out in the food preparation area.

"It's probably in my office. On my desk somewhere. My inbox."

"You didn't throw it out?"

"No… I don't think so. I wouldn't have needed it anymore, so maybe, but I thought I hung on to it. In case he came back and wanted something else. Or as a souvenir of his visit." She took a deep breath, trying to keep her voice steady. "Thinking that I would want to record and remember him coming here, doing the review. I might want to put it in a scrapbook or journal if I ever got around to making one."

She shook her head. But now this was a nightmare. She wouldn't want to remember it. She wouldn't look back on it fondly as the event that made her baking career—a highlight of her professional life.

How could she have ever thought that it could turn out well? With the trail of broken chefs and closed restaurants Montgomery had left behind him, what were the chances that he would give Auntie Clem's Bakery a stellar review? That people would flock from all over Tennessee and the United States to taste her gluten-free products?

She scrubbed at her eyes and rubbed her forehead, a tension headache gathering right in the center of it.

How could she be mourning her lost dreams when a man was dead? Killed by something she had given him. She had packed those muffins into a box and wished him well and, instead of enjoying the taste test, he had died at her hand. Terry might as well lock her up now.

"If strawberries were not on the card he gave you, you can't be blamed for his death," he told her consolingly. "It isn't your fault."

"Why did you say that strawberries were on his card? I saw it and Vic saw it." Erin visualized it, trying to see every word on it in her head. The colors, the layout, the various items listed so that she would not give him anything that might kill him. "Gluten, nuts, some fruits, but not strawberries."

"We saw his wallet cards. There were some in his luggage in the room. They did include strawberries."

Erin shook her head.

She knew she would never have given him those muffins if he had handed her a card stating that he was allergic to strawberries. Why would she? She didn't want to kill anyone. It would be the end of her career if she did so. As well as seriously curtailing her freedom when she was locked up in prison.

"Talk to Vic."

He looked toward the front of the bakery. "We'll wait until she's closed. I don't want to interrupt her duties."

Neither of them would be able to go back to serving customers after hearing the news of Montgomery's death. Erin knew Terry was right about that.

"Why don't I call his office?" Terry offered. "Maybe he had more than one card."

"And he gave out one that didn't include all his allergens?" Erin demanded.

That didn't make any more sense than anything else.

Terry shrugged. He pulled out his notepad and checked a

number on it, then dialed his phone. He put it on speakerphone while it rang. It was picked up after just a couple of rings.

"Montgomery Meals and Reels," a woman announced crisply. "Mavis speaking."

Terry announced himself. Mavis had apparently already been given his name and had known to expect his call.

"Yes, Mr. Piper. How can I help?"

"I had some questions about Mr. Montgomery's wallet cards. The list of allergens."

"Yes?"

"I found a stack of them in his room at the B&B. They included strawberries."

"Yes... do you think that's what killed him?" she asked with a catch in her voice.

"Well, that's the most likely scenario at the moment. But I'm not sure why he would be given anything with strawberries after giving someone his wallet card stating that he was allergic."

"It happens all the time. Even when Gerald would tell people he was allergic to a certain ingredient, he would be served something unsafe. Chefs would think that a little bit wouldn't matter or that he was just making up the fact that he was allergic to something to make the challenge harder. Or they would forget that the ingredient was in there. Some foods go by a lot of different names, and they didn't check the ingredients of the ingredients."

"The ingredients of the ingredients?" Terry repeated, baffled.

Erin opened her mouth to explain the woman's meaning, then closed it again and waited for Mavis's answer.

"Well, for example, if you were making a stir fry and sauce, and Gerald told you he was allergic to gluten or wheat, you might think that your stir fry and sauce was fine if you served it over rice instead of noodles, and not think about the fact that one of the ingredients in your sauce was soy sauce, and one of the ingredients of soy sauce might be wheat. You need to check all of the ingredients of the ingredients you put into the dish. Soy sauce isn't just soy. Potato chips aren't just potatoes. They might have all kinds of wheat or dairy ingredients but, as someone who does not have to deal with multiple allergies, you don't have to think about that. You just think potatoes."

"Ah," Terry said. "I understand."

"People just aren't careful about allergies," Mavis said. "They think that they aren't really a big deal. That people who have multiple allergies are just being dramatic or attention-seeking."

"There's no possibility that the bakery was given a card that didn't include strawberries on the list of allergens?" Terry prodded.

There was silence for a few seconds.

"Well…" Mavis didn't come back with a flat "no," which Erin took as a good sign. "Strawberries were a recently developed allergy. We had to add them in and reprint the cards."

"So it is possible he still had one of his old cards and gave it to the bakery."

"I really don't see how. We were careful to replace them everywhere. It would have been dangerous for him to be passing out incomplete information. Especially with how severe the strawberry allergy had become."

"What about the cards in his wallet?" Terry asked, looking at Erin questioningly.

She nodded to confirm that the card Montgomery had given to her had come out of his wallet.

"Yes, I changed out his wallet cards myself. I know that he had the new cards. Is that what these people are claiming? That they were given a wallet card that didn't include strawberries?"

"We're just investigating," Terry told her. "We don't have any statements to release yet."

"Well, I'll tell you," Mavis said with emotion filling her voice. "Those people ought to be charged with murder. I can't believe someone did this to him. They should be in prison for the rest of their lives."

Erin heard Vic lock the front door to the bakery and then she came through the kitchen door. She looked concerned about Erin and Terry not having returned from the kitchen. Then her gaze fastened on Erin.

"Oh, my stars. What's happened? What's wrong?" she demanded, her hand going to her throat.

Neither one of them bothered to ask how she knew something was wrong. Erin knew she must look like a wreck. She certainly felt like one.

She just shook her head, unable to speak the words. To break Vic's happy bubble and tell her the devastating news. Auntie Clem's would be ruined. They would all have to find work somewhere else. But worse than that, a man was dead. And Erin might be headed to prison for it.

"Gerald Montgomery is dead," Terry told Vic. "An allergic reaction to the strawberries in the muffins."

"Dead?" Vic's mouth opened and closed like a fish's as she attempted to find the right words. "Are you kidding?"

People always said that, going first to disbelief.

"I'm afraid it's the truth," Terry told her gravely. "I believe it was an accident. But we are conducting an investigation to sort out all of the details."

"Strawberries? Did he even know he was allergic to strawberries?"

"They were on the allergen card," Terry asserted.

"No siree," Vic disagreed. "Erin and I both read the allergen card."

Erin motioned to Vic, nodding at Terry. Vic had just confirmed what Erin had already said. They had two witnesses that the allergen cards had not included strawberries.

"We would never have given him the muffins if he had put strawberries on the card," Vic asserted.

"Do you have the card?"

"No. I gave it to Erin," Vic looked at her. "Didn't you show it to him?"

"I don't remember where I left it. Or if I threw it out. I thought I kept it, but…"

Vic looked toward Erin's little office.

"I can check—"

"Leave the office," Terry told her. "We'll check it out ourselves. We don't want anything touched."

"You think that we would mess with evidence?" Vic growled.

"I know I have to follow certain protocols," Terry said mildly. "We have to do everything we can to preserve the chain of evidence."

Vic folded her arms, her jaw jutting at a stubborn angle. "I wasn't going to touch anything."

"Of course not."

Vic looked like she wanted to argue further, but Terry wasn't giving her the opening she wanted. So she left it alone, giving a curt nod.

"We would never have given him those muffins if we had known about his strawberry allergy. And you know that we are very careful here about allergies."

"From what I've seen, yes," Terry agreed. "And you haven't had any accidents, as far as I am aware." He glanced at Erin for confirmation. She nodded. "That's a pretty good track record."

But Erin knew that wouldn't stop the rumors.

CHAPTER 11

"Y" ou should proceed with your usual closing procedure,"
Terry suggested. "Do I have permission to search your
office?" he nodded toward the closet-size room.

Erin hesitated. She didn't like other people to be in her office.
She didn't like other people to touch her things. She knew that it
was silly to be so worried about her privacy or the possibility of
someone else messing with her stuff, blaming it on her upbringing
in foster care, where she had never had her own place or her own
stuff that was safe from the other children in the home. She had
always known that at any time she could be moved to another
home and that she might be able to take nothing but the clothes on
her back with her. Sometimes she was allowed to throw a few
special things and changes of clothes into a plastic shopping bag or
garbage bag before she was taken out, but sometimes the parent or
social worker would pack while she was out of the house and she
wouldn't have any choice about what she took with her. Or she
would be taken in an emergency apprehension and would never see
anything from that home again.

It wasn't because she had secrets from Terry. None that would
be revealed by a search of her office at Auntie Clem's Bakery. Most
of her secrets were locked away in her head, with no written records

anywhere. That was the other thing she had learned in foster care. How to keep her thoughts and feelings locked up where no one else could read them. Her memories were her own if she were careful to share them with no one. Her private thoughts and feelings were no one else's business.

It didn't make for good relationship-building, and Erin was trying to share more of herself with Terry, Vic, and the other people she wanted to be close to. It was hard to be vulnerable.

And vulnerable was how she felt when she considered Terry searching her office. It was silly. There was nothing there but receipts, recipes, and newspaper ads. Nothing the least bit shocking or private. Nothing she needed to worry about Terry seeing.

"Erin?" Terry prompted. "I won't shut you down. I won't search the entire bakery. I just want to look in your office for that allergy card. It's a critical piece of evidence."

"I'm not even sure it is in there."

"I'll look. If it's not there, it's not there. I won't touch anything else. Whether it is there or not, I'll be in and out. Done in ten minutes and out of your way."

Erin swallowed hard. She glanced over at Vic, who was watching, but didn't jump in with any suggestions or tell Erin that she should or shouldn't allow the search.

"Don't tell me you're going to force me to get a search warrant," Terry grumbled. "For an allergen card you want to share with us to prove that you didn't know about his strawberry allergy. You *want* me to see it, Erin."

She nodded. "I know."

"So I'll look," he motioned again to her office. "And then I'll get out of your way."

Erin finally nodded. "Okay, but... shut the door."

Frown lines appeared between Terry's brows. "After I'm done, you mean?"

"No. While you're in there. Just shut it so I don't have to see you going through my stuff, okay?"

Terry nodded slowly. "Okay," he agreed. The frown lines didn't disappear. He hesitated, maybe thinking that she would give him more instructions or some explanation, and then he walked into her office and pulled the door shut behind him.

Erin tore her eyes from the door and tried to ignore what was happening inside. She couldn't see it, so it wasn't happening. But she imagined she could hear him rustling papers as he went through things.

"Why don't you put some music on while we close?" she suggested to Vic, trying to keep her voice light and casual, like this was something they did all the time.

"Sure," Vic agreed. "Any special requests?"

"No. I just need… I don't want silence."

They usually talked while they closed, so it wasn't exactly silent. But Erin didn't want to explain how jarring it felt today. At least as long as Terry was in her office, she needed music on.

Vic pulled a keychain-sized Bluetooth speaker from her purse and cued up a playlist. The kitchen, with its hard, reflective surfaces, immediately filled with sound. Pounding drums, harmonies, and a quick, energetic pace. It was just what Erin needed to get herself moving. She smiled at Vic in relief and gratitude and gave her hips a little shake.

"Perfect. Let's get to work."

Focusing on their usual closing routine and moving to the beat, she was able to shut out the worst of the thoughts about Terry looking for the evidence of her innocence. The tiny card that would prove to the world that she hadn't negligently killed the world's most famous food critic.

There was a lump in Erin's throat when Terry broke the news that he hadn't been able to find any sign of the allergy card in Erin's office. She nodded, forced a plastic smile, and pretended it didn't matter. Terry believed her anyway. He knew that she would never have been so careless. And Vic had seen the allergy card and read it and knew that it hadn't had strawberries on it. But of course they would both say that in the wake of Montgomery's death.

There would be other ways to prove her innocence. The facts of the case would be revealed and she and her bakery would be cleared and everything would go back to normal.

"I'll just check…" Erin said, and went into her office to check. There was no sign that it had been searched. Terry had carefully placed everything back just the way he had found it.

Erin was messier, ripping through stacks of paper and letting them fall back into place skewed and rumpled. She picked up bunches of paper and shook them violently to ensure that the card hadn't gotten stuck between the pages. But she knew that it wasn't there.

She could see at a glance that she hadn't left the card on her desk, where it would have been one of the top few items in her inbox. But she kept looking anyway. It must have fallen out. Gotten buried. Accidentally been clipped to something or slipped in between the pages.

After thirty seconds, she knew it wasn't there. After ten minutes, she had proven it several times over. She had checked every stack of paper, every file folder she had touched in the last week. Every drawer in her desk.

She grabbed her purse and, with tears burning in her eyes, returned to the kitchen.

"I'll see you at home," she told Terry calmly. "You won't be too late tonight? You don't have much more to do, do you?"

"No," he admitted. "There isn't much more that we can do today. We need to wait for responses on test results, people from his office, family members. An investigation takes time, even when it is something like this that looks like it was just… an unfortunate mishap."

Erin nodded. "You may as well get your sleep tonight. Be fresh in the morning."

She couldn't remember his shifts for the rest of the week. But his schedule would have changed. If there were a big investigation like this, his old shift schedule would be out the window while everyone put in all the time they could to break the case.

Terry nodded and looked at the clock on the wall. "I'll try to be home in an hour."

"Okay." Erin agreed. They all walked to the back door. Erin, Terry, and K9 went out first and turned to watch Vic arm the burglar alarm and turn off the lights before shutting the door behind her.

They would have to be extra vigilant. Who knew what kind of people might be coming by the bakery looking for a thrill after what had happened? She didn't want anyone to be able to get into the bakery to vandalize it, shoot some kind of on-the-scene video there, or steal something as a souvenir of the experience.

Erin climbed into the driver's seat of the yellow VW Bug, and Vic got into the passenger seat. They headed for home as usual, leaving Terry and K9 to find their way back to his vehicle and the police department offices or the B&B or wherever he was going next.

CHAPTER 12

*I*t will be okay," Vic said unnecessarily when Erin pulled into the garage. "Everything will turn out all right."

Erin nodded. "I'm sure it will."

She knew she couldn't bluff Vic. She would see through the facade and know exactly how Erin felt about the whole thing. And probably she was feeling the same way. She was just covering it up with talk about how everything would work out in the end because that was how God or the universe would make it happen. But Erin didn't believe in that stuff.

"Really," Vic insisted. "Everyone knows how careful you are. They know that you do this for a living, that you do it because you want to. You do it because you want to provide safe food for people, not because you want to make a million dollars. You would never jeopardize anyone's safety, and everyone in Bald Eagle Falls knows that."

"Unfortunately… this is going to have far-reaching consequences beyond Bald Eagle Falls," Erin pointed out. "This will be shared around the world. Everyone from here to Timbuktu will know what happened and that it was my fault."

"It wasn't your fault."

"Maybe I made a mistake."

"I saw that card. You didn't make a mistake."

Erin looked at Vic for a moment.

Vic held her gaze fiercely. "I saw that card," she insisted. "It did *not* have strawberries on it."

Erin took a deep breath and let it out slowly. "Unfortunately, there is no way for us to prove that now."

Vic followed Erin into her house rather than taking the stairs up to the apartment over the garage. She watched Erin disarm the burglar alarm there and turn on the lights. Erin was immediately targeted by a large orange cat with a raucous meow. Orange Blossom wound his way around her legs, yowling loudly and telling her how long he'd had to wait for her to get home and how his food dish had been empty all day.

Erin laughed despite herself. "You are *not* that hungry," she told the cat. "You aren't going to starve to death in a day. And I fed you this morning."

He kept complaining and, with him trying to trip her up, Erin made her way over to the pantry to get the can of kitty treats. She grabbed a few bits out of it and skimmed them along the floor. Blossom went rocketing after them and gobbled them up in an instant. After a few more, she filled his bowl, and he settled down to eat his dinner, his rumbling purr filling the room.

Marshmallow, the brown and white rabbit, made his way into the kitchen to see what all of the fuss was about. Actually, he knew what all of the fuss was about, since this was the way Orange Blossom behaved every day when Erin got home. Marshmallow waited patiently while Erin got a carrot out of the fridge and then hunched over it eating while Erin moved around the kitchen, putting the kettle on and looking through the fridge and cupboards without any interest in the contents.

"Gerald Montgomery is the one who is responsible for his own death," Vic told Erin firmly. "He is the one who ate alone even though he knew he put his life at risk by doing so. Montgomery is the one who chose a career putting his life on the line every time someone put a dish in front of him that he hadn't prepared himself. He's the one who told you *not* to tell him what was in the muffins and gave you a card that didn't list strawberries as one of his allergens. He should have asked you specifically about each of the ingredients that might make him sick. Read the ingredients list from the Bible himself. Looked at the card that he gave you to make sure it was the current one. It's his fault, not yours. He's the one who did not take care of himself."

It was a long speech. Erin watched the kettle and listened to it tick as it heated up, pondering Vic's words.

Everything Vic said was true. Montgomery had eliminated a lot of the safety nets that he should have kept in place. He had undoubtedly thought that if he had an allergic reaction, he could treat it himself. He had antihistamines for a mild reaction. He had epinephrine for anaphylaxis. How many auto-injectors did he carry? Erin knew that they might stop an allergic reaction for only fifteen or twenty minutes, and then he would need another shot. It took an hour to get to the city hospital. He might need as many as four or five shots to get him safely from the B&B to the hospital. Had he even considered that?

Or had he been flirting with death all along, just daring it to take him?

"He's had allergic reactions from foods he has tasted before. The woman at his office said so. Why would he keep doing this if it put his life in danger? Over and over again? Why wouldn't he take the proper precautions?" Erin asked.

Was it the same as Carolyn, who had refused to look different in front of her friends? To her, eating "normal" food had been about being accepted in her community. It had been more important for her to be normal and acceptable than it had been to protect her health. Even though she had been told that eating that normal diet could kill her, she had kept eating the food that would damage her intestinal tract. Her death had not been quick like Montgomery's, but had been long and drawn out over a period of months of starvation.

On the surface, Montgomery wasn't someone who had been obsessed with looking the same as everyone else. He was in-your-face. He was famous. He had millions of followers. But he had thrown up roadblocks to things that might make him look different in front of his fans. Refusing to disclose his allergies ahead of time. Insisting that his dietary needs be addressed on the fly, putting pressure on the restaurants he attended, which might result in mistakes or resentments and intentional sabotage. Had he just been a child inside, refusing to acknowledge his own vulnerability and mortality? Unable to fathom the consequences of his risky behavior?

"What are you thinking?" Vic asked, as Erin poured the boiling water from the kettle into the teapot and prepared to take the tea service to the table.

"Did they publish the recordings of the tastings where he had allergic reactions?"

"Yeah, they did. That's how I knew some of the ingredients to watch out for. Do you want to see? Hang on." Vic sat at the table and pulled out her phone to search. Erin put everything they needed on the table and sat down with Vic. She didn't have any appetite and her brain was whirling with a hundred different questions about Montgomery's death and what the police would be investigating. She picked a soothing ginger and chamomile tea. That would help to calm her digestive system and promote calm before bed and sleep in a few hours.

Vic drew in her breath sharply. About to pour the hot water into her cup, Erin looked at Vic to see what was wrong.

A problem at home, maybe. Willie was sick and needed to be taken into the city to see a doctor or be admitted to emergency. Or she had just remembered an appointment she was supposed to be at. Or that she had been planning to take her dog, Nilla, out for a walk right after work and now she might be faced with an unpleasant clean-up job when she returned to the loft.

Vic tapped her screen a few times, her face white and expression frozen. Erin didn't want to intrude, and waited for her to share what was wrong. Or to say that she had to go because she had something to take care of.

Vic stared at her screen for a few long seconds and then turned away, looking nauseated. Erin couldn't wait any longer.

"Vicky? What is it?"

"It's the video of Montgomery tasting our muffins," Vic whispered.

"What?"

"His company has posted the video of him tasting the muffins."

Erin gulped. "All of the muffins?"

Vic was staring at her phone, face as white as bone. "Yes, finishing with the Morning Sunshine Muffins. Including... his reaction to them."

"What? You don't mean..." Looking at Vic, Erin knew that she didn't mean that Montgomery broke out in hives on the video or expressed concern over the scratchiness in his throat.

Vic covered her mouth and shook her head. She didn't turn the phone to show it to Erin. Erin was torn between horror that the company would post such a thing and a need to see what had happened. She knew that she didn't want to see Gerald Montgomery die from anaphylaxis on the screen. That was just too horrible.

Erin took a few sips of her hot tea. Too hot. It burned her mouth and throat. But she was glad for the pain that made tears leak from the corners of her eyes.

"Are there... has anybody watched it? Do you have to search for the right thing to see it? Is it behind a membership wall?"

Vic shook her head. "The view numbers are in the six digits right now. Be into the millions before long."

Millions of people watching Montgomery die on the screen after eating Erin's muffins.

The ginger tea could not take away the nausea.

CHAPTER 13

*T*his is terrible," Vic said, staring at her phone, unable to take her eyes off the screen.

Erin reached over and took it from her. Not to look at it, but to get it away from Vic and turn it off. She did not need to keep watching it.

Vic clutched at it at first, then let Erin take it and watched while she turned it off. She sagged in her chair and put her face in her hands, murmuring words of what Erin thought might be a prayer to herself.

Erin put her hand on Vic's arm for a minute, then tapped Terry's contact record on her own phone.

Terry didn't answer. Erin hung up rather than leaving a voicemail message and called him again. There was no answer again.

Maybe he already knew. Maybe he was dealing with it and couldn't stop to take her call because it was more important to get the horrific video removed than it was to answer Erin's call. As far as he knew, she just wanted to know what he wanted for supper or something equally unimportant.

She found Sheriff Wilmot's number and called him. It went to voicemail. They were probably all in a meeting. None of them would answer. But someone had to be available for emergency calls.

Erin hung up and called the emergency dispatcher, though she felt guilty for doing so. It wasn't the kind of emergency where someone's life was in danger or a child was missing. But she knew the police would need to know about the video if they didn't already.

"Bald Eagle Falls emergency dispatch," a woman answered.

"It's Erin Price. Who is on call?"

"What's the nature of your emergency, Miss Price?"

"I need to get ahold of Terry or one of the others. About a piece of evidence in the Montgomery case."

"Leave a message on his phone."

"It's urgent."

"Is this piece of evidence in danger of being destroyed?"

"No…"

"Then they can deal with the case in an orderly manner—"

"A video of Montgomery's death has been posted online."

There was a second or two of silence as the dispatcher considered this.

"Is this the number you can be reached at?"

"Yes."

"Stay by your phone. Someone will call you right back."

Erin blew out her breath. "Thank you!"

She terminated the call and put the phone on the table beside her teacup. It would only be a minute or two, she was sure, before the phone rang and Terry or one of the other police department members was asking her the details.

"Are you okay?" she asked Vic, looking at her with sympathy.

"I hope never to see such a thing in my life again," she mumbled through her hands.

"I know," Erin agreed. She had seen things in her life too, things that she wished she could erase. To forget she had ever seen them, the images and all of the circumstances surrounding the memory wiped out of her mind. And not just the sights, but the smells, too, and the feeling of horror that went along with a gruesome discovery.

"Try not to think about it," Erin told Vic, picking out a bag of valerian tea and hanging it over the edge of Vic's cup. "Think about something else. Willie. You remember what it was like when you first met him? I know he's being a pain in the behind right now, but you remember what it was like in the beginning?"

Vic pulled her hands away from her face and looked at Erin like she was crazy.

"What?"

"Before you knew Willie really well? You remember how nervous you were about him? About how he felt about you?"

"Yeah…?" Vic said tentatively, clearly wondering where Erin was going with this. But it was just as Erin had told her. She wanted Vic to think of something else. Something with strong emotions attached to it so that it would hold her brain's attention and let her pull still further back from the video. If Vic kept replaying it mentally, it would be more likely to stay in her brain permanently, vivid and sickening. It would be less traumatic if she could pull back and move her mind on to something else.

"He's come a long way since then," Erin commented. "And you too. You're a lot more comfortable in your own skin now."

Vic's expression softened. She nodded her agreement. "Yeah, I am. I'm much happier with who I am now, and Willie has been a big part of that."

"I'll sure be glad when he's through the chelation therapy. Happy for you, I mean. He hasn't been much fun to live with the last little while."

Vic's gaze went to the window, likely checking to see if the lights were on in her apartment, or whether Willie was sleeping or out.

Erin's phone vibrated, making both of them jump. Erin took a deep breath and picked it up.

"Erin," Terry's voice was urgent. He didn't waste any time on preliminaries like asking her how her evening was going or what she was having for supper. "What's this about a video of Montgomery's death?"

"He always recorded himself during a tasting. He didn't want anyone else there, which was risky considering his food allergies and the reactions he'd had before, but he wanted to be alone."

"Yes, we know all of that."

"So I guess he recorded himself for the muffin tasting yesterday. And…" Erin faltered, but pushed herself on, wanting to be strong for Vic and save her as much mental pain as possible. "They got everything. His allergic reaction to the Morning Sunshine Muffins…"

"You saw it?"

"Vic did."

"Where is it? Who posted it?"

"Someone at his company, I guess." Erin looked over at Vic. "It was posted on the show's website?"

"I guess," Vic said, "and their social media. I just saw a video. I thought it would be one of the reactions that he had previously. He's always pulled through okay before…"

"On their social media," Erin repeated to Terry. "Vic said there were already hundreds of thousands of views."

Terry swore at this.

"How did they get that footage? It was Mrs. McClung who found his body, and she called us right away. No one else was allowed in the room."

"Then I guess…" Erin tried to think through the logical possibilities. "Maybe he did have someone with him? Or someone found him before Mrs. McClung and took the video but left him there…" She frowned. None of that made any sense. The company would have to know that the police would discover they had the footage and know that someone had been in the room. Maybe it was just someone who had happened by? But who would go into his room? And if they did, it wouldn't have been the production company that posted the ghoulish footage.

Vic was shaking her head. "It probably uploads to the cloud automatically. They can access it remotely. They don't have to be anywhere near the room."

Terry swore again. "Well, it will be fun trying to force them to remove it. We'll have to get a court injunction. That takes time, even in an emergency."

"Are you allowed to post something like that?" Erin asked. "Isn't it against the terms and conditions of the social media sites to post a video of someone dying?"

"Yes," Terry agreed. "We'll try that first. But getting them to pull it from their own site might be more difficult. And if it is still there, people will just keep downloading it and reuploading it to social media under different accounts."

"Have you seen the video?" Erin asked him.

"No. The video equipment was handed off to the forensic techies in the city for review. We're not allowed to mess around with electronics on our own. In case someone ends up destroying evidence."

"So now several hundred thousand people know more about how he died than the Bald Eagle Falls police department does."

Terry grunted, not sounding too happy about the fact. "We'll have to watch it before we get it pulled down. Have you watched it?"

Erin shook her head vigorously, even though he couldn't see her on the phone. "No way. I want to know what happened... but I don't want to see him die. Vic saw it. I know I don't want to."

Vic shook her head in agreement, her eyes looking hollowed out as if watching the video had affected her physically, drained some of the life out of her. Erin felt bad that she'd had to see it. All because Erin had suggested that she wanted to see footage showing what had happened when Montgomery had suffered an allergic reaction previously. If Erin had kept her mouth shut then, at least, Vic wouldn't have had to be the one to see it. She put her hand over Vic's, making an apologetic face. "Sorry," she mouthed.

Vic nodded her acknowledgment.

"We'll get right on this." Terry's voice was clipped. "Thank you for letting us know."

"Yeah. Of course."

"And Erin...?"

"Uh-huh?"

"I don't know when I'll be home. Don't expect me early."

He would probably be dealing with the video, Montgomery Meals and Reels, and the various social networking platforms that it had been posted to for hours. Terry wasn't the only cop in town, but Erin suspected that he and Stayner were probably the only ones with any technical savvy.

CHAPTER 14

*T*he next morning, fortified with plenty of caffeine, Erin looked at the Morning Sunshine Muffins they had baked the day before, still sitting on the counter awaiting their debut. She had planned to serve them as soon as Montgomery's tasting aired.

Well, now it had aired and she wasn't sure what to do about them. She couldn't serve them, could she? Serving the muffins that had killed Montgomery would be in poor taste.

Wouldn't it?

Vic followed Erin's eyes to the muffins and her mouth formed a grim line.

"What are we going to do?"

"Should we just throw them out?" Erin asked. "I hate to waste food, but… it's macabre, isn't it?"

"You still sold chocolate muffins after Aunt Angela died, didn't you?"

"Well, yes. But they weren't a special kind of muffin made just for her… they were just chocolate muffins. And everybody didn't see her die."

"Yeah, I guess that's a bit different."

"I can't just throw them out. I could freeze them for the home-

66

less shelter. Not call them Morning Sunshine Muffins. Instead, they can be… Strawberry Surprise Muffins."

Vic raised her brows. "Strawberry Surprise?"

Erin thought about Montgomery's surprise when he tasted the muffins and regretted the suggestion immediately. "No, no… Strawberry Compote Muffins."

Vic nodded. "That's better. Do you think they'll still know? They know that the donations come from Auntie Clem's, don't they? They'll hear about all of this in the news and know that the Strawberry Compote Muffins are what killed Montgomery."

"The administrators will know. But the diners won't. I think it's okay. I don't think they'll be upset about getting them, do you?"

"I think it will be okay," Vic said slowly. "Let's think about it, though, and make sure we both agree by the end of the day. We'll just leave them for now and put them in the freezer at the end of the day if we still think the same thing."

Erin nodded her agreement. "Yeah. No need to make a rush decision. They'll still be good at the end of the day."

They moved through the familiar morning routine. Erin was fighting brain fog after a very restless night. She hadn't settled down by the time Terry had gotten home and joined her in bed. Caffeine had helped to get her going, but she knew enough to anticipate a crash within a few hours unless she kept herself wired all day.

The caffeine also ramped up her anxiety. She knew it was going to be a trying day. Everyone would want to talk about what had happened to Montgomery, and some of them would have seen the video before it was pulled down.

How would people react? Would they be sympathetic? Accusatory? Even if they were nice to her, Erin knew she would feel guilty, embarrassed, and vulnerable. Maybe more so if they were nice. If people were rude, she could get angry and defend herself. She had done nothing wrong, after all. But she wasn't sure she could hold it together if they showed sympathy.

"You didn't set the timer," Vic observed as Erin put bread in the oven and walked over to the fridge for the next batch of batter. Erin looked at her, then the timer on the stove. Vic was right.

"Well, you just saved that batch of bread." Erin walked back to the oven and set the timer.

"You would have noticed," Vic said, brushing it off.

"On a normal day, maybe. Not today."

The first batches of baking were out of the oven, and Auntie Clem's was filled with the yeasty smell of freshly baked bread and the savory spices in the muffins and herbed pretzels and pizza shells. When Erin went to the front door, flipped the sign over to Open, and turned the bolt, she was surprised to see how many people were waiting for her to open.

Familiar customers stood around with their coffee cups as usual, getting the baking they would need for the week before work started, or a nice muffin or pastry to start the day. Their eyes were bright and excited and they were ready to ply Erin with questions, she could tell.

But there were other people there too. Faces that were unfamiliar. A group of young people was sitting on sleeping bags and blankets on the sidewalk, making Erin wonder how long they had been there. They hadn't been there when she had closed the night before, but they appeared to have been camped there for a few hours, anyway. They were like fans camped out in line to get tickets for their favorite band when they went on sale.

Erin looked at them for a moment through the glass, then opened the door to let her regulars in and ignored the trickle of strangers who mixed in with the group as she walked back to her place behind the counter to greet them and see what they wanted.

One of the young people pushed her way in front of everyone else who had been there waiting, snarling at them as if they had somehow stolen her place in line rather than the opposite. Her eyes went over the contents of the display case. She shook her head and pushed a lock of greasy black hair over her ear.

"Where are they?" she demanded. "The Morning Sunshine Muffins."

"Well…" Erin looked nervously at the other customers. "I didn't think anyone would want them after what happened."

"What do you think we came here for?" the girl asked, aggrieved. "It wasn't for a rice bran muffin, I'll tell you that!"

Erin felt a little embarrassed about the bran muffins in the display. There was nothing wrong with bran muffins, but the girl made her feel like she had been dishonest to put them out or that she was trying to fool people into thinking that nothing had happened the day before.

She didn't mean to cover up what had happened to Montgomery. That wasn't why she had left the Morning Sunshine Muffins in the kitchen.

"Well, I have some in the kitchen. I just didn't think people would want…"

"We all want the Morning Sunshine Muffins," one of the other young people said loudly, making sure Erin knew she'd better bring all the muffins out rather than just one. Erin glanced over the crowd. The strangers nodded in agreement.

A few of Erin's regular customers nodded too.

"It wasn't like something was wrong with them," the girl pointed out. "That wasn't why he died. But we want to taste… the last thing Gerald Montgomery tasted. We want that experience."

They didn't want the whole anaphylaxis experience; Erin could assure them of that.

But they wanted the Morning Sunshine Muffins. The muffins wouldn't be going to the homeless shelter at the end of the day.

CHAPTER 15

$\mathscr{E}$rin looked over the crowd of customers before stepping into the kitchen to get the muffins they had baked the day before. She was sure that the customers in this group would not be the only ones wanting to taste the muffins. If they wanted to, then everyone else would, too. She had badly misjudged in thinking that people wouldn't want anything that would remind them of Montgomery's death or how he had died.

It wasn't the first time she had misjudged how people would respond to a tragedy. Maybe by now, she should have figured out the way that people reveled in the news of an untimely death. She'd seen it enough times to have figured that out by now.

"I'm going to limit the Morning Sunshine Muffins to one per customer," she said as she looked them over. "And we'll get more in the oven as soon as possible. But we don't want to run out in ten minutes. I should have enough for everyone here, but if I do not, please come back this afternoon, and I'll have some more fresh out of the oven."

There were grumbles from a number of the visitors, but most of them nodded their agreement anyway. They could see how many people had come to eat the muffins. They wouldn't have camped out on the street if they hadn't thought the muffins would be in short supply and they would need to be there first thing in the morning to get a taste.

Vic nodded at Erin, telegraphing a look of understanding. Instead of one manning the counter and the other handling the till, they would divide their tasks between the kitchen and the customers. One would mix new batches of Morning Sunshine Muffins and get them into the oven while the other sold the finished product.

Erin was glad to get away from the eager eyes of the customers for a moment. She looked at the muffins, contemplating them for a few breaths. She could do this. She was a strong, capable person, and she had been running her own bakery for two years. She had gotten through worse challenges than this. She could put on a cheerful yet sympathetic expression and deal with the customers one at a time.

It should be a piece of cake.

She gathered the Morning Sunshine Muffins and collected them on a tray. She had known that there would be a run on the muffins after Montgomery's tasting. Now, it was time to put her plan into action.

Erin squared her shoulders and returned to the front of the bakery. People were chatting with each other, enjoying the warm bakery and the comforting smell of fresh-baked bread while they waited. Erin put the tray of muffins near the cash register, bumping Vic out of the way. Vic headed toward the kitchen to start on a new batch of muffins.

"Call around and see who else can come in," Erin told her. "I think we're going to need an extra baker or two today."

Vic nodded her agreement. "I'm on it, boss," she agreed.

Erin looked at the customers. "Okay, how many people are here only for a muffin and don't need anything else?"

Several people put up their hands or nodded their heads.

"Okay, I am going to sell one muffin to each of you and get you on your way as quickly as possible." She gave an apologetic look to her regular customers. "That will help to clear the bakery out quickly so that those who need longer to choose or have larger orders will have time to decide without feeling pressured."

Everyone seemed amenable to this. Not that it mattered. Anyone who had an argument about it would just have to put up with her plan of attack anyway.

The pushy girl who had camped out the night before was the first one at the counter and Erin didn't argue with her about having forced her way to the front of the queue. The best thing was to get her out of the bakery as quickly as possible. After paying for it, the girl held the muffin aloft, showing it off to everyone.

"The first Morning Sunshine Muffin to be sold since the one that killed Gerald Montgomery," she announced.

There was a murmur from the crowd. There was no cheer. It was more an expression of reverence than one of delight. The girl removed the wrapper from the cupcake and took a big bite. Everyone watched, not moving or saying anything. She turned it around to display the strawberry compote filling.

Everyone waited. The girl didn't have an allergic reaction or show any ill effects. She chewed, swallowed, and took another bite.

"It's really good," she told them in a calm, slightly wistful voice. "I think he would have liked it, if he'd had the time to enjoy it."

Was it a worthy last meal? Erin sighed and turned to the next person in line, quickly checking the single-muffin purchases through. People laid down twenty-dollar bills and told her to keep the change, not bothering to wait for her to ring them up. Many, like the first girl, unwrapped them and took their first bite or two in the bakery. A few gathered at the wrought-iron tables at the front of the store to have quietly murmured conversations.

Of the customers who remained after the single-muffin purchases, some were regular customers from Bald Eagle Falls whom Erin knew well, and others were not.

An Asian woman stepped forward with a friendly smile. "I'm Olivia Morgan," she announced.

"Nice to meet you," Erin said politely. "Are you from near here?"

"No." The woman laughed. "You've never heard of me?"

"Uh, no. Sorry, I haven't. I don't…" She was going to say, "watch a lot of TV," because she thought the woman looked like another TV celebrity and she obviously expected Erin to know who she was.

"You're a gluten-free baker," Olivia interrupted, shaking her head. "I would have thought you would have read one of my books. Tried out some of my recipes."

"Oh. Oh, *that* Olivia Morgan," Erin said, trying to act as though she were familiar with the woman's books. "Didn't you write…"

"*Baking Liberation: Set Yourself Gluten-Free?*" Olivia offered. "*Footloose and Gluten-Free?* I'm sure you must have read some of them. Anyone in the gluten-free baking business is bound to have read at least one of them."

"Of course," Erin agreed with a smile. She had heard the name before; she was pretty sure of that. She had developed her own baking methods primarily by watching other people in online videos and testing out the characteristics of the various flours and other ingredients that it was necessary to combine to replicate the properties of wheat flour. Before coming to Bald Eagle Falls, she wasn't a big reader and had only had what possessions she could fit into her suitcase and backpack. No books.

Olivia seemed to sense that Erin was not telling the truth and had not, in fact, read any of her cookbooks. Her smile dimmed, and she shook her head slightly. But she went on without pointing out to the world that Erin had never read any of them. After all, if Erin was now a famous gluten-free baker who had appeared on Gerald Montgomery's show and had invented the muffins that everyone was now flocking to taste and she hadn't ever even heard of Olivia Morgan, then what did that say about Olivia and her celebrity?

"What can I get you today?" Erin offered. "I'm afraid I don't have anything made from any of your recipes on offer today, but maybe you would be interested in…" Erin trailed off and looked down at the display case, unsure what Olivia's specialty was and what she would be interested in sampling.

"Well, let's try a variety," Olivia offered. "I'll have a blueberry muffin as well as the Morning Sunshine Muffin. And maybe one of those double chocolate chip cookies. They look good. A loaf of your regular white sandwich bread and then one of those artisan loaves... the rosemary and sun-dried tomato looks really tasty. What else do you sell a lot of?"

"The pizza pretzels are popular," Erin pointed to them. "And maybe a pastry? A turnover or tart?"

"Of course," Olivia agreed. "Get me a pretzel, whichever variety sells the best, and a lemon curd tartlet."

Erin gathered everything together and boxed it up for Olivia Morgan, famous published gluten-free baker.

"You should go next door to the Book Nook," she told Olivia. "See if they have copies of any of your books that you could sign. People always love getting signed copies..."

Olivia gave her a smile that seemed forced. "I'm not sure if the bookstore in a little place like Bald Eagle Falls would have much demand for gluten-free baking books. Especially with such a lovely gluten-free bakery right in town. People don't have to make their own."

"I suppose so," Erin agreed. "Well, I'll be sure to order some in now that I've met you. Replace my used copies and suggest them for those in town who want to do some of their own baking as well as buying from Auntie Clem's. People do still like to do some of their own baking as well. Some people really enjoy it."

"Do you?"

"Of course," Erin was surprised. "I love to bake."

"Some people don't, once they have to. Running a bakery can take the joy out of it."

"Oh, no. I still enjoy it. There are days when I wish I was just baking for myself again, because of the pressure of running my own business, but I still love to bake and experiment. In a business like this, you don't get ahead by just following everybody else's recipes."

After she said it, she wondered if she was being tactless,

somehow telling Olivia that she wasn't good enough or current enough to be of interest. She smiled and tried to reassure Olivia. "I mean, I always start with a basic recipe, but then I try out new stuff. Different ingredients, new techniques; soaking or fermenting or different oven temperatures…"

"I'm sure," Olivia agreed, looking irritated by Erin's explanation. As if she felt she were being patronized. "If you could just ring those up…"

Erin ducked her head, rang up the items Olivia had ordered, and gave her the total. Olivia paid.

"I hope you enjoy everything!" Erin said brightly.

She was a little nervous that Olivia would find her goods to be substandard or would tell people they were even if she didn't think so. Of course, she couldn't ascribe evil motives to someone she had never even met before. She could be totally misjudging Olivia; she didn't know anything about her. The woman had been friendly in her approach, and she had told Erin who she was, not pretended to be a regular customer and then ambushed her with a bad review like others might have done.

Olivia nodded coolly and left with her purchase. Erin turned to the next person in line, a bouncing Melissa Lee, who was obviously there to tell Erin the latest developments in the Montgomery case. There had been so many people that Erin hadn't even seen her come in.

"Oh, Melissa. How are you?"

"You wouldn't believe how tired I am." Melissa affected a yawn. "I was up all night worrying about this case and how it would affect you."

"Oh." Erin motioned to the display case to direct Melissa to make her selections. "Well, I don't think you need to be worried about me. I'll get through this."

"I knew how devastated you would be that Mr. Montgomery was killed by one of your muffins. It's too awful for words. And then to have the whole thing broadcast online like that. Did you watch it?"

"No. I didn't want to see it. Vic watched it," Erin glanced over her shoulder toward the kitchen. "It really freaked her out. I don't see any reason to expose myself to that, no matter how curious I am about what happened."

Melissa leaned forward. "I hear you. But I don't understand how you could *not* look. How do you resist something like that? I mean, don't you *want* to know? Can you just imagine it without checking to see if you were right in how you pictured it? I didn't want to watch it, but I couldn't not watch it. I had to look."

Erin shook her head. "What do you want? Like I said, I'm curious. But I'm too afraid to look. I don't want to see him die."

Melissa nodded sagely. "But it is evidence," she pointed out. "And if you want to solve what happened to Mr. Montgomery, then you need all the clues you can get."

"We know what happened to him. He had an allergic reaction to the strawberries."

"But why? Why wouldn't he tell you that he was allergic to strawberries, if they were that dangerous to him? They would be on his list, wouldn't they?"

"His office said that strawberries were on the list. And Terry said they were on the list he saw at the B&B."

"But not on the card that he gave you. You and Vic both said so. You wouldn't say that if it wasn't true."

Erin appreciated Melissa's support but knew that wasn't how law enforcement would look at it. They would be looking at ways to prove that she had intentionally poisoned Gerald Montgomery. They couldn't just believe what she had to say if it weren't substantiated by hard evidence. Maybe they would be more inclined to believe her since Vic supported her story, but anyone looking into the case would know that Vic and Erin were best friends, so of course they would back each other up.

Erin rested her elbows on the display case and looked at the customers waiting patiently behind Melissa. Or those who were not so patient, fidgeting and whispering behind their hands to each other.

Melissa looked at the people behind her and smiled, but decided she'd better make her selections and move out of the way.

"Okay. You still have a credit for the police department, right?"

Erin nodded. "Yes, would you like some pastries for them this morning?"

"Everyone has been working hard," Melissa declared. "Lots of hours put in on this case already. So I think they deserve a little something sweet." She looked slyly around her. "How about the Morning Sunshine Muffins?"

Erin just stood there looking at her. Melissa had presumably been there when she gave her little lecture on how she would only allow one Morning Sunshine Muffin per customer.

"Half a dozen," Melissa suggested. "That's only one per person, like you said."

"No, not one per person. One per customer. You can have one, but not every person in the department unless they all come in here personally. There will be more muffins later and over the next few days until the demand settles down. So... what would everyone like for breakfast today?"

Melissa rolled her eyes, but apparently decided there was no point in trying to cajole Erin any further on the Morning Sunshine Muffins. She sighed. "How about six Danishes and six assorted muffins? Including one Morning Sunshine Muffin."

Erin could imagine them cutting the Morning Sunshine Muffin into pieces so that everyone could examine one piece and then eat it.

But they could do whatever they wanted to with the Morning Sunshine Muffin, including sending it into the lab in the city to analyze the ingredients. Though of course if they asked, she would give them the list of ingredients. It wasn't that much of a secret. And they wouldn't bother asking her for the ingredient list because they already knew it was the strawberries Gerald Montgomery had reacted to.

"All right." Erin assembled an assorted Danish and muffin pack for Melissa, rang it up, and put the receipt aside to be charged against the police department's prepaid account. "And did you want anything for yourself?"

Melissa considered, then shook her head. "No, I'll just grab one from the box since I will be working there all morning today." She paused before leaving. "You really should watch that video, you know."

Erin shook her head. "No, I really don't think so."

Melissa laughed, her dark curly hair bouncing wildly, and she left.

CHAPTER 16

*V*ic returned from the kitchen. "Couple more batches in the ovens," she announced.

"Great, thanks for doing that."

Vic looked over the customers who remained. "You were able to clear people out of here pretty fast. How did you do that?"

"A lot of them just wanted one of the muffins. I took care of them first so that I would have more time to spend with everyone else."

"Good. How are we doing on muffin supply?" Vic looked at the tray on which the Morning Sunshine Muffins had been laid. "Just a couple left. We'll have some fresh out of the oven in fifteen minutes, so we're doing quite well. You want me to take till?"

Erin always felt more comfortable with Vic on the till. Both because she was better with the computer and making change quickly, and because she was good with the customers and made sure that no one left without feeling like they had been seen and their needs taken care of. Vic was just that good with people. Erin always felt like she was fumbling around in the dark, trying to figure out what people wanted when Vic knew instinctively.

And Vic seemed happy to deal with the till. She didn't think that Erin was just giving her the crap jobs that she didn't want. If neither of them had liked till, Erin would have been sure to change off with her regularly so that no one got stuck with the majority of the grunt work.

"Thanks, that would be great." Erin turned the cash register over to her. "Okay, who was next?"

She'd had a feeling it would be busy all day. It was a challenge to close down for their early lunch break. Vic had to man the door to let everyone out as they finished and not let anyone new in, advising them that they would be open in half an hour for the lunch rush. Eventually, they managed to lock the door and sit down on stools in the kitchen to take their own repast. She'd only had coffee and a piece of toast for breakfast and, by the time their lunch break rolled around, Erin was ravenous. She was in the mood for a treat, so she grabbed a couple of pizza pretzels as well as the sandwiches they had made. And another cup of coffee.

Vic eyed Erin, knowing she didn't usually have any coffee after her morning wake-up cup and that she'd already had extra coffee that morning.

"Are you trying to give yourself a heart attack?"

Erin laughed. "No. Just trying to come down gently." She inhaled the rich aroma of the fresh coffee. "If I don't have anything, then that post-caffeine crash is going to hit me in the middle of the afternoon and I'll be paralyzed. This will keep me going until I get home, and I might have another half-cup at supper."

"Having more coffee to avoid crashing sounds backward."

"I know, but it's what works for me. It's like weaning off of a drug."

"I guess it is, at that," Vic agreed, nodding.

They split up the sandwiches and pizza pretzels and were happy to take a load off for a while. Erin had comfortable shoes, but she still felt a lot of leg and foot fatigue by the end of the day if she put in both the morning and the afternoon shifts.

"Charley is going to come by and bake more muffins in the

afternoon," Vic said, "And Bella will be out of school early so she can take the last half of the afternoon shift. I figured that by then, we'll be ready to go home. Charley and Bella can close and we can crash."

Erin always felt guilty going home early, even if she was the boss and had made sure that everything was covered, but she knew Vic was probably right to arrange it that way. Neither of them had slept much, if at all, the night before. They would need to spend the evening unwinding and go to bed early to start catching up.

CHAPTER 17

When they finished their lunch and opened the door again, there was a lineup outside the door. The man at the front of the line looked disgruntled.

"What kind of business is this that closes in the middle of the day?" he demanded.

"An owner-run business that starts very early," Erin told him evenly. "And we need a break and our own lunch if you want the bakery to be open into the afternoon."

He stared at her for a minute but eventually nodded and backed down.

"Fine. I suppose you're running on limited staff. This is a small town and maybe the demand isn't as big as it would be in the city."

"Or maybe people here are more considerate," Vic suggested tartly.

The man's neck grew rosy. "I'm not being inconsiderate," he objected.

"Telling us that we can't take time for lunch? That we must be some minor league operation if we need breaks?"

He swallowed and gestured toward the door. "If you're open now…"

Erin opened the door and stepped back. Vic followed her example, making space for the customers to come in.

Erin looked the stranger over. She didn't think she'd ever seen him in town before. One of Montgomery's followers, she suspected. There to get a Morning Sunshine Muffin, and then she would never see him again.

He was tall and stylish, well-dressed; not the kind of guy she usually saw around the bakery. Most men who came in were dressed in work clothes, picking something up for lunch or break or on the way home to their wives. Or maybe dressed casually, stopping in for a cookie or a trail mix bar before or after a workout.

"What can I get for you?" she asked, indicating the baked goods in the display case. Things were starting to look a little spare as they kept making more muffins and didn't have a lot of time to refresh the rest of the baked goods. But the man didn't seem to care.

"I understand you're restricting purchases to one muffin per order."

Erin nodded. "For the Morning Sunshine Muffins, yes. Other muffins are not restricted. But we are limiting order to the Morning Sunshine Muffins until the supply and demand have stabilized."

"I guess that's what I'll have then. One muffin."

Erin got one of the fresh muffins out and put it into a single-serving box. "Can I get you anything else? Are you in town for long?"

"No, I'm not staying around. No reason to hang around here."

Erin nodded and smiled as if he had been friendly to her. "Were you and Mr. Montgomery friends?"

They were probably around the same age. Erin had no other reason to think they might have known each other personally. He was probably just a follower, as she had first thought.

"Friends?" His voice was gruff, resentful. "I should say not! I wouldn't associate myself with such an immoral, unethical fraudster."

Erin's mouth dropped open as she tried to think of a response to this. There were several gasps around the bakery at this accusation. Around Bald Eagle Falls, most of the church ladies tried to follow the maxim of "speak no ill of the dead."

"Well, I'm sorry to hear that," Erin told him lamely. She was just the baker. He certainly couldn't expect her to do anything about the past wrongs done by the dead man. She'd barely even met him. Practically all she knew about him was what she had learned from watching his shows. And he had produced those shows, so the chances that they would reveal any immoral or unethical behavior were pretty low. He didn't mind being portrayed as harsh, judgmental, or bad-tempered, but there were a lot of famous chefs who were those things. It was pretty much to be expected of a food critic.

"The man was a crook—a cheat. You can bet that over the next week, everyone will be writing about his life as if he were a saint. But I'll tell you, that was not the case."

"Well," Erin swallowed. "You're entitled to your opinion and can say what you like about him. I only met him one time."

"He built his empire on the backs of hundreds of honest and hardworking people. Creatives, chefs, bakers. People who put in the work and the time, only to have everything stolen from them by Mr. Magical Montgomery and his Meals and Reels mythology."

"Okay…" Erin drew the word out. "I'm so sorry for whatever happened to you. If you could pay over here, Vic will take care of you."

Vic encouraged him over and, even while Erin tried to help the next customer, she could hear him complaining to Vic, baring his soul as she tried to help him check out.

"My name is Mark Thompson, and I'm not the only one that fraud stole and plagiarized from."

"Can you plagiarize a recipe?" Vic asked.

"Of course you can. If it's someone else's and you copy it, that's plagiarism. Doesn't matter whether it is a book or a recipe."

Vic looked over at Erin. "Well, a lot of chefs get their ideas from other people's recipes, and then they make changes to it, the ingredients, the method… then it becomes theirs, right? I mean, there are going to be a lot of really similar recipes around. You can't tell who wrote the first one or who used whose as inspirations."

"I'm not talking about inspirations," Thompson argued. "He stole from me. Flat-out took my recipes and passed them off as his own. Copied my recipes, my ideas for setting up his company and TV tours. They were all my ideas, and he just decided to take them for his own."

Erin didn't think that ideas were something that could be protected. Company structure, concepts, viewpoints, how Montgomery conducted his tours and tastings, none of it could belong to one person.

But that didn't mean Thompson couldn't be angry about it. No reason he couldn't resent Montgomery just as much as if he'd stolen his wife or his manuscript.

Vic was nodding, clucking sympathetically, and trying to get Thompson to move on. Eventually, he found his way out of the bakery. There was a collective sigh of relief.

"Wow." Erin blotted her forehead with a napkin.

"Don't that beat all," Vic drawled.

"It sure does. I knew the guy wasn't very well-liked, but it seems like it might go a little deeper than that."

"I would say that is an understatement," Cindy Prost commented. "Seems like someone your boyfriend might want to make the acquaintance of."

Erin looked at her. "Terry? Why?"

"Seems like he isn't too broken up about Montgomery's death. Maybe he had something to do with... wanting him that way."

Erin shook her head, bemused. "But we know what killed Montgomery. It wasn't murder. It was... just accidental exposure to an allergen."

"Unless it wasn't."

Time seemed to stand still.

Erin stared at Cindy, trying to follow her train of thought. No one had suggested that Montgomery's death might have been caused by anything other than anaphylaxis.

Was there any other possibility? Could it have been poisoning?

What would make Cindy think it had been something other than what it had appeared to be? Did she actually know something? Erin glanced over at Vic.

"I didn't see the video. It *was* an allergic reaction, wasn't it? It couldn't have been... something else."

"It was an allergic reaction," Vic insisted. "It was just like you hear about. His throat swelled up; he had hives on his face, and he couldn't breathe. It just happened really fast. Like super-fast. He didn't have a chance to do anything about it, like he had when he'd had accidental allergic reactions before."

"You see?" Cindy shrugged as if this supported her theory of Thompson being the cause of Montgomery's death. "It happened too fast. Hadn't been like that before. So he must have gotten an extra-large dose of his allergen, or it was something even more lethal, like cyanide. It could have been, you know."

Erin was pretty sure that cyanide poisoning didn't look that much like anaphylaxis. Not from what she had seen on TV. Of course, crime TV wasn't a reliable source of medical information, but cyanide didn't cause hives, did it? Maybe an amateur observer couldn't tell the difference between his throat swelling from an allergic reaction and not being able to breathe due to cyanide poisoning, but the medical examiner would be able to tell, wouldn't he?

"I'm... no one has said anything about it being something other than an allergic reaction," Erin asserted. "I don't think... they're looking for suspects."

"They wouldn't have to look far, would they?" Cindy observed, and chuckled.

Erin's face burned. She knew better than to let Cindy get to her. Maybe it was because she was so short on sleep, but she wasn't willing to put up with Cindy's nonsense this time.

"If that's all you came here to say, then I think it's time for you to go now."

Cindy's mouth opened. "Well, no, I came here for..." She looked at Erin's face and perhaps thought better of asking for a

Morning Sunshine Muffin. She looked past Erin at the kitchen. "Is Bella here yet? I need to talk to her."

Erin looked behind her. She hadn't heard Bella come in, but checked to be sure. Cindy was Bella's mother and, if Bella had heard Cindy talking the way that she was, she would have had something to say about it.

"No, not yet. You can send her a text to give you a call. She's going to be busy when she gets here."

Cindy's eyes went to the Morning Sunshine Muffins and then back to Erin. She clenched her jaw, and then stepped back, toward the door.

"I'll talk to her later," she said in a clipped tone, then let herself out.

CHAPTER 18

*E*rin blotted her face with a napkin again. Despite the air
conditioning in Auntie Clem's, she was sweating heavily
after the interactions. She did not like confrontations. She wanted
the atmosphere in Auntie Clem's to be pleasant and friendly. She
wanted it to be a place where people felt happy and warm when
they arrived, where they could talk comfortably with each other or
Erin and the employees and experience being nurtured emotionally
as well as physically.

She looked at Vic and shook her head. "Things are a bit…
dramatic today."

Vic nodded, her eyes wide and round. "Things will settle down
now, I'm sure…"

Erin hoped she was right. She was used to dealing with gossip,
but Thompson's behavior was over the top, and Erin couldn't deal
with Cindy's digs after being stirred up by that conversation.

She took a deep breath and smiled at the next woman in line.
Another out-of-towner. A tall, slim woman with dark hair tucked
behind her ears, one strand lying loose across her cheek. Erin
reached for one of the Morning Sunshine Muffins.

"Hi, welcome to Auntie Clem's Bakery. Do you know what you
want, or did you need a minute to look?"

"You are despicable," the woman spat. "Do you have any idea what you have done?"

Erin froze, her hand hovering over the muffins. She looked for a way to defuse the situation.

"I'm sorry...?" She struggled to give the woman a warm, reassuring smile. "I'm just trying to sell some baking here..."

"You killed him. You don't even feel bad about what you did. All you care about is the money. A brilliant man died because of what you did, and you don't even care."

Erin swallowed. "Of course I care. If I had known Mr. Montgomery was allergic to strawberries, I would never have sold him that muffin. It's a terrible tragedy and I am very sorry for what happened."

"Oh, it sounds like it," she snapped. "It really sounds like you care about him. You're pushing those muffins like a crack dealer. Capitalizing on people's grief. Making this whole thing a circus and you're selling tickets to the show."

Erin tried to think of what to do or say to calm the woman down. She was obviously grief-stricken over the loss of Gerald Montgomery.

"I wasn't going to sell any more Morning Sunshine Muffins," she felt the need to defend herself. "It was the fans who asked for them. I wouldn't have... but there's a huge demand. People really want to... share something with him. To taste what it was he tasted before... you know."

"Before you killed him. Don't act like you didn't have anything to do with it. It was all your doing. You took him away from us. He was a brilliant foodie, and now he's gone. I can't believe you could be so cold and callous. Killing the guy just to sell a muffin. Despicable. That's what you are."

"Let's move things along," Vic said in a hard voice, lower and gruffer than normal, "It's time for you to leave."

"You can't kick me out of a public place. If you don't like what I have to say, that's just too bad. I have every right to say it."

"You can get out now or we'll call the cops."

"Do you even have cops in this town?" she challenged, nose wrinkling up as if she'd smelled something bad.

"The nice thing about such a small town is that they're always close by," Vic told her.

There was a short pause while the woman considered this information. But her brief contemplation about the possibility didn't make her any more cautious. "I don't care if you do have me arrested. I'm here and I'm going to say my piece."

Vic pulled her phone out of her apron pocket and dialed a number. Erin wasn't sure whether she was calling the police dispatcher or Terry or was bluffing, but the woman didn't seem to care.

"People like you should be locked up," Montgomery's fan told Erin venomously. "People can come and look at *you* and point and laugh. And you wouldn't be a danger to someone like Gerald, who deserved to live a long, fulfilling life and to keep contributing to the world like he was."

"I'm just a baker," Erin protested weakly. She knew she should be more assertive and stand up for herself, but she understood the woman was hurting. She had suffered a loss. Maybe she was a close friend or relative of Montgomery, thrown for a loop by what had happened, reacting before she had a chance to think about the appropriateness of her behavior. "I'm just trying to make sure that people who need a gluten-free diet have choices. I'm just trying to nourish people…"

"What did Gerald Montgomery ever do for anyone?" Lottie Sturm challenged the newcomer. "You think anyone other than you really cares about him being gone? He was the one who was only trying to bring everyone else down. He was happy to destroy other people for the sake of his pocketbook."

The two women faced off against each other. Erin clutched the counter, worried that they would come to blows. It was one thing if they had to get Terry in there to cajole a disappointed woman into leaving the store without causing any more trouble. It was quite another to have a fistfight in the middle of Auntie Clem's.

"Ladies," she protested. "I understand you're upset and disappointed... but this is not the place..."

"Who do you think you are?" the other woman demanded from Lottie. "What does this have to do with you? I was talking to the proprietor."

"I'm a customer, and you're not. So why don't you move on so the rest of us can get our baking?"

"I won't be treated this way!"

CHAPTER 19

*T*erry must have been close by when Vic called because he opened the door and marched in, the bells ringing loudly, and K9 close beside him, ready to take on any criminal he might encounter there.

The woman had turned to confront Lottie instead of Erin, so she was facing in the right direction to see Terry enter the bakery, his dark uniform and dog making it very clear who he was.

"I have a right to be here," she snarled. "You can't kick me out. You have no reason to detain or arrest me."

Terry's expression was inscrutable. "Is there a problem here, ma'am?"

"Yes, there's a problem. Why is this woman still here after she poisoned and killed Gerald Montgomery? Are the police here so incompetent that they can't even arrest her for that?"

"At the moment, Gerald Montgomery's death is considered accidental. We are looking into it, but I can't comment on ongoing investigations."

"An accident? She deliberately gave him those muffins. She wanted them to be famous, and now they are. Everyone wants one of the Morning Sunshine Muffins from Auntie Clem's Bakery now. They'll be taking orders from Japan and shipping them around the world next thing you know. His death is being made into a circus, with millions of viewers watching his death. And this woman is profiting from his death. Doesn't that tell you something?"

"Ma'am, I'm going to ask you to step outside. We can continue this conversation out there."

She folded her arms over her chest. "I'm not going anywhere. I came here to say my piece. And I'm not leaving until I'm finished. And I will decide when I am finished, not anyone else."

Terry raised his brows. He pulled out his citation book. "Can I get your name, ma'am?"

"Becky Chalmers."

"Do you have identification on you?"

"If I say my name is Becky Chalmers, that is who I am. You don't need my identification."

"It is an offense not to supply identification when asked for it by law enforcement officers."

She considered this for a moment and then dug into her purse. "I haven't done anything wrong," she asserted. "I have every right to be here."

"As a customer, ma'am. It doesn't appear that you are here to buy anything. The proprietors have every right to evict you or deny you entrance at their discretion. They don't have to have a reason or explain why. But if you come here or remain here after you are told to leave, you are guilty of trespassing. And I don't want to have to cite you for that."

His pen hovered over the page.

Chalmers found her wallet and opened it up to display it to Terry, taking several steps closer so he could see it. People moved out of the way to avoid being caught between them.

K9 growled when Chalmers got too close for his liking, and Terry hushed him. He looked the woman over.

"Do you have any weapons on you?"

"Weapons? Me? Of course not. I came here to talk. To tell that woman what she has done!"

"Are you sure?" Terry glanced down at K9. "My dog seems to think otherwise."

"Well… I have a weapon, yes, but I'm not going to use it."

"Drop your purse there, please, and put up your hands," Terry told her sharply.

The other customers drew farther back, worried. Erin reached out for Vic to herd her into the safety of the kitchen, but Vic stood her ground, one hand under her apron. Erin knew she used a bra holster and wasn't sure how easy it would be to draw with the apron on, but Vic was apparently prepared to do so. Knowing Vic, she had probably practiced the action regularly.

Chalmers didn't act as quickly as Erin would have liked but, looking at Terry, his eyes hard and one hand on his holster, Chalmers decided she'd better take him seriously. She lowered her purse to the floor and raised her hands.

"Where's your gun?" Terry demanded.

Erin wondered how he knew it was a gun or if he were just guessing. Chalmers might have meant that she had a knife or a taser. Some women carried personal tasers in their purses and might not have considered it a weapon since it was only for self-defense. Maybe K9 had given Terry a sign that it was a gun, or maybe Terry was assuming the worst. Better to be prepared for a gun than surprised by it.

"In there," Chalmers looked at the purse beside her. "In my purse."

"Kick it toward me. Keep your hands up."

She did so. The braggadocio was leaving her posture. She wasn't quite so brash and self-righteous now, maybe starting to comprehend the serious situation she was in.

Terry grabbed the shoulder strap and pulled the bag out of the way so it was beyond the woman's reach.

"Turn around and lace your fingers behind your head."

Chalmers obeyed.

"Get down on your knees."

"It's in my bag," she protested. "I don't have anything on me."

Terry didn't back down. "Get on your knees."

The woman was young and athletic enough to do so. Erin winced at how the hard floor must hurt her knees, though. As Erin got older, she found it harder and harder to be comfortable kneeling on anything.

"Lie face down."

"I can't do that with my hands behind my head."

Terry stepped forward. His hand left his holster and helped her transition from kneeling to lying prone on the floor.

Erin couldn't help but feel bad for Chalmers. She had undoubtedly not left home this morning expecting to end up face down on Auntie Clem's Bakery's floor with customers standing around her gaping as Terry frisked her thoroughly.

Vic's position relaxed and her hand came out from behind her apron.

Terry secured the woman and went to her purse to investigate it. He pulled out a handgun that was larger than Erin had expected.

"I didn't come here to shoot anyone," Chalmers protested. "I just came here to talk. I never threatened anyone or took that out of my bag!"

"Do you have a permit? Is it registered?"

"I've been using guns since I was a child. I know what I'm doing!"

"So it's not registered? Do you have a permit?"

"Not... as such."

Erin didn't even want to know what that meant.

"I'm taking you in on firearms violations. Do you want her charged with trespassing?" Terry asked Erin.

"No. I think... she's had a bad day. I don't want to make things worse." Erin tried to meet Chalmers's eyes as Terry lifted her to her feet. "I'm sorry about your friend. I hope you believe me when I tell you that I never meant anything to happen to him. I wouldn't have given him those muffins if I had known about his strawberry allergy. And as far as selling them... people want to buy them. It's an... homage to him. A way to remember his passing. I'm not doing it for the money."

She felt a twinge of guilt saying so, because she had put together a marketing plan to sell the muffins, fully expecting people to be interested in them after Montgomery released his review. And she would continue to sell them as long as there was a demand.

But she wasn't capitalizing on the man's death. She was just selling gluten-free baking, like she always did. She had marketing campaigns around Christmas and Easter and Founders' Day, and every other observance with a good hook to bring people in. She made different shapes of cookies and different recipes suited to each holiday. And now she was selling Morning Sunshine Muffins around Montgomery's death. She had to admit that it did sound a little ghoulish when she thought about it that way.

"No, I'm sure you're not making any money on it at all," Chalmers mocked. "You're just doing this out of the goodness of your heart."

"I can't just give them away. I would lose all kinds of money."

"Yeah, that's what I thought," she sneered at Terry as he marched her toward the door.

"I'll see you after work," Terry told Erin. "I'll be around for closing to make sure that nothing unexpected happens."

Erin appreciated it but, at the same time, dreaded the possibility that anything else could happen today. She just wanted it to all be over and for things to go back to normal. What was wrong with normal? Why had she been so excited about Montgomery patronizing Auntie Clem's Bakery to start with?

CHAPTER 20

$\mathcal{A}$fter work, Erin normally had some alone time to decompress and relax from the rigors of the day before Terry came home or it was time to go to bed.

And she was getting off early, as Vic had arranged extra shifts to come in so that she could get caught up on her sleep.

But Terry came by before Erin left to ensure that no one was hanging around the bakery or the house who shouldn't be. He walked a patrol around the block with K9, checking out both the front and the back of the bakery and making sure no one was lurking in parked cars nearby. He nodded, signaling that it was safe for them to go out to the car, and watched as they climbed in and buckled their seatbelts.

"I'll follow you home," he told Erin when she rolled down the window.

"You don't need to do that. You already checked to make sure that everything was safe."

"There could still be people around that I'm unaware of. I can only see so much."

"You don't think that Chalmers or someone else is really any danger, do you?"

"Let's talk about that when we get back to the house."

Erin hadn't been expecting all of the attention. He and the other law enforcement officers must think there was reason for concern if they were letting Terry off to watch over her, checking out her route as if she were a dignitary, escorting her home, and then sitting down to discuss the possible dangers.

She didn't like it.

It was good that she had a law enforcement officer who was so concerned about her, but she did not like the idea that he thought she was in danger.

Erin rolled up her window and drove home without any conversation with Vic, whose brow was wrinkled in a frown and seemed to be in her own world thinking things through.

When they got home, Terry suggested that Vic grab Willie and meet them in the living room so that they could all sit down for a talk together.

"Willie needs to be a part of this too?" Vic asked doubtfully.

"Best if everyone gets the same message. Firsthand news is always more clear and definitive."

Vic grumbled and headed over to the loft to see if Willie were there. Erin thought longingly of her bed and the afternoon nap she'd hoped to have. But it looked like this day was not going to go the way that she had hoped. She'd gotten their shifts covered at Auntie Clem's, but she still didn't get to relax.

"Should I make some tea?"

Terry shrugged. "I could use a beer."

Erin walked over to the fridge to get him one. "You're not still on duty?"

"Technically, no. Practically… I still want to keep an eye on things here and see if we can make any progress. I can manage one beer without it affecting my judgment."

He must have had a pretty rough workday. He normally would not have a beer unless he were truly off for the day and just planned to couchsurf with Erin. Or maybe while they were on a date. She didn't think there was any danger in his having a beer; as he said, he wouldn't be impaired by just one. But it was out of character.

Vic returned with Willie, who also helped himself to a beer despite Vic's glare. He wasn't supposed to be drinking until he was fully recovered from the heavy metal poisoning and chelation. Erin didn't know how significant the risks were, but she knew Willie had been told no alcohol.

CHAPTER 21

They all sat down in the living room.

"Did Vic tell you what happened at the bakery today?" Terry asked Willie.

Willie looked over at her. "She said something about a customer causing a fuss, but... it didn't seem like anything concerning."

"It wasn't," Vic agreed. "The woman was angry and upset, but no one was in any danger."

"That's not quite accurate," Terry said. "She had a concealed, unlicensed weapon. She would not listen to reason and was behaving erratically. All of those things together present a very serious situation."

Vic shrugged. "One crackpot."

Terry took a swig from the beer bottle. "The problem is that she was not just one crackpot. Montgomery seems to have had a whole following of crackpots. And they are all intent on getting to Auntie Clem's Bakery and eating a Morning Sunshine Muffin."

Erin laughed. "Could be worse things."

"Could be. Most of them will just buy their muffin and leave. Film themselves tasting it, post it to social media as hashtag Morning Sunshine Challenge, and go back to their lives. But you get some like this woman from this afternoon, who are not happy with just buying a muffin and who blame Erin or Auntie Clem's for killing Montgomery, and that's a whole different story. She wasn't much of a threat—unless she decided to use that gun."

Willie was leaning forward, elbows on knees, listening to Terry intently. He looked at Vic, nodding his agreement. "This isn't the kind of thing you want to ignore."

"But we can't have an armed guard on duty at the bakery."

"I'm there," Vic said. "I'm there for at least one shift most days, and I'm armed. I can take care of any threats."

Neither Terry nor Willie looked happy with that.

"It will blow over," Erin said. "In a day or two, it will all trickle off, just like it always does when there is a death. It won't keep going on for weeks or months."

"Are you planning to close down until it does?"

"Well, no. I can't do that. They're coming for the baking. Or at least the muffins. If I closed down… what good would that do? It would just get them riled up."

Terry shook his head grimly.

"How is the case coming along?" Willie asked. "You must be ready to put it to bed soon. It's pretty clearly an accident. An open-and-shut case."

"There are… complicating factors."

Willie grunted. "Like what? Seems to be a pretty straightforward case to me."

"Well, for one thing, the number of enemies this guy had. The number of people who were quite happy for him to be dead. There are online forums on which it is discussed in extensive detail."

"What is discussed?" Erin asked.

"The best way to kill him."

"Oh." Erin looked at Vic, then at Terry. She hadn't anticipated that.

"Yeah. And a lot of those methods involve his allergies. Somehow slipping him something that he is allergic to."

"That's horrible." Erin couldn't believe someone would discuss such a thing openly, even if the forum was supposed to be private and password protected.

"Has the medical examiner identified cause of death?" Vic asked. "Was it an allergic reaction?"

"Yes, it was. A massive allergic reaction that occurred too fast for him to be able to get help. He did manage to get his auto-injector but, by the time he injected, it was too late. It wasn't able to reverse the reaction."

Vic nodded.

Erin had wondered why he hadn't used his auto-injector. Now she knew. He had. But unlike the magical effects epinephrine always had on TV, a single dose wasn't always sufficient to reverse a reaction. Or time ran out and it was too late to recover.

"What else?" Willie asked. "The fact that people wanted him dead did not make this a murder instead of an accident. It's an interesting fact, but…"

"There is also the fact that Erin and Vic swear that strawberries were not on the wallet card listing of allergens that they were given. The corporate office confirmed that strawberries were a recent addition. Older wallet cards would have omitted strawberries as a trigger."

Erin tensed. Neither man acted like they doubted it was true. They seemed to believe that if their partners said it was true, it was.

"So he accidentally gave them an old card," Willie offered with a shrug. "That's believable."

"The office manager said that she changed over his wallet cards personally. She took the old ones out and put the new ones in. So how did Montgomery give them an old one?"

They all considered the possibilities.

"Maybe she is mistaken," Erin suggested. "A year or two ago, when I got a new credit card, I accidentally cut up the new one instead of the old one. I had to get them to send me another one. I've talked to a ton of people since then who have done the same thing. So maybe it was the same. She takes the old cards out of the wallet. Something distracts her. She puts the old cards back into the wallet and trashes the new ones. It could happen easily."

Terry nodded. "Yes," he allowed. "But there were no old cards in his room. Everything we could find listed strawberries."

Erin immediately wanted to defend herself and assure him that the card they had received from him had not had strawberries on it, even though he hadn't accused her of anything. She bit her tongue, but it was hard to keep from objecting.

"So he just had one of the old ones left," Willie said. "It was in his suit pocket, not his wallet. Or he had them in two different slots in his wallet and the executive assistant didn't realize it and only replaced the ones in one slot. There are a lot of different possibilities. If you've had two different versions of the same card printed, that will happen. You'll end up leaving the old ones somewhere without realizing it." He shrugged. "How many times have you had new business cards printed, gotten rid of all the old ones, and then two years later more of them show up somewhere? The briefcase you use for business conferences. A coat you haven't worn lately. A monogrammed card holder in a drawer that you never bother to carry with you. It's like they reproduce."

Terry sighed and sat back. He took a pull on his beer. "Maybe I'm imagining things," had admitted. "There are a lot of strangers in town; we're getting all kinds of calls from reporters, his office, other jurisdictions, and fans to find out what we're doing about it. People who think that there was foul play. That he was killed intentionally. We have this woman showing up in the bakery yelling and carrying a weapon. Maybe I am just reacting to outside pressure."

"How many people knew that he was allergic to strawberries?" Erin asked tentatively. "I don't think it could be really well known because we researched it before he came here, trying to figure out what was safe and what wasn't. Vic watched a lot of his old shows and I watched a few. We did a bunch of searches and avoided anything that it seemed like he didn't eat or that he was reported to be allergic to. Montgomery had this thing about people not sharing his allergies. I wondered if the list he gave us was a complete fiction. Like if it was just part of the game. An additional challenge to see who could stick to it and who screwed up."

"That would be a dangerous game if you really were allergic to multiple foods," Terry observed.

"Yeah. I know. I keep wondering why he didn't just put the list on his website. Let everyone know. Why keep it a secret? The only thing I can come up with is that he was ashamed of it. Felt like it meant he wasn't a man. But it was really risky behavior."

"Some people get off on risks." Willie leaned back in his seat and rubbed his forehead. He was obviously fatigued and fighting a headache. And he hadn't yet had supper. Vic would need some time to make him something. Alcohol on an empty stomach probably wasn't doing him much good.

It reminded Erin how tired she was. She was also hyped up and was afraid that when she finally did get a chance to crash, she would lie awake staring at the ceiling, passing a long, sleepless night as she tried to figure out whether someone had intentionally killed Montgomery.

"Maybe he liked the feeling of risking his life whenever he tried a new food," Willie said, eyes closed. "Maybe that's why he did it by himself instead of with someone who could help him if he had a reaction. Maybe that was why he decided to do it in a town without a hospital. Where the nearest hospital is an hour away."

"He was suicidal?" Erin asked.

"A risk taker. Not necessarily suicidal. Maybe he just liked the rush of danger."

A quote came into Erin's mind. For a few seconds, it floated just out of her reach and she tried to pin it down and to remember where it came from. Peter Pan, she thought. Maybe.

To die will be an awfully big adventure.

erry looked at his watch. "I'm going to head back to Auntie Clem's for closing. Just to ensure there is no more trouble and everything gets locked up properly."

"Charley is there. She'll make sure."

Terry grimaced. Charley was not his favorite person and he obviously did not trust her to ensure that everything was properly secured at the bakery. It could have had something to do with the fact that before they had met, Charley had been operating on the wrong side of the law, part of the Dyson Clan, an organized crime family. Or at least, dating a member of the Dyson clan. She was pretty young and Erin didn't know exactly how involved she had been in any illegal activities with the Dysons. Enough that she knew her way around a gun and had been in and out of trouble with the law. But she hadn't done any time, and Erin thought that said something about her.

"Charley is fine closing up," Erin insisted.

"I'm sure she is. But I'm also going to make sure. Just part of my services as the friendly town law enforcement officer." He stood up and hitched up his duty belt. "I'm sure they will feel much safer with Officer Piper on the scene."

It wouldn't hurt anything, so Erin didn't argue it any further.

What harm was there in his keeping an eye on things? There *were* a lot of strangers around town since Montgomery's arrival.

"Okay. We'll have dinner when you get back. I think that right now… I might have a hot bath or a nap. I haven't decided which one yet."

"Better not be a nap in the bath," Vic warned. "You don't want to drown yourself."

"I wouldn't drown. That only happens if you are drunk or something. Otherwise, the water wakes you up!"

Vic eyed her, shaking her head. "Don't do it. Pick one or the other or I'm going to have to supervise."

Erin gave a sharp laugh at the suggestion. "You need to go back to your apartment and feed Willie." Erin gestured to him. "Can't you see that this poor man is wasting away?"

Willie chuckled and opened his eyes. He tried a forlorn expression. "She's right, darlin'."

Vic laughed and motioned for him to join her. They went in their separate directions, leaving Erin alone with the animals, trying to decide her course of action.

"Erin?"

Erin startled awake, splashing the water and realizing that it was cooling down and the tub needed to be refilled if she were going to stay in any longer.

"I'm not asleep!" she told Terry, who was poking his head in the door. "I was just thinking with my eyes closed."

"It's time to get out. Why don't you come cuddle on the couch? Or head to bed. You don't want to fall asleep in there."

Erin moved drowsily. The water swirled around her, waking her up more. She rubbed her face.

"Yeah, I'll come cuddle," she agreed. She might just fall asleep on the couch and stay there. "How was everything at Auntie Clem's? Went smoothly?"

"There are still too many outsiders hanging around. I don't like it. But they were able to close without any incidents. And I made sure that the burglar alarm was set and everything was locked up tight."

Erin nodded. They'd had a break-in recently and, while Terry thought it was because the burglar alarm had not been set, Erin was sure that it had been, and that the burglar, a professional thief, had known how to bypass it. Beaver had told her that it wouldn't be that hard for someone who knew the system. But Terry felt better having supervised the closing and seen for himself that the burglar alarm had been set, and it didn't hurt to have him double-checking and making his presence known. Outsiders would notice that the police were keeping a close eye on the bakery and its employees and would be less likely to cause any trouble.

If they were actually there to cause trouble. Erin hoped that most of them were just there to try out the muffins and not to threaten her. Even Chalmers hadn't threatened to use the gun she carried. She seemed shocked that anyone would even think that. Erin thought she just felt better having a gun in her purse for self-defense, even if she never used it.

In a few minutes, Erin was out of the tub, had slipped into her comfy nighttime t-shirt and shorts, and joined Terry on the couch while he surfed for a movie to watch on the TV. Erin was wider awake than she had expected to be. Maybe the almost-nap in the tub had been all she needed to refresh herself for the rest of the evening.

"I made a snack," Terry pointed out unnecessarily, pointing to the chips, pretzels, and drinks he had assembled. Not really a good replacement for supper, but Erin didn't have the energy to make anything and Terry probably didn't either. They both just wanted to sit down and relax after a long and taxing day.

Half an hour into a drama that Erin wasn't following very well, K9 suddenly sat up, ears pricked, and looked toward the door. Erin looked out the window and waited for someone to approach the front door and ring the doorbell. She couldn't see anyone, but K9 could clearly hear someone out there. He got to his feet, sniffed the air under the bottom of the door to get their scent, and paced back and forth, waiting to be let outside.

"What's going on out there?" Terry asked him. "Something wrong, K9? What's going on?"

K9 sat down and whined to be let outside. Since his dog run was out the back of the house, not the front, Erin knew he didn't just want to go out to relieve himself or play with Nilla.

"Terry, do you think something is going on?"

He got up from his seat on the couch and went over to the door. K9 stood up when Terry put his hand on the doorknob, alert and waiting to be released. Terry patted his hip before appearing to remember that he was no longer wearing his duty belt.

"I'll be right back," he muttered, and went down the hall to the bedroom to retrieve his gun. Erin watched K9, worried about what might be going on. She had brushed Terry's concerns off as an over-reaction, but maybe she had been wrong.

Terry returned. With his gun in one hand, held down and out of the way, he used his other hand to slowly open the door, telling K9 to stay where he was so that he wouldn't dart out.

"Somebody out there?" he called, holding the gun out of view, inside the house. Not like some cop show on TV where he would have jammed it out the door ahead of him without knowing who might be in the yard.

Erin heard the yell of "murderer!" and some shouting back and forth that she couldn't make out.

"Get out of here, or you're going to end up in jail," Terry warned. Erin stood up to join him, but he caught her movement in his peripheral vision and motioned her to stay back.

There was laughter and more catcalling, and then whoever was out there seemed to have run off, footsteps and laughter and shouting fading off into the distance.

Terry muttered something under his breath and started to close the door again; then, something caught his attention, and he stepped out onto the front steps to look at the other side of the door and the front of the house. He swore.

"What is it?" Erin asked, moving forward, then stopping

because he had told her to stay put just a moment before. She pressed him further. "What's going on? Who was it? What did you see?"

Terry called K9 out of the house and nodded to Erin. "It's okay. You're safe. Our friends just decided to buy some eggs before coming over here."

"Oh, really?" Erin shook her head. "Why would anyone do that?" She joined Terry on the steps to look at the mess the raw eggs had made when they had struck the house.

"I guess they wanted a concrete way to express their displeasure," Terry advised.

K9 sniffed at the vandalism and began to lap up the raw eggs that were within his reach. Erin giggled. K9 was going to think that the vandals really were his friends. They had brought him this nice treat of raw eggs.

"I'll get the hose and rinse off the ones K9 can't reach," Terry advised. "Why don't you just relax while I take care of it? It's easy to clean up while it's fresh."

"Did you see who it was?"

"Out-of-towners. No one I recognized."

"More Montgomery fans."

"I guess so."

"Do they think I killed him on purpose?" Erin shook her head. "How could anyone think that? Why would I do such a thing? How would that benefit me?"

"Well, you are getting a lot more business, especially people who want to buy the new muffins."

"Really?" Erin rolled her eyes at Terry. "Don't you think I would have gotten a lot more business if I'd actually managed to get a good review from him? A positive review would have been better than him dying."

"You don't expect people to be logical about it, do you?" Terry asked. "They aren't acting from a place of logic. They know that you're the one who gave him the muffins he was allergic to so, therefore, you must have wanted to kill him for some nefarious purpose."

Erin shook her head. "I can't believe people think I would do something like that on purpose. My whole reason for running the bakery is so that people with gluten-free diets or food sensitivities have a variety of good food to choose from. I didn't set up shop to murder people."

Terry shrugged and walked over to the end of the house to get the garden hose, which he uncoiled so he could wash off the rest of the raw egg.

As he'd pointed out, the fans weren't acting logically. It was all just an emotional reaction.

Hopefully, in a few days, all would be forgotten and everything would return to normal.

CHAPTER 23

*S*unday was Erin's day to rest and relax, to take some time
away from Auntie Clem's and make sure she was prepared
for the next week. Auntie Clem's was closed every Sunday. Everything in town was closed on Sunday for the sabbath. But they did
hold a ladies' tea following Sunday services, for the women to get
together and gossip and have some tea and treats. Erin rather liked
the tradition now, though she had been a mite put out initially
when the church ladies had insisted that, atheist or not, she couldn't
run her business on Sunday, but that they expected her to reinsti-
tute the ladies' tea that Clementine used to hold at the tea shop
that had been the predecessor to the bakery.

Most of the time, Erin had other employees run the ladies' tea
so that she had all Sunday off. But she had been worried about
problems from the Montgomery fans when they discovered that the
bakery was closed and they were being barred from ordering more
Morning Sunshine Muffins. And that only the usual attendees of
the ladies' tea were being allowed to attend.

With Sheriff Wilmot on the back door and Terry screening
attendees at the front and only allowing Bald Eagle Falls residents
in, they had managed to keep the disruption to a minimum.
However, Erin was still happy when it was finished. She could go

home and sit down with her planner to work through the next week's activities and make sure she stayed on top of the birthday orders, holidays, specials to be advertised in the weekly paper, and whatever else she needed to keep track of.

She let out a long breath of relief, settling into the little attic office in her house, which was the perfect retreat away from the busy world. Terry and Vic both knew that if Erin was in the attic, she was not to be disturbed.

She had her cup of tea, planner, colored pens, highlighters, and flags. An hour or two of solitude in her attic room, and she would have everything laid out for the upcoming week. Things would undoubtedly change, but that was just the nature of planning. She would do her best and then adjust as real life happened.

Erin arranged her pens the way she liked them and opened her planning binder. She started to flip through the planning pages for the previous week, recalling how she had expected the week to unfold and evaluating how many of her set goals she had been able to achieve and where things had not worked out as expected. Gerald Montgomery dying had definitely not been in her plans.

But she had still been a part of the show. There had been a tasting but no review, and she had made the new muffins available to the general public, so those things had unfolded as expected. There had been a bigger run on the muffins than she had anticipated, and they were still going strong. Montgomery's fans were making a pilgrimage to the town where he had died and eating the last thing he had eaten as a way to connect with his memory and to honor him.

Erin's finger caught against a smooth card tucked into the front pocket of the planner a couple of times before she turned the pages all to a closed position to see what it was.

Gerald Montgomery's allergy card. Erin held her breath as she inched it out of the slot, sure she would see what everyone had told her must be there—the inclusion of strawberries in the list.

She pulled the card all the way out and read it another time.

She had read it three times before she could believe what she saw.

"Terry?"

She wasn't usually one to bellow across the house. She didn't like shouted conversations and preferred to be in the same room as the person she was talking to.

Terry didn't even hear her over whatever game he was watching on TV.

Erin whistled. "K9," she called, "get Terry."

A moment later, she could hear Terry chastising K9, trying to get him to lie down and be quiet. But then his manner changed. The sound was muted on the TV.

"Erin? Are you okay?"

"Come up here. I need to show you something."

She could imagine his rolled eyes. He sighed heavily as he got up to deal with whatever Erin wanted to show him, sure that nothing was more important than his game. It was his day off. Time to relax, not to deal with an addition to his honey-do list. But he didn't make any complaint as he walked down the hall and up the pull-down stairs.

"What's up?" he asked in a flat voice, attempting but not quite succeeding in hiding his irritation at his game being interrupted.

Erin pointed to the card on her desk. Terry got closer to see what it was, and his brows shot up.

"Where did you find it?" he demanded.

"It was in my planner. I guess I tucked it inside and forgot about it."

"You've touched it?"

"Around the edges. Sorry, I didn't think about fingerprints until I got it out and realized what it was."

"That's okay. I have your fingerprints on file. We can eliminate those and see if we pull anyone's prints other than yours and Mr. Montgomery's."

"And Vic's. He handed it to her first."

Terry sighed and shrugged. "That's a lot of people handling it. But maybe we can find a print that doesn't belong to someone with a good reason for having handled it."

"Does that mean you think it was intentional? That someone made sure that we got this card instead of the right one?"

"Well, no. The simplest explanation is that it was just a mix-up. An accident. Like we discussed before, it's easy to mix up two nearly identical cards."

"It doesn't have strawberries on it," Erin pointed out. She knew that he'd already looked at it and doubtless noted this fact, but she felt the need to draw attention to it. She and Vic were vindicated. Montgomery *had* given her a card without strawberries on it.

"No," Terry agreed. "It is one of the old cards. Identical, with the exception of strawberries."

"He should have looked at it," Erin told herself. "He should have looked at it before he handed it to us to make sure that it had been updated."

Terry nodded. "He should have been more careful. I know that his fans are trying to put this all on you and say that you did something wrong, but the responsibility was on Montgomery himself. He should never have eaten unfamiliar, untested food alone. He should have kept his auto-injectors closer at hand. He shouldn't have been so far from a hospital. He should have checked to make sure he gave you the right card, even read the list of items to you out loud and then noticed that it was missing strawberries. He should have looked at the list of ingredients for each food he ate instead of being surprised."

Erin nodded. She knew all of that was true, but she couldn't help feeling like she was just as guilty as Montgomery for what had happened. It had been an accident, but she could have done more. She could have insisted that he read the ingredient lists. She could have specifically asked about strawberries, which she knew had high histamine levels that could aggravate someone allergic to multiple foods, even if they hadn't been identified as a specific trigger.

She was sure there were other things that she could have done. But she had been flattered by Montgomery being there to review Auntie Clem's and hadn't wanted to do anything that would jeopardize the review. When he had said she shouldn't tell him what was in the muffins, she should have anyway, as a responsible baker who knew she was dealing with someone with multiple allergies.

She could have called them Strawberry Sunburst Muffins. Nothing in the bakery should be a surprise.

"It isn't your fault," Terry repeated. "He should have been more careful of his own health."

"I know."

Terry's expression told her he understood that even if she didn't admit it, she still felt like she was the responsible party.

"This shows that it was accidental and not malicious or negligent," he told her, pointing to the card.

"But you never thought it was."

"Of course not. After getting to know you, I knew there was no way. That's just not you. And if you did want someone dead—and I have no clue why you would want Montgomery dead—you wouldn't do it with food. I just know that."

Erin couldn't imagine how she would kill someone if she wanted to. She wasn't a violent person, and stabbing or shooting seemed far beyond her abilities as a moral and compassionate person. It was one thing to protect herself. But premeditated murder? She couldn't see herself ever doing it. But if she did, Terry was right; she would never intentionally feed someone poison or an allergen.

"Leave it there," Terry instructed, pointing to the card. "I'm just going to grab gloves and a bag."

He went back down the attic stairs.

Erin took a picture of the card on her desk and texted it to Vic.

Vic immediately texted back a stream of startled emojis.

You found it! She texted after the emojis. *Where was it?*

In my planner

A laughing emoji. *I should have known*

The planner is the key to all knowledge Erin agreed.

CHAPTER 24

*E*rin went to the bakery with a lighter heart the next day. Despite her worries about people still thinking that she had killed Montgomery intentionally or had been careless in giving him something she should have known was an allergen, she was happier just being cleared in her own mind. Whether anyone else believed her or not didn't matter.

The fans would keep coming to the bakery; some would believe her and some would not. If they didn't, they were just wrong. Too bad for them. Erin wasn't responsible for what anyone else thought.

She had always been a people pleaser. At least as long as she could remember. She wanted people to believe her, to like her, and to think the best of her. But she was beginning to see that none of that really mattered. She could live with it as long as she knew she had not done anything wrong. And as Terry had said, Montgomery was largely responsible for his own death.

Erin was in the kitchen of Auntie Clem's when her phone vibrated with a text message, so she took a moment to pull it out and check to see what the message was. She would never do that out in front of the customers. She asked her employees not to text or do other things that would distract them while working in the kitchen but, as she had finished her kitchen tasks and was just heading to the front, it seemed like the ideal time to take a quick peek at the message.

It was from Melissa. She must not have been able to get away from the police department and didn't dare let anyone hear her phoning Erin to tell her the latest news.

Erin's eyes flashed over the words.

ME's decision is in

Erin knew that Melissa was hoping for a reaction. And that she should not encourage this kind of gossip and drama from Melissa.

But she wanted to know. She had to know. And that was exactly why Melissa had texted her.

She hesitated, not leaving the kitchen and taking her place at the counter. She decided to take one more minute before resuming her place at the counter.

What?

Melissa kept her hanging, not answering immediately. Had she been interrupted by someone she didn't want to see her texting? Or was she trying to increase the tension?

Erin refrained from any response to try to hurry Melissa along. If Melissa wanted Erin's reaction, she would have to spill the beans. And she had to do it before Erin went back out front.

Finally, her phone vibrated again.

Accidental death

Erin gave a sigh of relief. That was it, then. The case was over. It was decided. It was an accidental death, and she didn't need to worry about the police coming after her. They knew that it had just been the perfect set of circumstances that had unfolded to cause Montgomery's death. They knew Erin had been given the wrong information about his allergies and had no way of knowing it was strawberries.

It was all over.

~

She couldn't stop thinking about it, but she kept reminding herself that the case had been decided and she didn't need to worry about it anymore.

Charley was working the afternoon shift and Erin told her the results. Charley pursed her lips and looked thoughtful, but didn't raise any objections.

"So you're okay now?"

Erin nodded. "Yeah. I'm good. Everything is decided. I don't need to worry about anything."

Charley indicated the customers with her eyes. "Only about any more wackos."

"I'm sure we won't see too much more of that. People will get bored with the muffins and move on to the next big thing."

"Probably… sooner or later…"

"Soon," Erin said. "We've seen… *unusual deaths* here before, and once people have had a chance to talk about them… they just kind of drift away again. People only stay interested for a few days, and then they move on to something else."

Charley nodded. She had been involved in her own case and had seen Erin work her way through several more since then. She knew the pattern as well as Erin.

"Did you drop this?" One of the customers Erin didn't recognize bent down to pick up an envelope from the floor.

Erin frowned at it. "No, what is that? Does it have a name on it?"

The woman turned it over and back again. She handed it over the display case to Erin. Erin took it and saw that her name was handwritten on one side. She shook her head and put it into her apron pocket.

"I have no idea what that is. I'll take a look at it later."

She sold the woman a Morning Sunshine Muffin, and the next couple of people too. Then, a familiar face, Mary Lou.

"What can I get for you?" Erin asked. "Do you want one of the —" Erin started to point out the Morning Sunshine Muffins and then stopped herself. "Oh! I never did give you your reserved Morning Sunshine Muffin. What happened to that? Someone must have taken it, but it was labeled with your name…"

Mary Lou held up a hand to stop her. "No, it's fine. Don't worry about it. I told them to give it to someone else. I really... didn't want it after Mr. Montgomery..." Mary Lou shrugged, looking away. "After he passed, I really didn't have any interest in having one of those muffins. I'm sure they're just fine. They sound perfect, but I couldn't. Not knowing that they had caused a man's death."

"Oh. I see. I understand."

"I'm sure they're fine," Mary Lou repeated. "I'm not big on sweets and, after hearing the news, I really didn't have any appetite for them."

"That's actually how I expected *everyone* to respond," Erin said with a small laugh. "I didn't think I'd have this big run on them. It really surprised me."

"It seems... a little morbid, to be honest," Mary Lou said with a note of relief in her voice that Erin hadn't overreacted to her rejection of the Morning Sunshine Muffins.

"I thought so too," Erin agreed. "I mean, I'm happy to make them and have people buy them. But I didn't expect so many people to want them. Not because they're a great muffin, but because someone died after eating one." Erin shuddered. "It's more than a little creepy. But if that's what people want..."

"Give them what they want," Mary Lou agreed. "I've learned to be a salesperson at the General Store. If people want a particular product... sell them that product. If there is a run, get more. Encourage fads, challenges, viral sales, whatever. If that's what people want to spend their money on, then give it to them."

"Yep," Erin agreed. She had learned the same thing. She couldn't predict what would be hot but, if people came in demanding Morning Sunshine Muffins, she would give them Morning Sunshine Muffins. "Now, what can I get for you today? What would *you* like?"

Mary Lou looked over the offerings. "Two loaves of bread, twelve rolls, and... how about brownies? Roger and Joshua both like brownies."

"Sure," Erin agreed. "How many do you want? Four?"

Mary Lou wouldn't likely eat them herself. So Erin calculated two each for her husband and son. Mary Lou was frugal, but liked to get them a little treat each week. Just something small to make them happy.

"Yes," Mary Lou nodded. "That should be good."

Erin packaged up her order, and Mary Lou counted the money out for Charley on the counter next to the cash register.

~

Erin didn't think about the envelope again until they were nearly finished closing. Her hand touched her apron pocket and she felt the envelope and looked down at it again.

"Oh, right." She pulled it out and looked at the handwriting again. She didn't recognize the writing. Who would have written her a note and then carelessly let it fall to the floor in the bakery? Had she handed it to Erin or placed it on the counter for her, and Erin had been thinking of other things and brushed it to the floor while filling the next customer's order? She couldn't remember anything like that happening. She didn't recall seeing the envelope until the customer had handed it to her.

"What is it?" Charley asked as Erin slid her finger under the flap to tear it open.

"I don't know. We'll find out in a minute here…"

She slid the folded white copy paper out and flicked it open. There was only one sentence handwritten in block letters in the middle of the page.

I did you a favor

Erin shivered despite the heat of the kitchen.

"What is it?" Charley repeated, approaching her this time to look at it. Erin held it for her but, when Charley reached for it, Erin pulled it back, not letting her touch it. Charley read it and looked at Erin's face.

"Who did you a favor? What's that about?"

"I don't know. It doesn't make any sense. But what if it's about… Montgomery's death. What if it means…"

Erin didn't finish the sentence. Her brain was already racing ahead, calculating all of the possibilities.

"Montgomery's death? You mean that someone intended for him to die?" Charley asked, shaking her head and frowning, brows knitted together.

"I don't know. What else could it mean? It sounds like… it almost sounds like a threat. Or the beginning of some blackmail scheme. 'I took care of your problem. Now it's your turn to take care of mine.'"

"But there isn't any demand."

"Maybe that's coming next."

Charley shrugged and nodded, agreeing that it was possible.

"You'd better call your sweetheart, then."

Erin realized it was true. She resisted the idea. The Montgomery case was closed. Why cause trouble?

"But there hasn't been any threat or ask, so maybe I should just wait until there is. And I don't know who left it for me. It could be anyone. Shouldn't I wait until we know who sent it and why?"

"Sure, if that's what you want to do," Charley said. A little too fast. Erin always had to check herself if Charley agreed with her too quickly.

"I can't really tell the police anything yet."

"You have physical evidence." Charley indicated the piece of paper. "They could test the paper. Test it for prints or DNA. Analyze the handwriting. Match it if they can find a suspect."

Charley was right, unfortunately. The police department would want to analyze the letter.

If they believed it was related to Montgomery's killing or another crime. But they believed that Montgomery's death was an accident. The ME had just closed the case on it. Why reopen it again without any evidence that it was something else? Anyone could have left the letter. It didn't have to be someone who had any connection with Montgomery or his death. She had seen the kind of things his fans did, things that made no sense to her.

They came into the bakery throwing around accusations, calling her a murderer. They egged her house. And they came to buy the muffins that had killed their idol, as if it were some kind of sacrament that would transform them and bring them closer to Montgomery even in death.

How could she make sense of someone like that? How could she predict their behavior or what they intended by leaving her the note?

Erin sighed. "I guess I'd better let Terry know. But maybe he won't want it."

"Maybe," Charley said, though it was clear from her tone of voice that she didn't think this likely.

Terry answered his phone almost instantly when Erin called. Maybe he had been watching the clock and worrying that she would run into trouble around closing.

"Erin. How's it going?" His voice was deliberately casual.

"I'm fine. Everything is fine," she assured him immediately. "I just… Charley thought I should call you. I got this strange letter… message… I don't know what it means. But it isn't threatening. It isn't clear what they intended by leaving it here…"

"What letter? What are you talking about?"

"It was just something that was left in the store. It was on the floor. And I'm not worried about it. I know the Montgomery case is closed, so you don't want anything else that might be related to that, right?"

"Well, if it is, then I guess we need to know about it. What does it say? What makes you think it has something to do with Montgomery's death?"

"It just says, 'I did you a favor.'"

"I did you a favor."

"Yeah."

"And that's it?"

Erin nodded impatiently. "Yeah. That's it. Like I said, it doesn't mean anything… or I don't know what it means…"

"Charley is right. I should probably have a look at it. At least log it into evidence, just in case."

CHAPTER 25

*T*erry took the message into evidence and promised to check it for fingerprints or other clues, but he didn't seem to think it was too important.

"There are a lot of crackpots in town right now, making the pilgrimage here after Montgomery's death, wanting to walk in his footsteps." Terry shrugged and shook his head. "Can't say I understand it or his popularity. From what I have seen, he wasn't a very pleasant person and had a lot of enemies. But he had his fans, too. This…" he indicated the unfolded sheet of paper. "This is probably nothing. Just a prank. Someone who wants some attention. He wants to see if we panic over it. But… we will follow up on it, just in case it is serious."

"But you don't think it is," Erin looked over at Charley. Just as she had expected, Terry didn't think it was anything of importance. He said they would follow up on it, but that probably didn't mean anything more than checking it for fingerprints.

Charley made a face at Erin. "I told you that you should call him."

"But they're not going to do anything about it."

"Erin," Terry frowned and used an exasperated tone, "I told you that we *would* follow up on it."

"Yeah. But you don't think it is anything to be concerned about."

"Well, no. But that doesn't mean I won't take it seriously. We will still follow up on it."

Erin shrugged. She wasn't expecting much. "You don't think it has anything to do with Montgomery's death."

"I don't think…" Terry's brows knitted as he tried to put together the words he wanted. "It may be *because* of Montgomery's death. It may be one of his fans. But I don't think that anyone did anything to cause his death. It was just an accident, an unfortunate set of circumstances. You know that. It was determined to be an accidental death. The police department and the medical examiner's office in the city agree on that point."

"It *could* have been engineered."

"Whose idea was it to put strawberries in the muffins?"

Erin opened her mouth, then closed it again. She thought about it. "Well… mine."

"And what was the one thing left off of the allergy card?"

"Strawberries."

"So unless *you* took strawberries off of the allergy card, this wasn't engineered. No one meant for this to happen."

"They might have taken strawberries off the list and just hoped that sooner or later someone would feed him strawberries."

"And that he wouldn't know it? That they wouldn't be billed as strawberry compote muffins? What were the chances, really, that someone would feed him strawberries not knowing about the allergy and that he would eat them not knowing that they contained strawberries?"

Erin had to admit it was a stretch.

Whoever had written the note was just playing games with her. Or they had meant something completely different, and she just thought it had something to do with Montgomery's death because that was what was foremost in her mind these days.

"Okay… you're right. I don't see how anyone could have engineered that."

Terry nodded, satisfied. "I don't want you worrying about

this, Erin. I know we have had a lot of crime in Bald Eagle Falls since you moved here, a lot of violence and death, which is unusual for a little place like this. But not every death is a murder. This was just an accident and you don't need to worry that it was anything more. It was unfortunate, but you can put it behind you. Okay?"

Erin nodded. "I'll try. I think... I don't know. Maybe it is a little bit of PTSD still. You know... hypervigilance. Thinking that there is danger where there is not. Maybe from the other deaths. Maybe just from the way that I grew up, with my parents' death and then growing up in foster care, where I couldn't really trust anyone else to keep me safe."

"Well, you're with me now. And I promise I will keep you safe. I would tell you if this was something to be worried about. But I don't think it is. I think that we still need to be careful of all of the visitors in town, especially the ones who are riled up over his death. But whoever wrote this message, whether they intended you to think that it was from someone who had something to do with Montgomery's death or not, I don't think they did. I can't see how anyone could have influenced enough of the factors involved in this case to have caused his death."

"So you don't think this has anything to do with Montgomery's death."

"I don't think that person had anything to do with Montgomery's death."

"I was afraid that they were going to ask me to do something for them. Since they did me this favor, whatever it is."

"How would killing Montgomery be a favor to you?" Charley asked. "It doesn't benefit you at all. In fact, you've got people calling you a murderer and throwing eggs at your house."

"Well... it has gotten me a lot of business with people coming here to taste the muffins."

"But how could anyone predict that? They didn't do it for you."

"They could still see that it was a benefit afterward and then decide to use that against me. Or... to get something from me. I don't know yet." Erin looked at Terry. "Do you think I'll get another one? Telling me to do something that is... illegal or unethical?"

"Maybe, maybe not. It probably depends on how you respond to this one. If you don't appear affected, maybe they just let it go. I don't know if they intend to follow up with a 'part two.' You can't expect these cranks to act logically."

"I know," Erin agreed. But she was wondering whether it really was a crank, or whether it was someone who had planned everything out carefully.

Terry had convinced her that if Montgomery's death had been intentional, the killer had been very clever in setting it up.

CHAPTER 26

I love it when we can get to the community market," Vic declared. She took a deep breath of air laden with the scents of baking, scented candles, flowers, and fried food. "There's nothing like a country market to whet your appetite and make you glad to be alive."

"And to make you spend your money," Erin added.

Vic grinned. "Well, you don't have to, but how else are you going to get a taste of those little fried donuts and the harvests coming in from the fields? If you get those fresh fruits and veggies, it offsets anything bad you eat."

"It is a lot of fun," Erin agreed. "And a great way to get super fresh ingredients. I'm going to put fresh blueberries in the muffins this week instead of frozen. They're so ripe right now that they practically pop when you put them in your mouth. So sweet and juicy…"

Vic mimed wiping her face with the back of her hand. "You're making me drool!"

"I love fresh berries."

"I'm hoping the Jam Lady might be back in business this year. I sure have missed those wonderful jams since the Jam Lady went out of business."

Erin thought about Mary Lou's husband Roger, the cook behind the Jam Lady label, though very few people knew it. She didn't know if he still had the ability to make the wonderful, flavorful jams that he had made before he'd had to go to the institution for treatment. Now that he was back, on fairly heavy medication, she could only hope that he would still able to produce another batch of his beautiful, jewel-tone jams.

"That *would* be good," she agreed. "Good news for everyone."

Vic nodded.

They made their way down the line of stalls, examining all of the wares. Everything from fresh fruits and vegetables to preserves and handicrafts, to quilts and furniture and harvest tools that cost hundreds of dollars. They really did have everything. It was hard not to go all -out and spend way too much money. Erin had learned that she needed to be critical and fight the urge to get everything that looked good.

It was midafternoon and the weather was hot despite the umbrellas and awnings that shaded most of the booths and tables from direct sunlight. Erin had her water bottle with her but, before long, she was looking for somewhere to refill the bottle and get into an air-conditioned space for a while.

"Maybe we could stop in at the General Store."

"They have a booth," Vic pointed out.

"I know. But I need to get out of this heat."

Vic refrained from saying, "But it isn't even hot out." She looked at Erin. "You're looking a mite red," she admitted. "We'd best get out somewhere cool for a bit."

Erin led the way to the General Store, and they entered. Like Auntie Clem's, the shop had bells over the door that tinkled quietly when Vic and Erin entered.

They browsed until Mary Lou came out from the back room to see who was there.

"Oh, Erin and Vic. I didn't know you were stopping in today."

"We were at the market, but I was getting overheated," Erin explained. "I need your air conditioning."

"It's always nice to shop out-of-doors," Mary Lou observed. "Until you need to get away from the out-of-doors."

Vic chuckled. "Ha. You're right."

They continued to browse through the shelves of the General Store, which boasted a wide variety of practical and decorative items, some of which were made or sourced locally and others special-ordered. Erin could always count on being tempted by something when she went to the General Store. Like going to a candy store, toy store, or little corner market when she was a kid.

"It's funny, we were just talking about Jam Lady," Erin told Mary Lou. "Wondering whether there would be any new stock coming in."

"Well, you never know," Mary Lou said. "Not yet, but… things change from one day to the next. I'm never quite sure what to expect. I am hopeful that he will improve enough to start cooking again… but as it is…" Mary Lou looked around the store to ensure no other customers were within hearing distance. "He can't be left in the kitchen. And for one of us to be there to supervise… well, we need the time."

"We sure would love it if he could produce another batch," Erin told her with a warm smile. "But of course we would never push. It all depends on what he can do and what you have the time and energy for."

Mary Lou nodded her agreement. "And how was the market? Were you enjoying yourself? Before you got too hot?"

"Definitely." Erin lifted her canvas bag bulging with goodies. "Too much!"

"Ah, that's good. I look forward to whatever ends up in your baking."

"Me too. I like my own baking just a little too much," Erin confessed, putting a hand over her stomach, which was definitely thicker than it had been when she had arrived in Bald Eagle Falls.

"You work hard," Vic dismissed. "You look just fine."

Erin rolled her eyes and looked for a way to change the subject. She wished she could stay as slim as Vic, but her body had other ideas. She didn't want to complain to Vic, who had body image issues of her own to deal with. But she didn't think she looked "just fine."

"It's too bad that strawberries are out of season. We've been going through so many in the Morning Sunshine Muffins. I still have some more preserves that we bought earlier in the season. But we'll be out soon."

"How long do you think this run on the muffins will last?"

"Who knows? It's crazy. I had no idea so many people would want to eat Gerald Montgomery's last meal." She shook her head.

"You might be able to pick up some more preserves at the B&B. Mrs. McClung was saying that she had such a bumper crop. She put up dozens of jars."

"Oh, I'll check it out! Thanks for the tip."

"If you're going over there…" Mary Lou hesitated.

"What?"

"I just have an order for her. She hasn't been able to stop by to get it yet. Like you, she's been overrun by sightseers and hasn't been able to get away."

"I'd be happy to take them over," Erin said immediately.

Vic looked at her with surprise. They had planned to spend several hours at the market, not running other errands.

"You don't have to come," Erin told her. "I was just thinking… I've never actually been there. Maybe Terry and I will take a little vacation there one day. Who says you have to go out of town for a getaway?"

"I thought it was implied in the name," Mary Lou said dryly. "A getaway?"

"Well, we would get away from the house and hopefully away from work for a day or two."

Vic was looking at Erin with a frown. "I've never heard you or Terry talk about going to the B&B."

"Well… I guess we haven't talked about it around you."

That didn't clear up the frown on Vic's face, but she didn't argue. Mary Lou looked thoughtful.

"Maybe there is something else you wanted to check out at the bed and breakfast,"

"Oh," Vic's face suddenly lit with understanding. "You want to snoop."

Erin's cheeks got hot. She couldn't very well deny it. But she didn't like the slant that the word "snoop" put on it. "I just want to... have a look around. See where it happened."

"What is that going to tell you?" Vic demanded. "You aren't going to find out anything new by looking around there."

"Who knows?" Erin shrugged. "Maybe it's just morbid curiosity, like all of the people coming to buy muffins at Auntie Clem's. I want to be where he was. I want to have a look around. I know I won't be able to figure anything out... but I still want to see."

"What is there to figure out?" Mary Lou asked. "Montgomery was killed by an allergic reaction."

"I know, I know," Erin agreed, not wanting to have to argue it with anyone. She had already been thoroughly put in her place by Terry.

There was no way that the allergic reaction could have been planned. No one had known what Erin was making. Nothing had been added to the muffins to poison Montgomery. He had just had a reaction to one of the ingredients Erin had included. And she hadn't known because he had given her the wrong card. It would never have happened if she had not been given the wrong card.

But no one had put the wrong card in his wallet intentionally. And no one had known that by doing so, Erin would give Montgomery something with strawberries in it. She rarely put strawberries in muffins. It wasn't a common muffin ingredient.

"I know it wasn't deliberate. It wasn't poisoning or something that anyone set up. But I still want to see, to understand what happened."

Vic was standing slightly behind Erin, and Erin had the feeling that Vic had made a gesture or facial expression to Mary Lou, warning her not to push it any further. They were humoring her. Letting her have her crazy theory in hopes that sooner or later, she would drop it on her own.

"I would be happy to help by taking your order to Mrs. McClung," Erin told Mary Lou firmly. "And I can ask her about strawberries and see if I can buy some extra preserves from her. If she has that many, she probably won't mind parting with a few jars."

She looked at Mary Lou and then back over her shoulder at Vic. Neither of them disagreed. Erin had two perfectly legitimate reasons for going to the bed and breakfast. It didn't matter whether she was just curious or had serious theories about how Montgomery's death could have been staged. She didn't need any other reason.

"Well, that would be a big help to me," Mary Lou declared. "Thank you so much for your kind offer. You make sure you stay inside here until you have cooled down enough to be outside again. And let me fill your water bottle."

Erin handed it over with a smile of gratitude.

They continued to browse and chat until Erin felt cool and relaxed and didn't think she would have problems walking over to the B&B with Mary Lou's delivery. Erin bought a few little items from the General Store to pay her way for standing around using their air conditioning for so long.

CHAPTER 27

$\mathcal{E}$rin had never been inside the bed and breakfast. She had only heard it referred to. Of course, most of the Bald Eagle Falls residents had never actually stayed there because, as Mary Lou said, when people wanted a getaway, they left town. They got away.

Since the closing of the Inn, the B&Bs had picked up the slack and, from what Erin heard, were usually booked up.

The house was similar in age to the one Erin had inherited from Clementine, but it was two stories tall, with bedrooms upstairs instead of on the main floor. Probably twice as many square feet as Erin's house.

She recognized the curly-haired woman who answered the door, looking questioning.

"Mrs. McClung. I brought you over a delivery from the General Store. We were just over there, so I thought I would pop by with it."

Mrs. McClung took the box from her slowly. "You're Erin Price, aren't you, the baker? You aren't working at the General Store now?"

"No, we were just saying hi to Mary Lou. She said that you had a bumper crop of strawberries this year."

Mrs. McClung looked even more confused by this segue.

"Yes, it was a very good year for strawberries."

"I am running out of strawberries, and she suggested you might have a few extra jars you would like to get rid of."

"Oh!" Mrs. McClung laughed and shook her head. "I had no idea what this was all about. So you came here to give me the delivery and find out if I had any strawberries you could buy?"

Erin nodded. "That's pretty much it," she agreed. Of course, she was still hoping to go in and look around but, if Mrs. McClung didn't invite her inside, she would have to find another credible excuse to ask.

"Well, that was very nice of you." Mrs. McClung opened her door wider. "Why don't you come in while I get you a few jars? You too, Miss Victoria."

Vic gave her a smile and followed Erin into the house. She looked around.

"I've never been in here before. This is very nice, Mrs. McClung."

Mrs. McClung looked at her and didn't say anything. Erin had found that some of the Bald Eagle Falls residents really didn't know how to talk to someone who was transgender, or disapproved of her and didn't think they should speak to her, as if they might somehow be contaminated with her "sin." At least she had invited Vic into the house and hadn't made her wait on the porch.

Mrs. McClung left them to go find the jars of strawberry jam and Vic rolled her eyes at Erin.

"Sorry," Erin apologized. "Some people are just... stubborn."

Vic nodded. "I'm a bit stubborn myself sometimes," she admitted. "Can't blame others for the same fault."

Erin snickered. Vic being a "bit stubborn" was like saying that Everest was a bit tall. She and Willie had some real set-tos when they disagreed, neither one willing to back down.

Erin glanced around to see if anyone else were around, maybe other guests of the B&B, but they seemed to be alone. She wandered around a bit rather than staying at the door where Mrs. McClung had left them. Vic watched her but didn't raise any objection about how rude Erin was being snooping around while Mrs. McClung fetched the strawberries.

Erin went to the bottom of the stairs but couldn't think of a good excuse for ascending them to look at the other rooms. Mrs. McClung returned with a box containing several jars of strawberry preserves. She looked askance at Erin.

"I was wondering about coming here for a sort of a date night," Erin said, not waiting for her to ask. "You know, a sort of a couples getaway. I know it's silly, vacationing in town instead of going somewhere more exotic, or at least to the city," she said, remembering Mary Lou's argument, "But I don't like to be too far from the bakery in case something goes wrong, and you know how Officer Piper has to be on call at all times…"

Mrs. McClung forced a smile. "Well then, going somewhere in town sounds like the perfect solution," she agreed.

"Do you think I could see the rooms? At least, the ones that aren't in use right now?"

"I don't know. I don't usually do tours. There are pictures on the website."

"Oh, of course," Erin acknowledged, but she didn't return to the front door. "What was it like having all of the police here? That must have been a unique experience."

"Yes, it certainly was," Mrs. McClung admitted. "I can't say I've ever had a guest die before. I guess it must happen sometimes, especially in bigger places. Big hotels. But it's never happened here before. I didn't know what to do. Who do you call when something like that happens? It isn't exactly an emergency, is it? Nothing the police or doctors can do when the man has been dead all night."

"How did you know he'd been dead all night?"

"Well, heavens… people were calling me trying to reach him all night. Very rude, some of them. They said he wasn't answering his phone and I should wake him up and make him talk to them. Do you think it's my job to wake guests up to make them answer their phones? Ridiculous!"

Erin nodded and made encouraging noises.

"But he didn't come down for breakfast in the morning, and it was getting late. The people from his office were getting upset about it. When he checked in, I told him that I clean the rooms at eleven every morning. By that time, breakfast is over and people are up. They're either sightseeing or want to get started on their trip to the next place, so they want to get an early start. People don't usually stay in bed past ten."

"So you finally decided you'd better check on him and make sure he was okay."

"Yes. I wish now that I had done it sooner, but I really can't breach a guest's privacy that way. People come here to relax and turn off. Honeymoons," she nodded to Erin, reminding her of her fictional plans to come there with Terry. "You can't just interrupt people because they're not answering their phones and certain other people don't like it."

"I would expect my privacy to be protected, too," Vic agreed.

Mrs. McClung gave her a look that clearly stated that Vic would not be allowed to register as a guest at the bed and breakfast. No such hanky-panky would be permitted while she was in charge of the place.

Vic's face got pink, but she didn't say anything.

"What time did Mr. Montgomery get in? And when did people start complaining that he wasn't answering his phone?"

"He was here early in the evening. He brought home a box of goodies from the bakery and didn't offer to share them. He went up to his room. He didn't go out for supper, but I guess he had all those pastries to eat."

"And then people started complaining that he wasn't answering his calls…?"

"A couple of hours later, I guess. Eight, maybe."

"Who was trying to reach him?"

Mrs. McClung favored her with a glare. "Your boyfriend may be a police officer, but I don't think you are, Miss Price."

"No, I'm sorry. I didn't mean to pry. I'm just another of those annoying rubberneckers, I guess. A curiosity-seeker. It is just so bizarre to think that he died right after I saw him. Right after he bought my muffins."

"Because one of them poisoned him," Mrs. McClung pointed out.

"Not poisoned," Vic objected. "He had an allergic reaction to it. There wasn't anything toxic in it. Just... for him."

"Yes, and he was poisoned by it, wasn't he?"

"How big are the rooms?" Erin tried, hoping that if she asked enough questions about them, Mrs. McClung would tell her just to go upstairs and have a look.

"The size of standard bedrooms. There are pictures on the website."

"And Mr. Montgomery's must have been the largest? The master bedroom?"

"Yes."

"Do the rooms all have their own keys?"

Mrs. McClung gave her an odd look.

"Yes, of course. How else would guests keep their rooms secure? I mean, we don't have people wandering in and out of guests' private rooms, but you can't ensure that if they don't have any way to lock their rooms."

"Are they regular keys or key cards like at hotels?"

"Regular keys. And a chain on the inside. We want people to feel safe."

"But Mr. Montgomery didn't have his chain on?"

"What makes you say that?"

"You were able to get in... you didn't say you had to break down the door or get someone to help you with it, so I assume the chain wasn't on."

"No, it wasn't."

"Where are the keys kept? The ones that have not been given out to guests?" Erin assumed there were at least three keys per door. Two keys for double occupancy and a key for Mrs. McClung herself. Maybe another for the maid. Or maybe there was a master key that opened all of the doors, and Mrs. McClung had one, and a part-time maid, and a handyman. There might be half a dozen people who could get into each room easily.

"The keys are kept in my locked drawer," Mrs. McClung said, wrinkling her nose at Erin as if she smelled bad. She pointed at a writing desk. A little faux antique number with a large keyhole on the front of the drawer that could probably be popped open with the long, slim letter opener on the writing surface.

"Did Montgomery have any visitors?"

"He had a TV crew. I don't know how many people. They were coming and going the whole time he was here."

"Or until he came back that evening. Were they coming and leaving from his room after he came back with the muffins?"

"I was told that he was not to be interrupted after that. It was his *artistic process.*"

By her tone of voice, she didn't like artistic people much better than transgender people. Erin rolled her eyes to make Mrs. McClung think that she identified with her on this point.

"I'll bet he was a pain in the neck. All of those artist types are, aren't they?"

Mrs. McClung nodded her agreement. "They always need something else. Making demands. It's like they don't understand that this is my *home.* I'm happy to give them a room and make them breakfast. I keep my house nice and clean and welcoming for them." She spread her hands to indicate their surroundings. "But I'm not a servant. I'm not there to see to every request and serve them hand and foot. *Get me an aspirin for my headache. Take these flowers out of my room. I thought this was a fragrance-free facility.*" She rolled her eyes and shook her head. "Fragrance-free? Where did he even get that?"

It was an odd comment. "Is that what Mr. Montgomery said?" Erin asked. "People with multiple allergies often have environmental triggers. But if you don't advertise the B&B as fragrance-free, I don't know where he would have gotten that."

"Somehow, it's *my* fault that there are flowers in his room? They came to him from his fans. I mean... talk about privilege. I'm supposed to read his mind and know what to put in his room and what not to. Of course I will put any deliveries that come while he is out into his room. I'm keeping them safe and ensuring he gets them right away, and then I'm a bad guy for putting flowers in his room. Good heavens."

"He got a flower delivery?"

"He was getting deliveries all day: flowers, wine, cards, chocolate. I don't know what all of them were. From the time that he booked the room, they were coming. I don't know how so many people knew where he would be staying. It was supposed to be a secret, or so I understood. He made the booking, and no one was supposed to know which days he would be here."

CHAPTER 28

*I*t must have been very exciting to know that such a famous person was going to be coming to the B&B," Erin observed. "I'll bet you were tied in knots trying to make all the arrangements to make it perfect for him."

"I wasn't supposed to go to any trouble for him. Just keep things the same as they always were. They didn't want anyone tipping people off that something unusual was happening. They weren't even supposed to know he was coming to Bald Eagle Falls, but someone obviously leaked that."

Erin nodded. "Yeah, I heard about it from a couple of different directions before he came. That's how I knew to be prepared for him at the bakery."

"By preparing something for him that he was allergic to?"

"Well, no. I didn't know Mr. Montgomery was allergic to strawberries. That wasn't included in his list of allergies, so I didn't know to avoid it. I wanted to make something special for him, and the strawberries this year were so good…" Erin motioned to the bottles of preserves that Mrs. McClung had brought out for her. "It just seemed like a great choice. Something that I didn't usually use in muffins, so it would be a surprise and so nice at the end of the summer. I looked through all kinds of recipes online to figure out what to make for him. And Vic and I watched videos of his past shows online."

Erin tilted her head toward Vic to try to keep her in the conversation despite Mrs. McClung's apparent opinion of her.

"And the videos didn't mention anything about him being allergic to strawberries," Erin went on, "Just like he didn't tell you ahead that he was allergic to flowers or fragrances."

"It would have made things so much easier if he had just been upfront about all that stuff from the start," Mrs. McClung's voice was aggrieved. "To expect me to know anything without telling me... well, that just wasn't fair. If he didn't want flowers in his room, he should have let me know. They were *his* flowers."

"Exactly. How were you supposed to know that?"

"He complained about everything. A light in his room was flickering. His neighbor was playing music he didn't like. He kept getting phone calls. Could *I* help it that he got phone calls? On *his own* phone? How is that my problem? He says he's never had issues like that before. So it must be my fault?"

"Issues like what?" Vic asked, unable to resist participating in the conversation.

"Some prank calls. I don't know. Do you think I asked him for any details? I just nodded and made sympathetic noises, but I couldn't do anything about the calls he got on his phone. He should complain about those to his phone provider or to whoever at his office was giving out his phone number. That woman is here." Mrs. McClung rolled her eyes upward, indicating the rooms on the floor above.

"What woman?"

"The one from his office. The one who is so demanding, constantly calling me up to make sure that I've made this or that arrangement. After telling me that I wasn't supposed to do anything special to prepare for Mr. Montgomery's visit"

"Is that Mavis?" Erin took a stab at it. She remembered the name from Terry's conversation about the business cards.

Mrs. McClung nodded. "That's the one," she agreed. "Mavis. I could think of a lot of other names for her, bless her heart. The woman was a thorn in my side. *Is* a thorn in my side. When is she going to go home? Mr. Montgomery isn't here anymore, so why is she here? Shouldn't she be back at his office taking care of things there? There isn't anything for her to do here,"

"Why *is* she here?" Erin asked curiously. It did seem strange that anyone from Montgomery's office would stay at the bed and breakfast.

"She says she needs to be here for public relations, because of all the fans. Do you know those people keep showing up at the door? Expecting to get a tour of the house? Thinking that I'll take them up to look at the room he died in?" She shook her head in disbelief. "What ghouls! I was afraid I wouldn't be able to rent that room out anymore after someone died there. You know how buildings get a reputation for being haunted, or for being bad luck. I wouldn't want someone else to think that it was a death room, that if they stayed there, they might die."

"That's exactly what I thought about the muffins," Erin told her. "I didn't think I would be able to sell the Morning Sunshine Muffins. Everyone would think they were murder muffins. But they all want them. Everyone who comes into town to mourn Mr. Montgomery's death, or whatever they are doing by coming here."

Mrs. McClung nodded vigorously. "I didn't think I would ever be able to rent that room out again. Or I would have to change its look completely and change the name so no one would know it was the same room."

"But you've already rented it out?" Erin guessed.

"I've had so many inquiries after it that I hardly know what to do with myself. But I don't want to rent it to all those ghouls. What if they rip it all up for mementos? Take the lamp and the bedsheets and the clock? You know how these people are."

"They'll strip it like piranhas," Vic contributed.

"The company has still reserved it, so I haven't had to make a decision about it. But what would you do? They're offering outrageous amounts for it. I could redecorate it for what they're offering to pay. They can have the lamp and the clock for that price; I'll just get a new one. But what if they damage it structurally? Or do some damage that takes hundreds of dollars to fix?"

"It's still reserved by the production company?" Erin asked.

"Yes, that Meals and Reels. Until next week."

"And Mavis is staying in his room?"

Erin supposed that eliminated any hope she had of being able to see the room where Montgomery had died.

But did she really want to? Maybe it was best if she didn't have the option. She wouldn't have nightmares about it.

"No, she is staying in one of the other rooms. The one that he died in is still sitting empty."

"And it's the big one? You don't think I could see if it is what I want for my getaway with Officer Piper?" Erin suggested. "You can come with me, and I promise I won't strip it down. I just wanted to see if it would be… suitable."

Mrs. McClung frowned. "Maybe some other time."

CHAPTER 29

*E*rin nodded slowly. "I guess you're probably run off your feet with all this stuff. I don't want to add to your work."

Mrs. McClung nodded. She motioned to the box of strawberry preserves jars. "We can settle up for these." Her eyes went to the box Erin had brought from the General store. "And I do appreciate you bringing this over for me. That was a very nice thing to do."

"Mary Lou knew how busy you must be and wanted to make sure you got it," Erin said with a nod.

Mrs. McClung ran a key through the tape at the top of the box to slice it open, then pulled it open. She took out a couple of fat white candles and held them up to her nose. "I just love these vanilla candles that the General Store carries. They are so nice, give a room such elegance and atmosphere."

"I'll bet Montgomery loved them."

Mrs. McClung shook her head. "Fragrance-free. That means no scented candles. No flowers. No room freshener. Even the sheets were too heavily scented from the laundry detergent. Can you imagine that? Not being able to use laundry detergent?"

"Well, they do have unscented detergents. But a lot of people like scented sheets."

"They smell *fresh*," Mrs. McClung agreed. "If they don't smell like anything… people think they haven't been washed. They are always washed between guests. Always. But if people can't tell, they get upset."

"You can't win," Erin said sympathetically.

Mrs. McClung put the candles aside and peeked into the box to see what else it contained, but she didn't remove anything else.

"The strawberries are five dollars a bottle."

"I'll take all I can get."

"Six jars in there and, when you run out, give me a call and see how much I've got left. I'm sure I won't be through my stocks before you are ready for more."

As Erin settled up for the jars of preserves, there was the sound of footsteps on the stairs, and she looked up, expecting to get her first look at Mavis from the production company but, instead, it was a face she had seen before.

"Olivia Morgan," Erin said effusively. "The cookbook author! I didn't know you were staying here."

The woman looked pleased at being recognized. She looked at Erin for a moment before placing her.

"The baker. What are you doing here? You live here in town, don't you?"

"Yes, I just needed to pick up some more strawberries, and Mrs. McClung had a bumper crop from her garden this year."

"Well, that was lucky, wasn't it?" Olivia asked. "Well, not for Gerald Montgomery."

Erin felt like she'd been kicked in the stomach. "None of us knew that he was allergic to strawberries."

"No, I guess you didn't," Olivia agreed.

"So you're staying here?"

"Yes. Nice little place. A bit rustic, but sometimes you want to get away from all of the pressures of the city. Be somewhere you can chill and enjoy the country atmosphere. It's a nice little place. Mrs. McClung puts on a nice spread for breakfast, so that's one less thing to think about during the day. I'm going to leave her with one of my recipe books so that she can see how easy it is to prepare gluten-free baking for any guests that follow a special diet."

"Or she could just get baked goods at the bakery," Vic pointed out. "Which is entirely gluten-free."

Olivia looked at her for a minute, then turned back to Erin without acknowledging Vic's comment.

"Do you think I could see your room?" Erin asked. "I've never stayed here and I'd love to see one of the bedrooms, but they are all booked up."

"Well, of course," Olivia agreed. "I'm just on my way out right now but... well, I guess you could grab a quick peek before I go."

She turned around and climbed the stairs. Erin followed close behind her. Vic followed a few steps behind, leaving Mrs. McClung to watch them from below. But apparently, she didn't need to do anything upstairs and didn't see the need to supervise the visitors when Olivia herself had taken them up to show them the room.

Olivia used her key to unlock her door and opened it. "There you go," she offered. "It isn't anything unexpected. Once you've visited a few of these places, they all look the same. Some different quirks from one to the other, but mostly white bread..." She lifted her eyebrows. "And not gluten-free white bread."

Erin chuckled. She wasn't quite sure what Olivia meant, but smiled along with it anyway. She looked around at the room, which wasn't that different from a hotel room, with some homey touches. There was a bed, writing desk, flat screen TV anchored to the wall, a quilt rack which probably held the colorful quilt displayed there twelve months a year, and a small table with two chairs. Breakfast would be in the dining room downstairs, but Mrs. McClung didn't offer three meals a day so, if guests wanted to take it to their rooms, they had a place to eat it instead of sitting on the bed getting crumbs in the sheets.

There was a bud vase with a flower, some doilies, little shelves and plaques on the walls with funny or sweet sayings. The bed wasn't just the usual sheets, cheap blanket, and scratchy bedspread that Erin was used to seeing at cheap hotels; it was spread with a bright, hand-stitched bedspread and sheets that looked expensive.

Olivia caught her eyeing the unmade bed. "I wasn't expecting anyone," she said, laughing at herself. "My mother taught me always to make the bed... and I hardly ever do."

"It looks comfy," Erin observed. "How is the noise? Do you hear everything your neighbors say in the next room?"

"It's not soundproofed, but it isn't too bad. I've had a lot worse in hotels. These old houses were well-built with heavier materials. Not as much deadening as concrete walls, but not paper thin."

Erin thought about Montgomery complaining about the noise. Who had been next to him? One of his camera crew? A stranger? A fan who had managed to figure out where he was going to be staying in time to book the adjacent room before anyone else could?

"So, it's just you up here now?" she asked Olivia, knowing it wasn't the case.

"Oh, no. Not just me. One of Montgomery's staff is staying here, and she and the rest of the crew are coming and going at all hours. There's supposed to be a curfew, you know, so that you aren't keeping the other guests up, but it doesn't seem like it applies to Mavis from Meals and Reels." Her tone was sarcastic.

"I guess Mrs. McClung feels like it is a special case."

"I won't be here much longer. I'll be happy to get home, I guess."

"Why were you here? Just for a vacation? To see Mr. Montgomery?"

"You don't know him at all, do you?" Olivia questioned. "I mean... you don't know anything about him. The kind of person he was. It was like he went out of his way to bring other people down. I was doing great with my books and becoming known as a gluten-free chef. Had a good gig at a respected restaurant. And then he comes in, and..." Olivia trailed off and shook her head.

"He did what Gerald Montgomery does," Vic suggested from the doorway. "Insulted your cooking skills and wrecked your reputation."

Olivia nodded and spread her hands out in mute appeal. "I couldn't believe it. I hadn't ever done anything to hurt him. He had no idea who I was. I was just some faceless chef who had prepared his meal. He said… it was bland and tasteless. I can assure you it was not! He was out to get me. He wanted to hurt someone, and I was just a convenient target."

"I'm sorry." Erin touched her on the arm, just lightly, then let her fingers trail away. "That must have been really hard to deal with."

She tried to reconcile what Olivia said with her actions.

"Then… why were you here? Why would you follow him and stay at the same place?"

"I wanted another chance. I wanted him to taste some baking, to see that he'd been wrong about me. He just happened to be in a bad mood when he tasted my food before. So I hoped to get him to… give me another try."

Erin had a feeling that Gerald Montgomery didn't give anyone a second chance. You had one shot to impress him and, if that failed for some reason—whether because the food was bad or he was just a jerk in a bad mood—then that was it. You got what you got. Erin was glad she hadn't known more about him and his reputation before he had arrived. She would have been a wreck when he showed up at Auntie Clem's. It had been bad enough when she had thought he was just hard to please.

"But then you never got your chance. Did you stay here hoping someone else would take over for him? That you could get someone else on his crew to review it?"

Olivia shrugged in a way that Erin thought meant that had been her hope, but it hadn't worked out. She felt bad for not recognizing Olivia's name when she had first shown up at Auntie Clem's and for saying that she didn't work from cookbooks. Olivia had been through the wringer with Montgomery's review and was trying to get her name out there now. Erin's ignorance had just made her feel worse.

"Well, sorry it didn't work out," she sympathized. "I hope you can see some success… now that he's gone. Maybe people will forget about all of his reviews now. Move on to the next famous critic or chef."

"We can all hope so," Olivia agreed.

She motioned to the door, indicating that they should go. She had said she was on her way out, so Erin didn't want to hold her up any longer.

"Which room was Montgomery's?" Erin asked as they walked back into the hallway.

"The one in the middle. That one," Olivia indicated a doorway at the end of the hall, "is where Mavis is staying now. I think there might be a connecting door between them, but I'm not sure. I haven't gotten in to take a look."

Erin looked at Olivia, wondering if she were implying that Mavis or someone else from the crew might have had access to Montgomery's room from another direction. But it didn't matter. Montgomery's death had been ruled an accident, not homicide. There was no way anyone could have known that Erin was going to serve him muffins containing strawberries.

"Thanks for letting me see your room. I appreciate it."

"You should go over and talk to Mavis. I'm sure she could answer any questions that you have about how Montgomery died."

"I don't really have any questions…"

Olivia gave her a look that said she didn't believe a word of it, and then continued down the stairs.

Erin looked at the door. She was right there. Olivia had said that she should talk to Mavis. Erin assumed that Olivia and Mavis must have talked in the hallway or over breakfast, and Olivia knew what kind of a person Mavis was and how she would respond to questions from Erin about Montgomery.

She hadn't gotten the feeling that either Mrs. McClung or Olivia liked Mavis from Meals and Reels. But that didn't mean that Mavis couldn't answer a few questions. She had helped Terry with his questions about the allergy cards. She was probably the stereotypical type A personality—driven and efficient, but pushy and not terribly considerate of anyone else.

Erin could handle that.

CHAPTER 30

a re you ready to go?" Vic asked, taking a step toward the stairs.

Vic hadn't wanted to go to the B&B to begin with. She had wanted to go shopping at the market. Then she went into the General Store with Erin to make sure that she cooled off and was okay. Then she came over to the B&B even though Erin told her that she didn't have to. Probably to keep Erin out of trouble and ensure she didn't get too overheated on the way over there or the way back, carrying a box full of jars. Erin hadn't considered how awkward and hot it might be to walk back to the bakery with a box of jars of jam. They wouldn't be light, and it wouldn't be any cooler out.

Vic probably wanted to get back to the market before everything closed.

"If you want to go back, go ahead," she encouraged. "I think... I just wanted to ask a few more questions." Erin took a few uncertain steps toward the door at the end of the hall.

"More questions?" Vic shook her head and followed Erin. "What about? We already know what happened. I mean, you could watch the video and see it with your own eyes. I saw it, and I'm telling you, no one killed him. He had an allergic reaction and he just couldn't stop it. It all happened *so fast*," Vic got glittery-eyed as she considered it. "I never saw anything like it."

"I don't want to see it. I know that it was just an allergic reaction. But... someone sent me that message saying they had done me a favor. And what else could they mean?"

"How could killing Montgomery be a favor to you if it was actually done on purpose? Unless they knew that he was going to give you a bad review? And why would he? Your baking is fantastic. Everyone loves the muffins. He wasn't going to give you a bad review. So killing him... was probably the worst thing they could have done for you. They should have let him broadcast how good the muffins are. People would flock to Auntie Clem's. Killing him with your muffins had a better chance of shutting you down or putting you in prison than triggering this pilgrimage of everyone coming to taste the muffins."

"Is someone there?" came a voice from within the room.

Erin and Vic looked at each other, trying to decide what to say. There were footsteps, and the door opened.

Erin had been expecting an older, gray-haired woman. Mavis was an old name. Erin didn't think she'd ever met anyone under sixty by that name.

But the woman who opened the door was young, in her thirties, earnest-looking. In a dark gray tailored suit and white shirt, she looked like Erin had predicted—a type A corporate executive—just a very young one.

"Can I help you?" she demanded. "I didn't hear you knock."

"Uh, we hadn't yet," Erin said, feeling awkward. "We were just trying to decide whether or not to disturb you. I know you must have a lot to do here. Things are very disrupted. But..."

Mavis looked questioning, waiting for Erin to get to the point of what exactly she wanted. Why was she standing outside Mavis's door discussing whether to disturb her?

"Okay, well... I'm Erin Price."

Mavis looked at her for a minute as if she had no idea who that was or why Erin was there. Then the light came on.

"Erin Price. Auntie Clem's Bakery. You're the baker that Gerald was supposed to be reviewing."

"Yes," Erin agreed, looking down. "It was my muffins… my muffins that he was eating when… it happened."

"Your police chief said it was an accident," Mavis said. "Case closed. No one blames you for what happened. I'm just as guilty for what happened as you are."

Erin shook her head. "Why?"

"I was the one who had the new cards made up and put them in his wallet. I told that detective who came by. If there were still old ones around that didn't list strawberries on them, then I am the one to blame. I was supposed to have swapped all of them out. And I thought I had. I don't know how he managed to give you an old one. He must have had some in his pants at home or somewhere I never thought of."

She threw her hands up, tears welling in her eyes. "It was my fault."

"He should have noticed, and he should have told me," Erin said. "He shouldn't just rely on someone else doing it. It was his life that was at stake. And he shouldn't have stopped me when I was going to tell him what was in the Morning Sunshine Muffins. He said he wanted to be surprised. But if he hadn't stopped me, it never would have happened. I was about to tell him they were filled with a strawberry compote. If he hadn't stopped me, he would have known."

"Oh, what a mess. Who would ever have thought that something like this could happen."

"Were you with Mr. Montgomery for long?"

"No, only a few months. And I was the one who insisted that he had to have the allergen cards so that he wouldn't end up sick or in the hospital from an accidental exposure."

"Did you like working with him?"

"Well… he wasn't the easiest guy to work with, I'll admit. But if you ignored the personality… and the criticisms…" Mavis gave a little laugh. "Well, it was a good job."

Erin wondered what would be left to be good about it. Maybe

when Montgomery was away and out of her hair, there were other parts of the job that Mavis liked. Or perhaps it paid well. She hoped so. Mavis was young and inexperienced; maybe she didn't know how to be assertive with Montgomery and insist that she be paid what she was worth.

"Will you be staying on with the company now that he is gone?"

"I don't know yet. We'll have to see what happens. I assume they'll get another personality to take over for Mr. Montgomery, but he may come with his own staff, and then I'll be gone."

"How much longer will you be in Bald Eagle Falls?" Vic asked.

"Well, I guess that now that the police investigation is closed, I'll be moving out of here pretty soon. I needed to be here to take care of anything the police or anyone needed. The company wanted to make sure that we were fully cooperating with the police and to control messaging."

"Do you think we could see Mr. Montgomery's room on our way out?" Erin asked as they turned back toward the stairs.

Mavis frowned. "Why would you want to do that?"

"Well, I suppose it might sound a little gruesome," Erin admitted while trying to figure out how to make it sound less so. Did she really want to see the place where Montgomery had died? It was better than seeing the video of him dying. She had no desire to see that. "I just... want to be able to put it all together in my mind. What happened to him. It all started with my muffins... I wish it hadn't. I wish this had happened to him somewhere else, with someone else's strawberry dish. Or maybe he would have seen the strawberries in something else. But I just..."

Mavis didn't seem to need a more coherent explanation. Maybe the fact that Erin was vague and rambling was to her benefit.

"I suppose," Mavis said reluctantly. "It isn't like it's a shrine or still a police scene or anything like that. It's just... a bedroom. And it's booked until I tell Mrs. McClung the company doesn't want it anymore."

Mavis exited her room and walked past Erin and Vic in the narrow hallway to the middle bedroom.

"Did Mr. Montgomery complain a lot?" Erin asked. "Mrs. McClung said something about the noise, but it seems pretty quiet up here."

"I think that other woman, the gluten-free author, kept doing things that irritated him. I doubt she was that loud. That was before I got here. He kept calling me and telling me that it was untenable. The noise, the smells, people coming and going all the time, his phone constantly ringing." She shrugged. "He was a celebrity. What did he expect?"

"His phone?" Erin repeated. "What did he expect Mrs. McClung to do about the phone? Do you mean the phone in his room kept ringing?"

"No, his cell phone. That wasn't a complaint he made to her. Or if he did, you're right; there isn't anything she could do about it. But he wanted me to track down who kept calling and hanging up on him. It was his personal cell phone and no one was supposed to have the number, but someone must have gotten it, somehow. He lost his wallet one night, so maybe he had something in there that someone traced... I don't know. It's not like I am a cop or some CSI tech. I asked the phone provider for a list of the numbers he'd been talking to, but the one that kept hanging up on him was a blocked caller. It didn't show who it was on his phone activity statement either. The phone company says they don't share information like that. If it's blocked, it's blocked. Only the police can subpoena it."

Mavis put her key in the lock and opened Montgomery's bedroom door.

CHAPTER 31

*E*rin looked around. She didn't know what she had been expecting. There was nothing menacing about the room. It was bright and pleasant. The same type of furnishings and decorations as she had already seen in Olivia's and Mavis's rooms. Old fashioned, homey, the restful atmosphere Montgomery had probably sought.

It wasn't dank or dusty. Erin had been braced for the smell of death, even though she knew it had been several days since Montgomery's body had been there, and he had only been there for a few hours after death.

"Can I go in?"

Mavis shrugged. Erin entered the room and moved slowly around, taking in her surroundings. She didn't know what she was looking for. Nothing, really; she just wanted to reassure herself that, as everyone kept telling her, this had not been an intentional death. No one could have known or predicted it. No one could have planned it.

Montgomery's suitcase and equipment were still there. Mavis would take them back with her, presumably. And give them to whom? Was there a next of kin? Someone to take his personal things and whatever money he had made? Who benefited financially from his death?

Erin imagined Montgomery in that bedroom, sitting down at the table, which was slightly larger than the one in Olivia's room, and setting out the muffins for tasting. Had his auto-injectors been close at hand? Across the room in his luggage? What had made this allergy attack so fast and severe that even with his epinephrine at his table, he'd been unable to stop it?

And why hadn't he had anyone with him? He'd had a camera crew and a number of people who had come into the bakery with him. Why not keep one of them on hand during the tasting of any unfamiliar food to make sure that he was safe and didn't come to harm?

Erin heard the stairs creaking and footsteps as Mrs. McClung made her way up. She flashed a quick look at Vic and decided they had seen enough of the bedroom and it was time to get out of there. She didn't want to give the proprietor any reason for concern. They were out of the room and shutting the door when Mrs. McClung reached the top of the stairs.

Erin smiled at Mrs. McClung reassuringly. "We were just coming back down."

The woman did not return her smile. She looked around as if to see what havoc the two young women had been raising since they had come up with Olivia and then not gone back downstairs again.

"This is a private residence," she pointed out. "I did not give you permission to have the run of the place. I told you earlier that you could look at the bedrooms on the website. You didn't need to come up here. There's no reason for you to harass my guests. I can't understand why you would do such a thing."

"No, we weren't doing anything to harass them." Erin looked at Mavis for her to confirm that they hadn't been doing anything intrusive. "We just… I thought I would talk to Mavis while we were up here. We didn't even knock on the door; she just heard us talking and came out to see what was happening. I didn't mean to disturb anyone."

Mrs. McClung looked significantly at the door to Mr. Montgomery's room. "And you had to go in there? Why? Don't try telling me that you just wanted to have a look at it because you might want to honeymoon here with your sweetheart. I wasn't born yesterday, you know. I know when someone tries to pull the wool over my eyes."

"We just wanted to see it," Erin said. She didn't have a good explanation. She didn't even understand why she found the need to go in there and have a look around. She knew what had happened. If she wanted to, she could even see a video of what had happened. The police and the medical examiner had ruled it an accident, and that was the best outcome for her. She didn't want to be held responsible for having given Montgomery something that had harmed and ultimately killed him. So what was she doing messing around now? Giving them a reason to look at her further?

"I'm sorry. I didn't mean to cause you any problems. I didn't think there was any harm in just looking at the room."

"My guests have their right to privacy. That room is still rented by someone else. Not either of you." She turned and looked at Mavis. "And not even you. You just work for the company that has it booked. You have the right to be in there if there is something you need, but that doesn't mean you have the right to let other people in there, not without the approval of your company. Why would they want Erin Price in there?"

Mavis blushed. She shrugged her shoulders and looked down. She had looked young before; now, she looked even younger. She looked like a child taken to task for helping herself to a cookie before supper. Shamefaced that she had taken advantage of the privileges she had been given and had made a wrong choice.

"Now," Mrs. McClung said heavily. "It is time to take your jars of preserves and go. I appreciate you bringing me my delivery from the General Store, but I hope not to see you again any time soon."

Erin felt her face getting red. She didn't like being treated like a child in front of the others either. She had thought that she was being subtle about her investigations, but she had obviously not been. Mrs. McClung had seen right through her, and probably everyone else had, too.

"Yes, of course," she agreed, heading down the stairs with Vic as if this had been their next planned move, not that they had been caught with their fingers in the cookie jar and had them slapped. Vic looked embarrassed enough for them both, and none of it had been her idea. Erin felt bad for leading her into trouble, and murmured an apology on the way down the stairs.

Mavis returned to her room. They heard it click shut behind them as they returned to the main floor.

As they reached the front room, there was a quick knock on the front door, and then it opened. Erin saw Terry on the threshold with K9.

"Mrs. McClung?" Terry called before seeing them all there. "Oh." Terry's lips thinned and his face tightened as he looked at them. "Erin. What are you doing here?"

"I just brought Mrs. McClung a delivery and was picking up some more strawberry preserves," Erin told him quickly, picking up the box filled with jars. She glanced around. "What are you doing here?"

"There's been a complaint."

Erin looked back at Mrs. McClung, her face flaming even hotter. She had called the police on them? Even knowing that Terry was Erin's partner?

It was bad enough that she had called the police, but then for Terry to be the one to answer the call... Erin tried to swallow her embarrassment.

"We were just leaving."

"Good. You and I can talk about this later." Terry looked back over his shoulder. He groaned and shook his head. "And you have the press to deal with, too."

Advancing to the door, Erin saw a reporter and camera crew approaching the house. She had seen them around town, but she had refused to talk to them at Auntie Clem's and had sent them on their way. Now she didn't have the advantage of being able to kick them off her property. And she couldn't even jump into her car and escape, because it was still parked back at the bakery, where they had left it while shopping at the street market.

Erin looked at Terry for help, but he just shook his head. What was he supposed to do about it? He was there as a law enforcement officer responding to a complaint, not as her friend or romantic partner. He couldn't take either of those roles in front of the reporters. He didn't need the Bald Eagle Falls police department taking any flak because he had treated a possible offender like a friend.

Erin marched past Terry and K9 with the box of jars. She flinched at the furnace-like summer heat. Vic followed in her wake. Erin didn't imagine Vic felt any better about the situation than Erin did, and none of it had been her doing.

"Miss Price," the reporter called. "What are you doing here at the bed and breakfast where Gerald Montgomery was killed? Why would you want to be here after what happened? After what you were responsible for?"

"I wasn't responsible for his death," Erin protested, over Vic's declarations of, "No comment, no comment!"

"It was your Morning Sunshine Muffins that killed him. Isn't that true?"

"It isn't my fault because he never told me he was allergic to strawberries. And that's been proven. I turned in the card he gave me to the police, and they can confirm that it doesn't include strawberries."

"Has that been proven?" the reporter immediately asked of Terry, turning the microphone toward him. Terry gave Erin an angry look.

"Gerald Montgomery's death was determined to be an accident. That's all the police department has to say about it."

"But just *how* accidental was it?" the reporter pressed. "Shouldn't Miss Price have known his allergies before cooking for him? Wouldn't that have made more sense?"

"I can't speak for Mr. Montgomery or his company's practices," Terry pointed out.

"You have been in contact with his company during the course of the investigation, haven't you? What did your investigation show? Was there negligence on the part of Auntie Clem's Bakery staff?"

"If you don't want to be sued for slander, I would be very careful what you say."

"It was only a question. We haven't made any accusations of wrongdoing."

"You're blocking the sidewalk," Terry told the reporter and his crew. "If you would please step aside and let people through."

Under Terry's stern eye, they did move aside and make room for Erin and Vic to walk by them to head back to Auntie Clem's.

The box of jars was already heavy and Erin knew that by the time she got back to the bakery, her arms would be aching and she would be soaked with sweat. She really didn't like Tennessee summers.

CHAPTER 32

*E*rin knew she was going to be under fire when she and Terry both got home that evening. They were in the kitchen, where Erin had hoped to make a cup of tea that would help to keep things calm and civilized. But Terry had been embarrassed by being called to the scene where it had appeared that Erin was the guilty party, and by having to face the press over the incident. His ego wasn't going to be soothed by a cup of tea. He wouldn't sit down with her, but paced back and forth across the kitchen trying to deal with all of his burning energy.

"What were you thinking, Erin?" he demanded in frustration. "I can't understand you going over to the bed and breakfast and making trouble over there. What was the point of that? The whole thing has been declared an accident. You are in the clear. There will be no consequences. And then... this. I don't understand you at all."

"I wasn't... I didn't go over there to make trouble," Erin said hotly. "And I wasn't doing anything wrong. I just took a delivery over to Mrs. McClung and asked her about getting more strawberries. The rest... just happened. I was there anyway. I just talked to the people who were there, who knew something about Mr. Montgomery and what had happened. I wasn't doing anything to bother anyone. They talked to me freely. It was only Mrs. McClung who got her panties in a twist."

Erin had never even used the phrase before. That just went to show how upset she was about the whole thing. She shouldn't need to defend herself. She hadn't done anything wrong.

"It wasn't Mrs. McClung. Just because someone didn't tell you to your face that you were bothering them or file a police complaint, that doesn't mean that you *weren't* bothering them. It just means they were too polite to tell you to take a hike."

"Olivia and Mavis were *fine* with me talking to them. I wasn't pushy. I just asked them a few questions…"

"You shouldn't have been there and you shouldn't have been asking any questions. Why can't you let this go?"

Erin hated raised voices. She hated confrontation. That didn't mean she was a shrinking violet and couldn't express her opinion, but she hated arguing with Terry over anything.

"Because it was my muffins that killed him!" she growled at him. "Why can't you understand that?"

"It was an accident. It wasn't done intentionally, I know that. The police department knows that. It's been declared an accidental death. So why would you want to stir things up more?"

"I don't want to. I want to… understand it. I want to know what happened and understand why it happened, because it doesn't make any sense to me. I know how to cook for allergies. I know how to take care of people. This shouldn't have happened!"

"Of course not," Terry said, dropping his volume and trying to sound sympathetic. "I understand that it was a shock. It was a terrible thing, and you would have done anything to avoid it. But it happened. It was more Montgomery's fault than anyone else's because he didn't take proper precautions. But you need to put it behind you and stop making everybody else miserable. You're getting the press and others in town stirred up, thinking that there was more to it. And there wasn't. It was just an accident."

Erin gritted her teeth, trying to ignore his tone and deal with what he was telling her. She knew it was true. She had been obsessing too much over Montgomery's death, and there was nothing she could have done to prevent it. It had been Gerald Montgomery's responsibility to tell her what he was allergic to, not hers to figure out or guess at. She had followed the directions he had given her and that should be the end of it. She had been worried that the police would find that she had some culpability in it or the company or estate would sue her.

All those worries had been resolved, but she still felt like she needed to do more. Everyone else was satisfied with the answers that the medical examiner and police department had provided. Why couldn't Erin be?

"I just… I don't know. I don't understand it myself," Erin told him, shaking her head.

Terry looked in the fridge and then slammed the door shut, frustrated by her responses. Erin knew he wanted to solve the problem, to fix things for her, to actually do something to make everything better. But he couldn't do that. No one could.

"I'm sorry," Erin told him.

"You don't have to apologize for your feelings. I just wish I could… you need to understand that even if you aren't happy with it, you can't keep pursuing this. You can't stir everyone else up. We want this to blow over and things to return to normal. As long as you are providing the media with fodder and his fans are coming here for muffins… it isn't going to happen. Can't you just let it go?"

Erin opened her mouth to respond, though she didn't know what she was going to say to him. But there was a quick knock at the back door, and Vic burst in.

CHAPTER 33

*S*trands of her hair were pasted to Vic's face. Even when Erin had been soaked in sweat that afternoon, Vic had looked as cool as any southern belle. But now, everything was in disarray, and her eyes were wide and frightened.

"Vic! What is it?" Erin sprang to her feet, the lethargy she had been feeling a moment before disappearing in a flash. She was on her feet before Terry finished turning around to look at Vic.

"It's Willie. Something is wrong. I need to take him into the hospital, but…" Vic shook her head. "I can drive, but you know I don't have a… car." At the last moment, she looked at Terry and replaced "license" with "car." She didn't have either one, but Erin could see that she had been about to say she didn't have a driver's license, but then didn't want to admit it in front of Terry. As if Terry hadn't already figured it out.

"We'll drive," Erin said immediately. "I guess one of the trucks. The bug is too small." She looked at Terry. "We could use your lights and siren."

"Of course," Terry agreed. "Do you want me to drive it around back?"

Vic nodded. "Yeah. That would be really helpful. Thanks. I'll bring him down."

"Do you need help?" Erin asked Vic.

"No... I don't want too many people on the stairs; someone will trip and fall down."

Erin nodded. The staircase was steep and wasn't made for three people walking together. She hoped that Willie could walk on his own, not wanting him to rely on Vic for support as they descended the stairs. There was a sturdy railing.

Terry left by the front door to get his truck. K9 was immediately at his heels, eager to know what was going on, ears pricked up alertly. Erin shut the door behind him and locked it. Then she went out the back door, setting the burglar alarm and waiting anxiously for Vic to bring Willie down the stairs.

Willie was able to walk under his own power. He held on to the handrails on both sides of the stairs, moving down them slowly ahead of Vic. Erin could hear Vic arguing that she should go first to help Willie if he fell. Willie, in turn, argued that he didn't want to fall on her and injure her. Two hard-headed people wanting to help each other.

When they reached the bottom of the stairs, Erin could see why Vic was so concerned. Willie was pale, with a number of welts on his face and neck. He was scowling and didn't give Erin his usual reassuring smile. Once he was at the bottom of the stairs, Vic hurried forward to steady him in his walk to the truck, which Terry was pulling around the back. Willie struggled to maintain his balance but, with Vic's support, he managed to stay on his feet. She wasn't carrying his weight, but providing a steadying shoulder.

Terry jumped down out of the truck to give Vic a hand. "Let's get him into the front seat. That will be the quickest to get him in and out of."

"I don't need help," Willie protested, swatting at Terry's hand to start with, but then taking the proffered shoulder a few seconds later. "It's just a headache," he insisted. "They said that was one of the side effects of chelation. I'll just sleep it off."

"You've been trying to sleep it off all day," Vic told him sternly. "This is serious. I can feel it in my bones. I'm not going to let you argue me out of this."

Willie allowed them to guide him into the cab of the truck. They boosted him up onto the seat.

"Erin, why don't you and K9 take the back," Terry suggested. "I'm sorry, I just think it's best if he is in front with me and Vic."

"Of course it is," Erin agreed. She had CPR and first aid training, but Terry's training was more extensive than hers, and Vic had a better chance of recognizing the instant anything changed and worming out of Willie what he was feeling.

Erin climbed into the back seat and called K9 to her. He sat on the seat beside her and watched the activity in the front seat with interest. As soon as Vic's door was shut, Terry reversed the truck and flipped on the lights and siren, heading for the highway.

He waited until he was on a straight section of the road before looking at Willie and asking him a few questions to evaluate his condition.

"So, you've been having headaches?"

"It's perfectly normal," Willie said, slurring slightly. "I've been having headaches after every treatment. And between treatments. In fact, I have a headache almost all the time."

"But this one is worse," Vic contributed. "It isn't usually this bad. He's been nauseated and throwing up."

"That's all part of the treatment. Sometimes it hits me the wrong way. This isn't the first time I've been sick from it." Willie rubbed his forehead slowly, but it didn't seem to be giving him any relief.

"What else?" Terry asked. "You look like something that crawled in from the swamp."

Willie chuckled at this. He fingered one of the welts on his face. "They said I could have rashes or hives. My system is full of toxins. It's not unusual to have a skin reaction to the toxins or chelation agents."

"Any trouble breathing?"

"No." Willie's head shook back and forth ponderously, as if it were very heavy. "Breathing just fine."

But Erin had noticed him breathing hard when he had come down the stairs. It wasn't surprising that he would be tired climbing up the stairs, but it was unusual for him to get out of breath going down a single flight of stairs.

Terry's foot was pressed to the gas pedal, and they were moving down the highway faster than Erin would have been comfortable driving. As Terry asked Willie questions, his attention was split between the road and his passenger's condition.

"They're gonna tell you everything is fine," Willie told Vic. "I should have just stayed home and slept."

"You've been sleeping all the time lately," Vic told him, "I'm kind of worried about it, if you want to know the truth."

"Sleep is the best thing for me. The body's way of healing."

Vic didn't repeat that it had been too much. That would just aggravate Willie further, but she glanced back at Erin to see what she thought. Erin shrugged. She happened to agree that the amount of time Willie had been sleeping lately was excessive. But people who were sick often slept. She agreed with Willie too, that it was probably what his body needed. That and good food to nourish and strengthen his body.

"How have you been eating?" she asked, thinking about his having a beer with Terry the other day. She knew he had been specifically counseled to stay away from alcohol.

"Vic's a good cook," Willie said. "Everything has been just fine."

"You've been following the instructions the doctors have given you for what you should be eating? Or not eating?"

Willie rubbed his forehead. "More or less."

Erin looked at Vic, but Vic didn't meet her eyes or make any comment on whether Willie had been following the diet instructions given to him by the clinic doing the chelation therapy.

"I'm doing what I'm supposed to," Willie told Erin, his eyes closed and head back. "You might think you would do better, but it's not easy trying to follow all the instructions. They said that the symptoms would be mild, but I can tell you they are anything but mild. And I'm no wuss as far as being sick goes. I'm not one of those people who whines and takes to his bed at the first sign of a sniffle."

"I know you haven't been feeling well," Erin told him. "I'm not trying to say that's because you haven't been 'doing it right.' Just wondering… if there's anything we can do to help. To make it easier on you."

"How about letting me sleep instead of dragging me to the hospital?"

Erin looked at Vic. Despite Willie's assurances that everything was fine and he just needed to sleep, he looked like death warmed over. And Erin knew that Vic wouldn't insist that Willie needed to be taken to the hospital without good reason. She had seen the look of panic in Vic's eyes when she had burst into the house. She was really worried.

"What is it you were the most worried about?" Erin asked her.

Vic hovered over Willie, watching him like a hawk. She stroked a lock of hair on his temple. "He's just not himself… he was having chest pains and palpitations. And the headache… it's not just a headache." She shook her head. "He hasn't had one like this before."

"I've had plenty of headaches," Willie said, eyes still closed.

"I know. And this one isn't like any you've ever had before, is it?"

"I just want to go to sleep."

Vic looked at Erin and shook her head helplessly. Erin nodded her sympathy and gave Vic's shoulder an encouraging squeeze. She didn't know what to do about Willie's symptoms, but they would be at the hospital in record time at the speed that Terry was driving. When Erin thought about Willie's pallor and everything else Vic had mentioned, she got a knot in her gut that wouldn't go away.

Willie was still. His breath rasped noisily. He had apparently gone to sleep as he had wanted to. Vic stroked his hair lightly so as not to wake him up. She shook her head.

"I worry about him so much. This whole thing has been much worse than they ever told us. I know they said that his levels of heavy metals were so high it was hard to believe he was still working normally and wasn't obviously sick. I thought he would just fly through the detox. He'd go from feeling a bit irritable and moody to being calm and mellow. I wasn't expecting all of the physical symptoms. It's like he's a chemo patient."

Erin didn't like the sound of Willie's breathing, growing louder and raspier. She touched his carotid and felt for his pulse.

Vic looked at her worriedly. "What is it?"

"I don't like his breathing. His pulse is… fast and irregular. If he's sleeping, it should be slow."

"I told you he was having palpitations. I was worried he was going to have a heart attack."

Erin nodded. "We'll be at the hospital before too long and they'll take care of him."

They were all tense and didn't know what to say to make the others feel better. Terry was occupied with driving, so it mostly fell to Erin and Vic to stay on top of Willie's condition. They listened tensely to his breathing, waiting for each new breath to be regular and whether it would be better or worse sounding than the previous one.

It seemed like it took forever to reach the city limits, even though Erin knew Terry had been pushing the truck as fast as he could safely go. Erin breathed a sigh of relief.

She remembered Willie running her to the hospital when she had been poisoned. He had sung to her, trying to keep her awake and alert. His singing had been terrible. But he had gotten her there in time for the doctors to treat her. And they would see that he got the treatment he needed too.

Terry weaved through the streets and, eventually, they reached the hospital's emergency entrance. Vic put her hand on Willie's shoulder and shook him gently.

"We're here, Willie. Time to wake up for a few minutes."

He didn't respond. Vic shook him harder.

"Come on, Willie. Wake up!"

Erin knew what it was like to try to rouse someone who would never wake up. Heart in her throat, she pinched Willie hard and he stirred, swatting at her. "Ow!"

Vic repeated that it was time to get out, and he managed to slide himself across the seat to the door and land without collapsing on the sidewalk outside the truck. Erin climbed out behind him. It was easy to see that he was leaning on Vic for more than just balance this time. Vic struggled to hold him up. Erin hurried to his other side to support him from there.

"I'm just fine," Willie protested. "Don't need to be treated like an invalid. I'm just fine."

But even as he protested, he leaned on Erin as well, and the two of them together were still straining. They staggered forward a few steps, and an orderly outside for a smoke break quickly put out his cigarette and grabbed a wheelchair. He efficiently settled Willie into it, quelling his protests.

"It's procedure," he insisted. Once Willie was sitting, the orderly grabbed the handles of the wheelchair to push Willie into the emergency department, walking briskly past the lineup at triage and swiping his card to get past a locked door to jump the queue. A few nurses and other professionals hurried in to help him, asking questions and leaning over Willie to check his vitals and talk to him.

Vic leaned against Erin, sniffling. "Now what?"

Erin took in a deep breath, sucking in the smells of antiseptic, cleaners, and the faint smell of fries.

"Now we wait and see what they can tell us. They won't be able to tell us anything right away. But they're going to need to ask you questions. Whatever Willie can't answer himself."

"He can answer all of them. They won't need me for anything."

But Erin had seen how Willie was and knew he would not be answering many questions. He might be able to answer the basics about who he was and that he was going through chelation therapy, but Erin didn't think he would be able to manage much beyond that.

"Come on. Let's get over to where they can find you when they need you."

She led Vic over to the triage area. The heavy nurse triaging patients looked at them and pointed in Willie's direction, raising her brows questioningly. Erin nodded in response. The nurse gave her a nod in return and continued talking to the patient before her.

When she had dealt with him and sent him back to wait in the chairs area, she motioned to Erin and Vic. Erin pushed Vic forward.

"They need to talk to you."

Vic looked over her shoulder at Erin as she stepped forward, looking uncertain and abandoned. But Erin knew how strong she was and that she would be able to handle it once the nurse started asking her questions. Erin went back to the waiting area and found Terry. One of the benefits of driving an emergency vehicle to the hospital was that he could park in the reserved area, nice and close to the doors. He didn't have to search for a parking space and pay an arm and a leg for it.

"They took him straight in?" Terry asked, looking past Erin to see Vic talking to the triage nurse.

"Yeah."

"That's Good. They'll stabilize him, and then can start to figure out what's going on with him."

"Do you think it's all because of the chelation therapy?"

"I'm sure that's probably the trigger—or rather, the heavy metal poisoning is. And that can cause all kinds of problems. I read all about it when we were looking into Fontainebleau's death. It can affect all of the body's systems."

"It's good we got him here when we did." Erin gazed toward the triage area. "I don't know what would have happened if they had waited any longer."

CHAPTER 34

*E*rin knew it would be hours before they would have any real news about Willie and what had gone wrong with his treatment. Terry offered to drive her home and then to return for Vic when she was ready to come home, but Erin shook her head. She wanted to be there for Vic, just as Vic was always there for her. And Willie was a good friend. She wouldn't be able to sleep without knowing that he was stable and out of danger. She wanted to hear that they understood what was happening and were treating him for it.

That was a lot to ask. How often did people get sent home from the hospital without the doctors having the slightest idea what was happening? Hospital shows on TV might give the impression that hospitals can always effectively diagnose and treat even the most obscure diseases, but real-life experiences were far less impressive. Erin knew plenty of people who had been sent home without a diagnosis or with the wrong diagnosis or treatment.

They would be able to help Willie.

He was important to Erin and Vic. The doctors would be able to find out what had gone wrong and teach them how to keep it from happening again.

She hoped.

In the meantime, Erin had to call the various employees to make sure that someone could cover for her and Vic in the morning. Erin would be back in the afternoon, she assumed, but those early hours would have to be covered so that Auntie Clem's could open on time in the morning and serve the early customers their morning muffins.

K9 lay by Terry on the floor, occasionally sighing or groaning and shifting to another position. He didn't like lying around, and Erin didn't suppose the cold hard tiles were much fun to sleep on. She took him outside a couple of times to stretch his legs and sniff all the interesting nighttime smells. She and Terry took turns. It was, Erin thought, a little like keeping a toddler entertained—a very smart toddler who didn't have much to say.

Eventually, Vic came out to the waiting room.

"The doctor said that I was right to bring him in," she told them, as if she needed to justify her actions, though neither Erin nor Terry had given her even the suggestion that they thought she was overreacting to Willie's condition. "He was having irregular heart rhythms, as well as the rest of the stuff. He shouldn't be having this bad a reaction to the chelation therapy, but some people do. Especially if the poisoning was very bad."

"And we know Willie's was," Erin put in.

Vic nodded. "They should have told us back at the beginning that the worse the poisoning, the worse the chelation side effects would be. Then, at least, we might have been prepared for some of what had gone on instead of being blindsided when they said that the side effects of chelation are usually mild."

Erin and Terry nodded. Erin leaned forward in her seat. "And his breathing? They got that sorted out? I was really worried about how he sounded. He doesn't always sound like that when he sleeps, does he?"

"No. A bit of snoring now and then, but not that breathing he was doing in the car. The doctors said it was anaphylaxis."

"Really? I thought that it would be a lot more severe if he had anaphylaxis."

"His throat was closed almost all the way by the time we got him here. They had to put a tube down to help him breathe. They said it will be taken out soon, they don't expect him to need it for a long time. But I guess not all anaphylaxis is fast like you see on TV. Or like it was for Montgomery. Sometimes it can take a few hours, and it doesn't always involve breathing problems." Vic shook her head to try to accustom herself to this new information. "I guess it's like a Hollywood heart attack. We expect it to look one way because that's how it is always portrayed in the media, but there are different kinds, and it can look really different."

Erin nodded. "Anaphylaxis is a life-threatening allergic reaction. It might be less obvious symptoms. If you have a reaction that causes symptoms in several body systems—skin, digestive, respiratory, circulatory—then it is considered anaphylaxis. But what was he allergic to? Did he have a different treatment than usual? Did they change things around?"

"They said sometimes it can be triggered by stress or exercise, not necessarily an allergen. Or that if he is stressed out, that could turn a normally mild reaction into anaphylaxis."

"I thought anaphylaxis was always caused by an allergy."

Vic shrugged. "Apparently not. I guess sometimes people get it just from exercise, like an asthma attack. Willie's had side effects from the therapy right from the start. I guess those can indicate a mild allergic reaction, but they don't worry about it too much if it isn't life-threatening or keeping him from getting further treatment."

"Maybe he should have gotten treatment for the side effects earlier."

"Maybe. But you know how men are." Vic looked at Terry. "They don't like to ask for help. Don't like to admit that they might not be able to handle things on their own. And Willie prides himself on not being a whiner about getting sick, like some guys."

Erin appreciated that Willie didn't become a helpless infant when he got a cold or flu bug, but he still needed to take care of himself and talk to his doctor about his symptoms.

"So why do they think this happened now? Was it all of the treatments adding up, or the amount of metals being pulled from his body now? Or do they think it is from a different allergen trigger or stressor?"

Vic sat in one of the plastic chairs across from where Erin and Terry were sitting.

"Doctor said that we might never know. They'll do their best to figure out the trigger so we can avoid it happening again."

"How are they going to figure it out?"

Vic flourished a stack of papers. "Questionnaire time. Full history since he started treatment, any previous medical history, especially any previous reactions or allergies, things that have been going on in his life lately. All of the medications he had taken, not just the chelation agents but any over-the-counter medications, herbs, vitamins, or alternative treatments. Changes in diet, samples of his dietary plan…"

"Wow. Can I see?"

Vic raised her brows and handed it over to Erin. "You want to fill it out too?" she teased.

"I don't think so." Erin was not sure why she even wanted to look at the papers. She wasn't a big reader, and there was a lot there to digest. She promised herself that she only needed to skim. She didn't need to read everything. "I just wanted to take a quick look."

Before the night was over, Willie was moved to a room so they could visit him briefly before heading back to Bald Eagle Falls.

He had more color in his face, Erin noted. The welts she had noted earlier, hives from the reaction, had disappeared. He was hooked up to a pulse oximeter so that his vitals were shown on the screen on the monitor beside him. Everything seemed to fall into normal parameters, except his blood pressure seemed slightly low. Erin knew that lower blood pressure could be normal for Willie, either genetic or because he was in good physical condition. With all of his physical work and caving, Erin assumed it was because his body was working efficiently, not because of anaphylaxis. They would be watching for any recurrence of those symptoms.

"Hey, Willie," she greeted, giving him a warm, reassuring smile. "How are you doing?"

"Feeling a lot better," he admitted. "Whatever they gave me is working."

"You're looking much better, old man," Terry observed. "Not like you're at death's door anymore."

Willie rubbed his head. "It wasn't *that* bad."

"Who do you think you're kidding?" Vic demanded. "You had to be intubated to keep you breathing. Your heartbeat was irregular. Your blood pressure was barely registering. If Terry hadn't kept the pedal to the metal and used his lights and siren, we might not have gotten you here fast enough. You should be thanking him for getting you here before you died."

"It wasn't that bad," Willie grumbled. "I would have slept it off."

Vic rolled her eyes and shook her head at Erin.

Men. So stubborn.

"How long will you be here? Have they given you any idea?" Erin asked Willie.

"I don't think it will be long. I don't need to be here now; they just want to monitor me for a while to make sure that I don't… start having trouble again."

"You'd better stay for a day or two," Vic told him sternly. "This was serious, and if I hadn't been home or Terry hadn't been able to get you here quickly enough, that might have been the end of the road for you."

"But I'm okay now. And we know what to watch for if it happens again. Time is money."

"Your business can wait for a day or two. What would have happened to it if you had died? Or been so disabled by this that you couldn't do anything anymore?"

"They charge an arm and a leg to stay here," he grumbled, "I'd be just as good recovering at home."

Vic shook her head adamantly. "You're staying here until I'm sure they've got everything sorted out."

Willie rolled his eyes. But Erin could see his affection for Vic and that he would do as she said and stay there until she was convinced that it was safe for him to go home again.

"What about one of those watches?" Erin asked. "A lot of the sports watches now will tell you if you are having heart trouble. I'm always hearing about how it saved this person or that one who didn't even know that they had a problem."

Willie's eyes gleamed. He was a tech guy, and the idea appealed to him. "I can get one of those. They can send out alerts, too. So even if I was asleep or couldn't get to a phone, it would let everyone know."

Of course, *everyone* in this case was Vic.

"That sounds like a good idea," she agreed. "But it doesn't replace doctors. You're going to have to have your heart checked. Make sure this was just a one-time reaction, not some disease or disorder needing treatment or regular monitoring."

Erin couldn't help grinning at the young girl ordering Willie around and telling him what he needed to do to take care of his health. Willie nodded his agreement and promised to get the help that he needed.

"I plan to be here for a long time," he told Vic. "On this planet, not in the hospital. I don't plan on leaving any time soon."

Vic nodded, her eyes glistening with tears. "You'd better. If you up and died, I would kill you!"

CHAPTER 35

*W*illie was home from the hospital, but Vic still wasn't ready to leave him alone, so the other employees covered her usual shifts during the week. The furor from Montgomery's death was starting to dissipate, with fewer Morning Sunshine Muffins being ordered each day and not so many strangers hanging around town.

Terry was happy to see that Erin had abandoned her obsession with what had happened to Montgomery and that things were getting back to normal.

Except that they weren't. Erin had managed to stay out of trouble and to keep Terry from noticing that she still had something on her mind. Or maybe he noticed that she was still troubled but just happy that she wasn't drawing attention to herself by questioning random Bald Eagle Falls residents or talking to the media.

But that didn't mean Erin was done.

"I've been thinking about Gerald Montgomery and how he had such a severe reaction to the strawberries," she said to Vic over tea one evening.

Vic raised her brows. "Oh? I thought you had decided to leave the subject alone."

Erin shrugged. "No. I know Terry doesn't want me involved in it, but…"

"But you are," Vic finished. She shook her head but didn't try to dissuade Erin. "So… you're wondering about his reaction. He was apparently *really* allergic to strawberries."

"But when we looked at his stuff online, that's not something he had ever reacted to before. So it had to be a recently developed allergy or one that had gotten more severe over time."

"Okay…?"

"And the videos where he'd had a reaction, he'd always been able to handle it before. I mean, I know we keep saying that it was his own fault because he didn't have someone in the room with him or have every ingredient checked like he should, but he'd never had a reaction that was that severe before. Had he?"

"I don't know if he ever had, but not on any of the videos we watched. And certainly, nothing that was *that* bad, or he wouldn't have been around to have another one."

"So it was a lot more severe than any reaction he'd had before. So fast and serious that the epinephrine didn't work, even though he took it."

Vic agreed. She took a sip of her tea. "But what does that tell us? We've known all of that from the start."

"There must have been factors that made it worse. Like Willie's reaction. All of those things that you filled out in the questionnaire that might have contributed to him getting so sick."

Vic's eyes widened. "Yeah. That makes sense. We were all wondering why he reacted so violently."

"All those things on that questionnaire—stress, exercise, another allergen that he was already reacting to…"

Vic nodded eagerly. "Let me pull it up…" She tapped and scrolled on her phone. "I took pictures before I gave it to the doctors so that I have a record and don't have to look those things up again down the line."

"Good thinking."

Vic scrolled through a few pages. "Okay… other things that

they said could make a reaction worse. Alcohol. He hadn't had any of that. Willie, I mean."

"Not that day," Erin pointed out. He hadn't been avoiding alcohol as strictly as he'd been told to. "Mrs. McClung said Montgomery had gotten deliveries. Including wine."

"Okay, so check that box for Montgomery. Medications that can make an allergic reaction worse… non-steroidal anti-inflammatories."

"Like aspirin or naproxen," Erin said, "He was complaining about headaches and asking for aspirin."

"And about the flowers and fragrances… the doctor said that if Willie was already having an allergic reaction to something, then a new reaction could be more serious."

"And *stress*. The show must have been stressful. Having to make a decision about how to review the muffins."

Vic wobbled her hand back and forth in a "maybe" gesture. "He thrived on that, really enjoyed that part of it. Even though it would have been stressful for me or you, that was the part that made the whole thing worth it."

"Hmm." Erin thought about it, pressing her lips together. "Yeah. You're probably right."

"But it did sound from Mrs. McClung's description like he was stressed. He was complaining about the fragrances and the music. His headache. The hang-ups on his phone."

"Right." Erin pointed to her. "So he *was* stressed. Stressed, drinking, taking something for his headache, reacting to other allergens…"

Vic nodded slowly. She stirred her tea absently while she considered it. "So it was like the perfect storm. All of those things together that would make an allergic reaction worse. So when he happened to be exposed to the strawberries in the muffins… it was a much more severe reaction than he would have expected. He thought he could handle any reaction with a shot of epinephrine and some antihistamines, but it was too severe this time because of all of the other factors."

Erin agreed. She sipped her tea, which was getting too cool and needed to be refreshed.

"So now you know," Vic said. "It wasn't just you. And it wasn't just Montgomery. There were all of these other factors too, things no one could have predicted. And it was all of them together that resulted in Gerald Montgomery's death."

"Yeah."

"So that makes you feel better? That you can relax and know that it wasn't your fault? It was just all of these chance things happening at once?"

Erin took another sip of her tea. "But *was* it all coincidental? Just by chance? What if it wasn't?"

CHAPTER 36

*T*here was still one other piece of the puzzle to put together. As Vic had told Erin more than once and Terry had also brought up, it had been pure coincidence that Erin had served Montgomery strawberries. Especially in muffins. She made plenty of blueberry muffins. That was a traditional flavor, but there were not a lot of strawberry muffins around. It wasn't something that she saw when she went to other bakeries or to the grocery store. She read a lot of recipes and looked at a lot of baking brands online, and it just wasn't a usual muffin flavor.

If someone had been trying to engineer Montgomery's death, they could not have been relying upon Erin to deal the fatal blow. Whoever the culprit was that had arranged for all of the other *coincidences* that Vic had noted, had to have another plan in mind. Had someone sent Montgomery something spiked with strawberries, perhaps the wine, without his noticing? Maybe the wine *had* been spiked with strawberry juice, but it wasn't enough to put him over the edge. Not until he'd had the muffins as well. Maybe just drinking the rest of the bottle would have had the same effect, and the mastermind had simply been lucky that Erin had stepped in with her strawberry muffins and finished the job.

She might have believed that, except that if she were right about everything else, Montgomery's death had been carefully planned. It had been a very detailed, methodical approach. Nothing left to chance. Except for the introduction of the allergen.

It didn't make sense that someone would plan everything out and leave the last step to chance.

So Erin sat in front of her computer in her tiny office at Auntie Clem's Bakery and tried to reconstruct in her mind the thought processes that had led up to her creation of the Morning Sunshine Muffins for Gerald Montgomery's tasting.

She had her browser history, and that was a good start. She wasn't a very technical person and she wasn't aware of any utility that could have shown her everything she had done in the days before she started experimenting with a recipe for strawberry compote surprise muffins. It would have been nice to have Willie's help with the project. He was very good with computers. But he was still recovering and she didn't want to do anything that might take away from his energy and the healing process. He needed to be at home in bed relaxing until Vic said otherwise.

Erin searched her browser history for the word *strawberry*.

There were more hits than she would have thought. Apparently, strawberries had been on her mind quite a bit. She narrowed the timeline and studied web pages that came up. She consulted several when looking for the best sugar ratios and cooking time for the strawberry compote. It was important for the compote to be sweet and thicken properly but to avoid overcooking the strawberries or losing the tartness of the berries. It was a balancing act, and she looked at other recipes for the starting point, which she then experimented upon.

Erin went back before that, looking for the genesis of her idea for the muffins. There were a few baking forums where she had discussed possibilities for an impressive muffin to serve to a critic. She had posted anonymously so that no one would know she was the one asking about it or that Montgomery was the critic in question. In those discussions, people had talked about several ways to incorporate strawberries into a muffin recipe.

Going further back in the browser history, Erin found a series of emails she had received the week before she started playing with ideas for a strawberry muffin.

- Before Strawberry Season is over…
- Everyone loves strawberries
- Strawberries in muffins? Yes, please!
- Surprise your guests with strawberries
- Win over even the toughest critic with these strawberry recipes

Erin stared at the subject lines. She didn't even remember receiving any of those messages. She was subscribed to a lot of baking newsletters and blogs and only read a fraction of the emails she received from them. It was entirely possible that all she had read of these emails was the subject lines. She might not have ever even opened them. But they had arrived in her inbox and she had read at least a portion of the subject lines in order to decide what to do with the emails. To read them, save them for later, or delete them.

She opened each of the emails in turn. They looked like what they appeared to be. Chatty, informative newsletters that attempted to sell a brand or to get readers to buy something based on what they had offered in the email.

But she didn't recognize the senders or the branding of the emails. They were not emails that she got regularly. She tried following links and searching the senders' names to get a better handle on who they were. Chances were, she had subscribed to them at some time or another. But too many of the links ended up with 404 errors, and she didn't recognize the faces or websites of the signatories she managed to find. Even though she got a lot of emails, that seemed odd. If she didn't ever read what someone was sending to her, she generally unsubscribed after a few weeks.

She tried the unsubscribe link in each email, but only one worked. The rest returned errors of "not found."

Erin clicked on the selection box for each email and forwarded them to Terry's police department email address.

Call me, she wrote to him.

There was no immediate response, but she didn't expect one. If everything was going well, he was on patrol somewhere with K9. If there was a lot going on, then he was at a trouble call and wouldn't be checking his email. She might have to wait until later in the evening or the next day for a response. And then she would have to explain herself to him, which she wasn't looking forward to.

Erin got up from her desk to stretch her legs. She kept reading about how dangerous it was to sit at a desk for hours on end. Bad for one's health. Increased rates of heart attack, diabetes, and other lifestyle diseases.

She checked the burglar alarm while she was walking around. The bakery was very quiet. Normally, she liked that. She loved the peace and quiet of sitting in her office in the deserted bakery, making plans for the upcoming week or reviewing how the previous week had gone.

But tonight, it was creepy. Erin wanted Terry to call her back. She wanted to know that he was okay out there and that no one was hanging around near the bakery to vandalize it, break in, or do her any harm. It had happened in the past, and she was vulnerable, there alone, even with the burglar alarm armed.

As she paced, she thought about who the email sender might be. What if someone had sent all of those emails to her to intentionally influence her choice of what to make for Montgomery's review? "Strawberries in muffins" and "Win over even the toughest critic" were not exactly subtle. But with those emails buried among others, and reading only the subject lines, Erin might easily have absorbed them subconsciously and then they had come to the forefront as she considered what kind of muffin to make for Montgomery's tasting.

Erin didn't like to think that she could be as easily manipulated as that but, when she looked at the history and considered how soon after those emails she had started experimenting with strawberry compote, she couldn't very well deny the possibility.

There was a sharp knock on the back door of the bakery. Erin's heart leaped in her chest. It raced as she pretended to herself she could walk calmly to the door. She looked through the peephole, one hand on her phone as she prepared to call Terry to get him to run off whoever had shown up now to harass her.

As much as she hated that he kept insisting she move on with her life and quit obsessing over the Montgomery case, Erin had to admit that it would be really nice if his rabid fans didn't keep showing up, either demanding muffins or calling her a murderer and saying she should die. Or both.

It would be nice to return to normal and not worry about them again.

She let out her breath slowly and unlocked the door. "Come on in." She let Terry and K9 enter and rearmed the burglar alarm. "I wasn't expecting it to be you. I'm glad it was."

Terry pulled out his phone and tapped the screen. "What's all this about? Why are you sending me these emails?"

"I think Mavis engineered Montgomery's death."

CHAPTER 37

*T*erry rolled his eyes. "No one engineered Montgomery's allergic reaction. We've talked this to death, Erin. No one could have done that. No one could have known that the muffins had strawberries in them unless you told them. No one could have engineered it."

"Did you look at those emails? Someone was sending me emails about strawberries. About putting them into muffins. About giving them to food critics. They were trying to influence my thinking!"

"It was strawberry season and you are on a million mailing lists. Of course you got emails about using strawberries."

"I know, that's what I thought too. But none of those are from legitimate mailing lists. Someone is trying to make it look that way, but they aren't. I thought maybe your forensics guys in the city could track down the IP address that is sending them, or whatever, and verify who was trying to get me to put strawberries in those muffins."

"The case has already been closed. We don't need to look into anything else."

"Listen. I think it was Mavis. She was the one who had easy access to his cards. She was probably the one who booked the B&B and then sabotaged Montgomery's stay so that he was stressed out and having a low-level allergic reaction to the flowers and whatever other fragrances, and a couple of other things that would increase his reaction. She might have told him it was a fragrance-free house so he would stay here."

Terry just stared at her.

"And why is Mavis still here?" Erin demanded. "She's the one who called the police about us being at the B&B asking questions, wasn't she? She calls the cops about us harassing people there and then tries to keep us there longer. She was the one who opened the doors and invited us in. And let us see Montgomery's room. She was keeping us there until the press and police arrived."

"Why would she do that? Keep you there?"

"So that she could get the police and the press involved, so that we would stay away after that. Embarrass us so we would stop asking questions." Erin realized she was implicating Vic in all of this. "Me, I mean. Vic wasn't in on me asking people questions."

"Why would she attract police attention when she wanted us to close the case?"

"You had already closed the case. Mavis didn't need to worry about that. She just wanted to keep us away."

Terry shook his head. "So you think Mavis, who worked for Montgomery, set him up? Made him think he had the new cards when he had cards without strawberries on them. Then emailed you to make you put strawberries into the muffins. And sat back to see what happened."

"*And* made him react more strongly to the strawberries by exposing him to stress, other allergens, and other substances that would increase his allergic reaction. That's why it killed him so fast, even when he tried to use his auto-injector to stop the reaction."

"How could she do that?"

Erin explained the various factors she and Vic had discussed: the wine delivered to him, aspirin for his headache, the phone hang-ups, and other stressors and allergens.

"I just don't know," Terry said, reluctant but not saying it was entirely out of the question, which was progress. "It all sounds a little… out there."

"Will you at least look into it? If those emails about strawberries came from Mavis, then you know something weird was happening, right? If they were all legitimate, then you just tell me. I'll accept it."

Terry smiled with good humor. "You will never accept it until you are completely satisfied that it was an accident. And I don't know if that is even possible."

CHAPTER 38

*T*erry promised he would look into the emails, extracting from Erin a promise that she, in turn, would not approach Mavis through any means, ask her any questions, or send her any messages, letting Terry take care of things through proper channels.

"If Mavis did have something to do with engineering Montgomery's death, then she could be dangerous. Not the type of person that you want to get involved with."

"No," Erin agreed. "I'm not going to do anything to put myself in her crosshairs. Right now… she has no reason to think I suspect her."

"Keep it that way," Terry agreed, voice firm.

Erin felt better knowing that he was looking into the emails. That would be a real, concrete answer. Not just Erin guessing about what was going on. She didn't have the technical know-how to tell where those emails had come from. Maybe it was just an inept mailer who had entered the wrong information in his links. Or let his web hosting account or security certificate expire. Or his server's web host had gone down for some random reason.

That kind of thing did happen. It happened all the time. Erin could just be looking for something that wasn't there. The mailer or mailers had just been looking at the bumper crop of strawberries that year and making suggestions accordingly, without knowing that their website was about to go offline.

Whatever the case, she was happy to have Terry looking into it. From the beginning, he had not considered Montgomery's death anything but a tragic accident, one that only involved Erin by pure coincidence. Now he was finally looking into it. She just hoped that it wasn't too late. They could reopen investigations, couldn't they? They did it all the time. They even looked at cases that had already been adjudicated and people were serving prison time for.

What if Terry was right, and Erin was just seeing conspiracies where there were none? What if she was seeing patterns or motives where there weren't any because she wanted to make herself feel better about being the cause of Montgomery's death? What if Mavis was completely innocent and Erin was just imagining things? The young woman had certainly not done anything that had seemed suspicious to Erin. She hadn't acted like someone who had just engineered the death of her boss.

But a sociopath wouldn't.

Vic was still looking after Willie and making sure he didn't jump back into work too soon. Erin covered extra shifts at the bakery and had the other employees come in more often to cover Vic's usual shifts. It was an extra hassle, but everyone was happy to help out despite the inconvenience.

It was the quiet point in the afternoon, when Erin spent as much time as she could in her office working on accounting and planning, and in the kitchen cleaning up and prepping for the dinner rush before closing. She could hear the bells if someone came into the bakery, unless she were running a mixer or blender, which she avoided.

The bells at the door drew her out of her contemplations about Mavis's possible involvement in Montgomery's death. Erin tried to push it all aside. She had customers to serve.

Walking out to the front counter, she saw Olivia.

"Oh, hello! I didn't expect to see you again. I thought you would be on your way home by now."

"I was supposed to be doing a tour, but they've delayed the next event, so I'm stuck here. Well, not stuck. I could go home in between, but I would be backtracking, and I don't really want to go home just to turn around and go back out again in another day or two. I thought I would extend my stay here, enjoy the fresh air and atmosphere, and be nice and relaxed and mellow for the next appearance."

Erin nodded. "Sounds like a plan. I'm sure you're not happy about having your plans disrupted, but it's nice to have another day or two to relax."

Olivia nodded. She looked over the offerings in the display case.

"The thing is, I've got itchy fingers. I want to cook. But I can't exactly take over Mrs. McClung's kitchen. I offered to make her and Mavis dinner tonight, but she seemed… rather horrified at the idea of someone else being in her kitchen to tell the truth. It was funny, actually. You would think a busy woman like her wouldn't mind having a nice home-cooked meal in her own kitchen. But…" Olivia shrugged. "I guess I can understand not wanting someone else to come into your territory, too. Her kitchen is her own private place, and some people really don't like other people touching their stuff."

"I wouldn't mind someone making me a home-cooked meal!" Erin laughed. "I'm always so exhausted by the end of the day; it's mostly just warmed-up soup or freezer meals."

Olivia smiled. She pointed to a rustic loaf of hand-shaped bread. "That looks lovely. If it was winter, I would suggest pairing it with a nice, hearty beef stew. But in the summer… maybe with a couple of salads and the bread toasted and topped with bruschetta…?"

"Yes," Erin agreed. "That sounds wonderful."

"How about it?" Olivia said. "I will come to your house and cook you an extra-special meal. All you have to do is sit back and enjoy it."

Erin considered. She knew that Terry was on the evening shift and wouldn't be home until it was nearly time for Erin to go to bed. She was always so tired at the end of the day. But maybe she wouldn't be if she had a chance to relax and be pampered by Olivia's top-notch cooking. Erin had looked at some of her recipes and demonstrations online, and it all looked delicious.

"That sounds really nice." She considered how she felt about someone banging around in her kitchen and decided she was okay with it, considering the outcome. "But I have pets… are you okay with a pesky cat underfoot? I would lock him up while you're there, but he's really loud and would ruin the evening."

Olivia laughed. "Yes, of course. I love cats. No dog?"

"No. Terry has K9, but he will be on duty. And there is a rabbit, but he won't cause you any trouble."

"Wonderful. Can I do it, then? Come by and cook for you when you're off?"

"Sure." Erin laughed. "It's an offer I can't refuse!"

"Awesome." Olivia looked happy about this development. Erin wondered if she would go stir-crazy and want to go to other peoples' houses to bake if she weren't able to do it for a week or two. She just might.

"I'll take that loaf, then." Olivia pointed.

"On the house, since you're providing the supper," Erin told her. "What other ingredients will you need? I have the basics in the kitchen, but if there is something in particular that you are thinking of…"

"No, I'm going to shop to entertain myself. What time are you off tonight?"

"I should be home about six-thirty. Does that work?"

Olivia nodded. "I'll see you then. What's your address?"

Erin gave her the details and packaged up the bread for her.

CHAPTER 39

$\mathcal{E}$rin was excited when it was time to head home. Vic was her best friend and they often saw each other multiple times a day. Erin could always talk to her and they shared everything. But Vic was busy with Willie's medical crisis, and she hadn't had time for Erin lately. Erin had been feeling alone and neglected, even though she knew Vic had a perfectly good reason for not being around.

The dinner date with Olivia was the perfect solution. Erin was looking forward to being pampered, not making her own supper, and having a great discussion with Olivia about gluten-free cooking, restaurants, cooking, and even Gerald Montgomery, if his name came up. Olivia got her kitchen fix and Erin got socialization and a free dinner.

Olivia was at the front door with bags of food a few minutes after Erin arrived. Erin shut off the burglar alarm and let her in. "This is going to be so much fun," she told Olivia. "Now, can I help you in the kitchen?"

"Just show me where things are and I'll get on myself. This is your chance to rest, remember? Just sit and chat with me and we'll have the time of our lives."

"Whatever you want," Erin agreed. She showed Olivia to the

kitchen and gave her a quick tour of the cupboards, pantry, and fridge. Orange Blossom came into the kitchen warily, not sure what he thought of a stranger being there. He yowled at Erin, telling her how hungry he was. Olivia would think that she had been neglecting him for days; the poor thing sounded so mournful. But then, she could see by his size that he wasn't actually on a starvation diet.

"Oh, he's lovely," she told Erin as she watched Erin feed him. Hopefully, that would quiet him down for the night and he would stay out of Olivia's way. Marshmallow pattered into the kitchen a few minutes later, ready for his supper as well.

"And this is Marshmallow," Erin introduced. "They are both rescues. Marshmallow was injured when we found him, and rabbits are really prone to going into shock, so that even if their injury is treatable, vets often lose them anyway. But he pulled through just fine and has been here ever since."

"He's very nice. And he gets along with Orange Blossom?"

"They're really funny when they get to play with each other. Blossom will chase him around the house until Marshmallow decides he's had enough, and he turns around, kicks Blossom in the nose, and chases him instead. If you've never seen a rabbit chasing a cat…"

Olivia's peals of laughter filled the kitchen. "That must be hilarious. I hope they do it while I'm here."

"I don't know. They might, but usually it's when it's just me and Vic around."

"That's the young lady you were at the B&B with, right? The two of you seem close."

"Yeah. She lives back there." Erin waved a hand at the loft apartment over the garage. "And we work together. So we're together all the time, but we love it. We don't get tired of each other and are happy just to sit around and do nothing together, too—planning, crossword puzzles, journaling, genealogy, whatever. But her partner had a medical crisis this week, so she's staying with him, making sure that he's feeling better before she comes back."

"Oh, that's too bad. What happened?"

"He's going through some treatments for a medical condition, and they think that he might have reacted to one of the medications, or it might just be the stress that he's under. He went into anaphylaxis, and that's never happened before so he didn't have epinephrine. We barely got him to the hospital in the city in time."

"That's scary. Especially after seeing Montgomery die from the same thing."

"Well, we didn't know at the time that was what it was, luckily. I didn't have to worry about that as we were taking him in. But I could tell that his breathing and pulse were bad. It was pretty scary."

"It must have been. I understand Vic's wanting to stay home to care for him for a while."

Erin nodded. "Okay, well, the beasts are fed, so the kitchen is yours. If you need anything, just ask." Erin sat down on one of the kitchen chairs. It was strange to be a guest in her own kitchen. She wanted to jump up and help Olivia with the preparations. But it was nice to sit back and watch someone else cook, too. Like having her own cooking show right in her kitchen.

"This is very cool," she told Olivia. "I've seen you on the internet, so it's like having Celebrity Chef right here in front of me. Tell me about what it was like running your own restaurant."

Olivia talked about it as she chopped and measured and stirred. She had clearly enjoyed the restaurant business, no matter how stressful it must have been. She spoke of her kitchen staff as if they were family, the same way Erin felt about her employees. They weren't just people who worked together; they really were her family, whether they were related like Charley, distant cousins, or not at all. They were the people she loved and trusted and spent her day with, and they didn't let her down.

Many of the challenges that Olivia had faced were similar to what Erin had experienced at Auntie Clem's. There were always supplier issues, customers who weren't happy, and malfunctioning equipment. But there was a lot more to deal with in a sit-down restaurant, dealing with thirty or a hundred diners there for an hour or two, supervising the prep of hundreds of orders in the kitchen, and ensuring people were happy.

But Olivia sounded like she had been right in her element. It had been her dream job, despite all the ups and downs.

"Things were going really well. All of the kinks worked out, stable employees, good location, everything working smoothly… and then along comes Gerald Montgomery," Olivia told her as she bussed serving dishes over to the table. She had spread garlic butter on the bread from Auntie Clem's; it smelled so good, Erin could hardly wait to dig in.

Olivia told Erin about each dish and its ingredients and preparation, though some of it was repeated from her comments as she had cooked. They dished up and tasted each of the salads Olivia had prepared and Erin raved about the bruschetta on garlic toast.

Olivia returned to her discussion about Gerald Montgomery.

"He shows up at my restaurant one day out of the blue. Like these guys do. They love a surprise. And you're supposed to pretend you don't know who he is, even though he is surrounded by cameramen and equipment. I mean, it's not exactly covert. So you're trying to prepare something for this critic, and to get everything just right, but not neglect anyone else's meals either, because if he hears other people complaining, that is going to go into his show as well."

"So stressful," Erin commented. Even just having Montgomery walk into Auntie Clem's, only having to deal with him for five minutes at the counter, had been stressful. She couldn't imagine what it would be like to have him in her restaurant for an hour or more, while still trying to maintain service to the rest of the customers as well.

"It was. And, of course, you aren't ever going to have a day when everything goes perfectly. Something is going to be off. He's going to be able to find something to complain about. And throw his allergies into the works as well…" Olivia shook her head. "Well, of course, I am the Queen of Gluten-Free Cooking; just ask my fans, so that part of it really wasn't a challenge. But he was in a bad mood, so it didn't matter what I did or said; he was going to find something negative to say."

They ate in silence for a minute.

"In fact, most of what he said was negative," Olivia confessed. "I can't think of a single nice thing that he said. Maybe that the gluten-free baking was 'adequate' or something to that effect. It was just... a roast. He called me out. Said I wasn't a good baker, or chef, that the cooking at the restaurant was bland, tasteless, and unimaginative. We *had* good reviews. People loved the place. It had a good reputation, regular clientele, good write-ups in the papers and foodie review sites. It was a good restaurant."

Erin indicated her food. "I believe you. I can see—taste—what you can do. This would be a hit at any restaurant."

Olivia nodded appreciatively. "We were doing so well. I thought when Montgomery came in that it would be a challenge, but we would be able to impress him and it would just be another feather in our caps. I hadn't dealt with him personally before, and I didn't realize how unreasonable he could be. That he wrote reviews based on how he felt at the moment, which wasn't anything to do with whether the food was good or not. If he was in a bad mood, he wrote a bad review, even if he didn't have anything specific to say about the food. He would just... burn everything down, if you know what I mean. Write a review that said that everything about the restaurant was bad."

Erin shook her head slowly. "That's terrible. A critic should be very specific, and his personal feelings should never enter into it. It should be a balanced, unbiased review. Not just some... drunken rage because someone cut him off in his car on the drive in."

"Exactly," Olivia agreed. She pointed at Erin and then emphatically thumped her finger on the tabletop. "That's exactly right. You hit the nail on the head."

"But other people didn't see that side of him. They thought that a bad review really meant that the restaurant was bad," Erin suggested.

Olivia sighed and nodded in agreement. "And that was the beginning of the end. Things went down pretty quickly from there.

He has—had—so many followers that word just spread like wildfire across the internet and into the real world. Before long, everyone was badmouthing the restaurant based on what Montgomery had said, without ever experiencing it themselves. Pretty soon, all the review sites had negative reviews and reposts of Montgomery's review. And the clientele just dried up. Even those who had been repeat customers before acted like we had the plague. They stopped coming. It didn't matter what advertising or promotional efforts we attempted, they wouldn't come back, and nobody new would try us out. We changed the name a few times, tried new promotions to bring people in, tried changing the cuisine and menu, but nothing we did made any difference. As soon as we reopened with a new name, it would be posted online and people would copy what had been posted before. We all put our own money into it and tried to keep it running, but eventually… none of us had anything left to put into it and we had to admit that it was dead. That dream was gone."

"I'm so sorry. That sounds just awful."

"And the reviews still follow me. Whenever I try to get a new job at a restaurant, they look me up, and they find the 'boring, bland, and uninspired' garbage and won't hire me as a chef. I've done some restaurant work, but it's impossible to get any traction or get promoted above line cook. My book sales bring in some money, but not nearly enough."

"Why won't people trust their own taste buds? Give you a chance, and if they like what you cook, hire you. Why does it have to be based on some stupid review that will never go away?"

"I wish I knew the answer to that. I've considered changing my name—not just using a pen name, but legally changing my name so that people will give me a chance."

Erin, who had gone by many different names in many different circumstances, could certainly understand that desire. Sometimes, a person just wanted to shed the past and start over again. To start with a fresh slate. What Montgomery had done to Olivia was reprehensible. It was awful that one person should have so much power over another's life.

"Now *you* are a good gluten-free baker," Olivia told Erin, indicating the serving dish with the toasted garlic bread. "You wouldn't want to be limited by a bad review from Gerald Montgomery. You wouldn't want the same thing to happen to you as happened to me."

"No," Erin agreed. "I guess I dodged a bullet on that one. I thought he would probably give me a good review but, even if he didn't, I could still weather it. I didn't realize how much weight people would give to someone else's opinion over their own."

"You're lucky that he died."

Erin made a face. "Maybe. But not so lucky that it was while eating my muffins."

"Do you think so? Seems to me like you've had quite a run on those muffins. On the social networks, they are still promoting hashtag Morning Sunshine Challenge. The people who can't make it here to eat one of your muffins are trying to duplicate the recipe and make them at home so that they can participate. You might not like it, but your muffins have become a touchstone for his followers. That doesn't hurt you."

"I've been lucky," Erin admitted. "But I'd just as soon it never happened."

"Sometimes fate has a way of stepping in."

Erin took a long sip of her tea, wondering whether to tell Olivia about her thoughts about Montgomery's death being engineered by Mavis at Montgomery Meals and Reels. She took another piece of garlic bread and considered.

"You look like you have something serious on your mind," Olivia said. "Is the bakery having problems? I thought that with all of the new business after Montgomery's death, things would actually be going pretty well for you. You're the only gluten-free baker in this part of the country. You've got a captive audience."

CHAPTER 40

*I*t's not that," Erin told her. "I am doing well, and Montgomery's followers have brought a bunch of business to the bakery. His death has definitely brought us more attention than we would have gotten any other way. I was thinking about Montgomery himself and that it's too bad it had to end that way."

"He was a nasty, judgmental person. You're better off having only had a very brief encounter with him. And with him bringing business after his death—I don't see how you can complain about that."

"I'm not complaining. Like I said, the bakery is doing well. It's just… I'm not sure that his death was as accidental as everyone thinks."

Olivia dropped her fork with a clatter. She quickly picked it back up and said nothing about her clumsiness.

"What do you mean, not an accident? Did you know about his strawberry allergy?"

"No. I didn't know about that. I wouldn't have given him something I knew he was allergic to. But I'm afraid that someone might have known that and tried to engineer things so I would make muffins with strawberries without knowing he was allergic."

Olivia shook her head, bemused. "How could anyone make you make him strawberry muffins? If they even knew in the first place that he was allergic to strawberries?"

"His office knew."

"His office? How many people knew that?"

"I know one in particular."

Olivia didn't answer at first, looking at her plate and worrying her salad with her fork.

"Which one? Mavis is the only one I know personally, and she seems like a nice girl."

"Yeah, Mavis. I know that she knew about the allergies because she was the one who made the new allergen cards and replaced them in his wallet. She says that she was the one who thought of doing the wallet cards in the first place."

"And you think that… she made a mistake on them? Put the wrong cards into his wallet?"

"I think she put the wrong cards in his wallet. But I don't know if it was an accident."

"Intentionally? You think that she wanted Montgomery to die? She was trying to make it so that no one would know about his strawberry allergy?" Olivia's voice rose, disbelief in her tone.

"I know it sounds crazy," Erin admitted. "I haven't had much luck getting anyone else to believe it."

"I'm not surprised." Olivia gave a little chuckle.

Erin's cheeks heated. She didn't want Olivia to think that she was crazy, but that was probably how she was coming off.

"I'm not just making it up," Erin told her. "I may not have proof—yet—but think about it. She was the one who had the best access to the cards. She didn't have to do anything but mix one or two of the wrong cards into the stack. So it would look like he only had the right ones, when Montgomery was handing out cards with the wrong information, making it more likely that people would make him something he was allergic to."

"Sure. But other people might have had access to his wallet. People he worked with, a girlfriend or wife, whoever he lived with. Or people lay their wallets down, maybe even leave them unattended for a minute or two. He wouldn't necessarily know if someone had been touching it."

"But the wallet isn't the only thing. I think they were trying to force Montgomery to have a more serious allergic reaction, too."

"How is that even possible?"

"Because of Willie's allergic reaction, we had a bunch of information on what can make a reaction worse. Like stress."

"And how would she cause him extra stress?"

"Phone call hang-ups. Someone kept calling him and hanging up. Who knows what kind of business stresses she might have caused him. She could have screwed up all kinds of arrangements for him. Mrs. McClung said that he had a lot of complaints. Things like expecting the B&B to be fragrance-free when it was never advertised that way. He was bothered by the smells of the flowers and linens and who knows what else. They gave him a headache and caused him extra stress. And he probably took aspirin, too."

"And is that bad? That would help, wouldn't it?"

"It could intensify an allergic reaction. And if the flowers and fragrances were causing him a low-level allergic reaction, then he's starting at a higher level of histamines. It wouldn't take as much to put him into anaphylaxis. He was already well on his way there."

"But you don't have any proof that Mavis was doing any of this."

"The flowers were sent from somewhere. Maybe we'll be able to trace who sent them. And there were the emails, too!"

"Someone was sending him threatening emails?"

"No, no. Someone was sending *me* emails."

"Why would they send you emails? And what effect would that have on Montgomery?"

"They were trying to get me to put strawberries into the muffins."

"Blackmail? But why would you do it if you knew he was allergic? Did you think that he wouldn't have a big reaction? That he would just get a little bit sick? But then he wouldn't give you a good review."

"No, I didn't. It was more subtle than that. Sending me emails about strawberry season, about putting strawberries in muffins, about silencing the critics with strawberry recipes…"

"Well, you certainly accomplished that."

Erin's cheeks flamed hotter. She hadn't even thought about how it would sound before the words came out of her mouth.

"I didn't mean that. I mean what the email said. That everyone would think they were great, that there wouldn't be anything about them to criticize. And I must have taken it all in subconsciously. I don't even remember reading those emails."

Olivia shook her head. "Well, I'm not sure how you would prove to anyone that you were subconsciously tricked into making something that Montgomery was allergic to."

Erin's phone rang and she took it out of her pocket to see who the caller was.

CHAPTER 41

erry's email dinged and he opened the inbox to see what he had received. Surprisingly, the techs from the electronic forensics lab in the city were getting back to him with preliminary results.

He opened the email and skimmed through it.

The first revelation was that all of the emails had come from the same sender.

Since all the emails had different headers and sender information, Terry had initially dismissed Erin's suspicion that they might all be from someone trying to engineer Gerald Montgomery's death as paranoia.

What were the chances that someone had been trying to engineer Montgomery's death? And even more, that they had succeeded? Erin's theories had sounded far-fetched.

He dug deeper into the report and tried to sort out what they had found. They needed to reach the sender's ISP to find out the name of the account holder. And what if it turned out to just be public Wi-Fi? Then, the address and account holder wouldn't get him anywhere.

Erin had suggested that the person who had set Montgomery up was Mavis, Montgomery's assistant, so that was who Terry needed to talk to next. Hopefully, she was at the bed and breakfast and not out sightseeing.

"Come on, K9." Terry stood up and gestured for K9 to heel. "Let's go check out the B&B."

～

In a few minutes, he was knocking on Mrs. McClung's door. She seemed confused as to what he was doing on her doorstep.

"I didn't call the police," she told him, shaking her head.

"I know. I'm here to talk to Mavis. Is she in?"

"Uh… yes, I believe she is in her room. It's the supper hour, and she should be going out to dinner soon, but she hasn't left yet."

"What can you tell me about her?"

Mrs. McClung looked at him questioningly. "What do you mean?"

"How much do you know about her? I know Mavis works for Meals and Reels, but that's about it. She arrived with Mr. Montgomery? As his personal assistant?"

"No," Mrs. McClung shook her head. "She didn't come here until after he died. To see to arrangements."

"Oh. She wasn't here at the same time as he was?"

"No. I had talked to her on the phone when she booked the rooms, but I hadn't seen her face-to-face. She was just a voice on the phone."

"Who was here with him, then?"

"I don't know. There was a whole mess of them. Camera crew, microphones, I don't know what all of those people are called. I never did understand all of those technical positions they list after a movie. Gaffers and grips and all of that. He had a lot of people, and they used the second room. Came and went. They didn't sleep here; they used it for equipment and meetings. Then after he died, they didn't need the crew here anymore, but wanted someone here to deal with… the body and the press, I suppose. There's a lot to do when someone dies. And it's more complicated when that person is out of town. Transporting the remains back to his family."

"And there has been a lot of press surrounding his death."

Mrs. McClung nodded her agreement. "It has not been fun trying to keep them out of here. They keep trying to sneak in, bothering me and the other guest and all of the fans who keep coming into town to see where he died."

Terry knew that Mrs. McClung had made several trespassing complaints. He and the others had each been there at least once to disperse a crowd or get rid of some fan who thought they had the right to go wherever they liked.

"They're quite a nuisance."

"You're right about that," the old woman agreed, nodding. "Think they should have the run of the place. Olivia said that I should just start charging admission for them to come and see where he died. I could make a lot of money doing that."

"I suppose you could."

"But I am not the type to take advantage of a person's death. That's just not right. They are ghouls. I'm not going to encourage that kind of behavior."

"Good for you." Terry nodded. "But I imagine it does make things disruptive for you. You can't escape them."

"Well, I'm sure it will only be a few more days now. You've decided it was an accident. I'm sure Mavis will be packing everything up and moving on. You have released the body…?"

"That would be the medical examiner in the city. I don't know what arrangements have been made. I assume it has been released. Mavis will be able to make arrangements for its transport."

"It's such a strange thing when you think about it. Dealing with the shell of the person you have lost. They aren't there anymore, but their husk is still important for our rituals. It's the last thing that we can hold on to physically."

"I guess so," Terry agreed. "I haven't thought much about it. I'm involved with the other end of the business. I'm not the one dealing with the body after it has been released. It must be difficult for such a young woman. I don't imagine she has much experience with that kind of thing."

"She is a very competent young person. But it has been very

hard on her. I don't think people have much compassion for a girl who just worked for someone who has died. But the tragedy has touched her, too. This is probably her first real job, and what happens? Her boss has a terrible accident and dies."

"You're right. I didn't think about how it must affect her personally. Though I gather he wasn't a very nice person, so it wouldn't be as bad as if she were close to him."

"That would be a real tragedy," Mrs. McClung agreed. "The poor girl. She thinks she can hide her red, puffy eyes with cold compresses, but I sometimes see her when she gets up in the morning before she's had a chance to put anything on them. I see how it's affecting her."

In Terry's experience, those who had intentionally killed someone did not generally spend the night crying their eyes out. Even if they felt guilty afterward, that usually led to increased drinking, agitation, or moodiness—not tears.

CHAPTER 42

"So Mavis wasn't even here before Montgomery died," Terry mused, thinking through Erin's theory. How many of the things she had suggested would Mavis have needed to be present for? Obviously, Mavis could have sent the emails from anywhere. She could have changed the wallet cards when Montgomery had last been at the office. Wine and flowers could have been ordered over the phone or internet from anywhere in the world. Nobody would be looking at them with suspicion. Would Mavis have needed to be present for any of the set-up Erin had suggested?

"Who was it that booked the room? I supposed that was done several weeks before he arrived."

"Yes. They had to make a reservation, but no one was supposed to know when he was actually going to be here. They booked it for a couple of weeks, but no one knew what day he would arrive."

"Including you?"

"Including me," she said with a nod.

"And was it Montgomery or Mavis who made that reservation?"

"It was Mavis," Mrs. McClung said with certainty. "And it was a good thing, with Mr. Montgomery canceling his credit card."

Terry had been looking at K9 and preparing himself mentally

to go upstairs and talk to Mavis, but Mrs. McClung's words pulled him back down to the present.

"What?"

"It was Mavis."

"No, what was that about the credit card?"

"His card was canceled. So he would not have been able to pay for the room."

"Why was his card canceled?"

"He had lost his wallet, so he canceled his credit cards and was in the process of finding out how to get his identification reissued."

"This happened right before he died?"

"A few days. Maybe the day before he got here. But it was turned in. He got it back. He was just missing his cash so it turned out he didn't have to get his identification reissued. But he'd already canceled his credit cards."

Terry pondered this new information. The wallet had been out of Montgomery's possession for long enough for him to notice its absence and start canceling credit cards. Certainly long enough for someone to add a couple of old cards in with the new ones, or take the new ones out and put the old ones back.

"I imagine he'd had plenty of practice getting cards reissued," Mrs. McClung told him. "He didn't keep track of it very well. He left it on the desk down here one day and I had to take it up to him."

"Really. Do you remember what day that was?"

"Some people are like that, you know, they don't pay attention to what they are doing. Leaving wallets, phones, keys—you wouldn't believe the number of times I have to return things to guests that they've just carelessly left here or there."

"Mmm-hm. Do you remember what day it was? That you found his wallet and returned it to him?"

She considered it for a moment. "Probably that last day. The day he died."

"In the morning or the evening?"

"Oh, the evening. Definitely. And there were so many people coming and going with that film crew of his. It was just chaos here.

He should have booked all of the rooms so that there weren't any other guests around to bother. I was very concerned about him upsetting Olivia. But she didn't complain. I guess what's good for the goose is good for the gander."

"What do you mean by that?"

"Well, because she was the one who had been making noise and bothering Mr. Montgomery the day before that." She widened her eyes at Terry and anticipated his question. "Playing her music. Opera, mostly. I went up to talk to her about it after a couple of hours, told her how inconsiderate she was being of the other guest and that she needed to wear earphones if she was going to continue to listen to it. But she just laughed. Said that she and Mr. Montgomery were old friends and he could deal with it." She rolled her eyes. "He kept complaining about it. I tried just to put him off to begin with, said that I had already talked to her, and if he wanted to try appealing to her directly, he was welcome to. I heard the two of them arguing, and him banging on her door, but she was not to be reasoned with."

Mrs. McClung shook her head.

"Up until then, I thought that she was very charming and an excellent guest. I can't understand why she behaved that way. But I guess some people are very particular about their music. She said that it was meant to be listened to in open halls, not on tinny little earphones. She had it on very late the night before he died. And then again early in the morning. Last night, she had it on again after dinner, but only for a little while, and Mr. Montgomery wasn't complaining, so…"

She trailed off, the blood draining from her face.

"Is that why he didn't complain about the opera music? Because he was dead? Oh, my stars…"

Terry patted Mrs. McClung on the arm and looked for somewhere for her to sit down. She looked like she might faint dead away.

"Try not to think about it," he told her, steering her into a chair. "Can I get you a cold glass of water? That usually helps."

She didn't answer. Terry looked around and found the kitchen.

He ran cold water into the sink until it was icy cold, then filled a glass and took it out to her.

"So it was Olivia who played the music that gave him a headache."

"Yes. He was whining and complaining like a baby. He couldn't work like that. He needed to have quiet and solitude for the tasting." Mrs. McClung stuck her nose up in the air and spoke precisely, obviously mimicking Montgomery. "If he wanted absolute quiet for his little show, he should have used a recording studio. In a bed and breakfast, people come and go, they talk, they play music, they make noise. It's a home away from home. Expecting it to be silent so you don't get any outside sounds on your tape is ridiculous."

Terry nodded. He waited for Mrs. McClung to take another sip of her water. She was pinking up again. "You're right. People need to be reasonable. Practical. If he needed a soundproof room, he should have booked a place with soundproofed rooms."

She nodded emphatically.

"And if they want fragrance-free rooms, then they should book a room that advertises that," Terry added, watching her closely for her reaction.

"Exactly. I would never go to someone else's house and insist that they remove all of the smells!" She looked affronted at the idea. "I understand that some people are very sensitive, but then those people should know to ask ahead and only book rooms in places where their *needs* can be accommodated." She sneered out the word needs.

"Mavis didn't say anything about Mr. Montgomery's allergy to fragrances on the phone when she booked the room?"

"No, course not. I would have told her that there wasn't any such thing here. Probably not anywhere. Can you imagine running an inn where no smells are allowed? What do you do when other guests are wearing perfume? Or if a child picks a bouquet of flowers? I'm supposed to clean anything without any chemical cleaners? How? It can't be done."

Terry agreed that very few people would probably meet a

rigorous definition of being fragrance-free. But other owners might be a little more open to it than Mrs. McClung. If Mavis had talked to her about Mr. Montgomery's environmental allergies, she would undoubtedly have gotten an earful.

"So what if he had a headache?" Mrs. McClung said with a shrug. "I have a headache most of my waking hours. I gave him some aspirin. If he's so sensitive, why doesn't he pack his own? It's ridiculous."

"Maybe he just forgot his at home."

"Or maybe he liked to whine and make people do things for him. I don't like to speak ill of the dead, but the man really was a pain in the neck. And I'm used to dealing with demanding guests. That one really took the cake."

"And then the cake took him."

Mrs. McClung snorted. "You really shouldn't say such things," she declared, fanning herself with her hand as if blushing. "It's very irreverent!"

"Well, some people deserve it and some people don't. It doesn't sound like he was too considerate of anyone else's feelings."

"He was difficult," she admitted. She looked up at the sound of footsteps overhead. "Oh, you see? I was right. She's getting ready to go out to supper now. You've missed your chance to talk to Mavis."

"I'll just ask her a question or two on the way out. Do you know where she is going to eat? I can walk her over."

"Probably the family restaurant. She has tried the Chinese already. And the hot chicken. These foodies, you know. They like to test them all, see what they're like."

Terry nodded. He waited while Mavis walked back and forth a few times overhead, getting ready, and then came down the stairs. She saw Terry and looked surprised.

"Oh, I didn't know anyone was here. How are you doing, Officer...? I don't remember your name."

"Terry Piper, ma'am. I was hoping to ask you a few questions. Maybe I can walk you over to your dinner appointment and we could discuss it on the way."

"Certainly," she agreed. "I always enjoy walking with a handsome gentleman." She smiled. "And his owner, too."

Terry laughed, looking down at his dog. "K9 seems very taken with you, too. And he has very good taste."

"Well, then, let's walk, shall we?"

K9 was looking at Terry hopefully with the repetition of the word "walk."

"Let's go, boy," Terry confirmed, motioning for K9 to heel and leading the way out the door.

He looked back at Mrs. McClung. "Is Olivia here? Or has she already gone out for dinner?"

"Oh, she's already gone out." Mrs. McClung confirmed what Terry had already guessed by the quiet of the house. Since Mrs. McClung didn't serve dinner, guests had to fend for themselves, and the supper hour was well underway. With Mavis out of the way, Mrs. McClung would have the house to herself and be able to relax for a while without worrying about her guests' needs.

"Where did she go, do you know?" he asked, wondering if he might be able to connect with her after talking with Mavis.

"Well, I believe she was going to cook dinner for your wife."

Terry looked at her in amusement. "I'm not married."

"Erin Price. She's your... partner, isn't she?" Her mouth twisted sourly on the word partner. Of course the old biddies didn't like the fact that he and Erin were living together outside the bonds of matrimony.

"Yes, that's right."

"Olivia was going to cook for her tonight. She was quite excited about it."

CHAPTER 43

*O*livia reached over and pulled the phone from Erin's hand.

"No phones at the table," she scolded. "That's rude."

So was taking someone's phone out of her hand. Erin stared at Olivia with her mouth open, wanting to protest but unsure what to say.

It was her house, her phone, her dinner.

But as Olivia had said, it was rude of her to talk on the phone while they were eating.

But Erin had only been checking to see who it was. Whether it was something important or just an unknown caller, a sales rep for some kitchen equipment company or a phone company trying to talk her into a new plan. She wouldn't have answered it unless it was really important, and then she would have explained that to Olivia.

Olivia laughed. "You should see the expression on your face."

"Well… I wasn't expecting you to do that."

"We're having such a good time together. I didn't want it to be interrupted by a phone call." Olivia looked down at the phone, waiting for it to stop ringing. "You know, at my restaurant, there was a no phones policy. You couldn't even have it out at the table. When you're eating a special dinner, something that you've paid for and that the chef has put so much time and effort into, you should give it your full attention."

"Of course," Erin agreed, turning her attention back to her meal, showing Olivia that she was willing to immerse herself in the experience and worry about the rest of the world later, when she was finished eating. Olivia put the phone down on the table beside her. It had stopped ringing and the screen was dark. Erin hadn't been able to see who it was before Olivia had snatched it, but suspected it was Terry. Maybe he was on his way home. He could share the dinner with her. There was plenty to go around.

She suddenly felt a little uncomfortable being alone with Olivia and wished that Terry were there to cushion her from Olivia and her intensity.

Olivia was an interesting person. She'd had some amazing experiences with cooking and restaurants, and Erin was fascinated with her encounters with Montgomery, giving her a little window into the kind of person he was. Erin could see that she had dodged a bullet with Montgomery dying before he'd had a chance to review the baking.

If he had come out with as negative a review as he had with Olivia, the results might have been the same. Maybe she would have been ruined, despite being the only bakery in town. She would be forced out and someone else would come in and take over and run a conventional bakery instead of a gluten-free one.

Running a gluten-free bakery had been an uphill battle for Erin right from the beginning. She'd had to fight for the reputation she had. Each and every sale was a win, overcoming people's resistance to eating something different that they considered strange, inferior, or faddish. She had to get people to taste it, to give it a chance.

It would have been much easier for her to open a conventional bakery. With Angela Plaint's death, the timing was perfect for her to take over from The Bake Shoppe, stepping into the void left by Angela's death.

"Everything okay?" Olivia asked.

Erin looked up from her food, forcing a smile. "Yes, I'm fine. Sorry. Off in my own little world there. This really is lovely. You're a good cook. And I love the concept of a simple meal from simple ingredients, but that blends together into something so…"

Erin had another forkful of salad and tried to think of the word she wanted.

"So complex, I guess. The way that all of the flavors and textures go together just the right way. You know, I'm always so tired when I come home from Auntie Clem's that I really don't have the energy to figure out what to make, let alone take the time to do it. I open a can of soup, pull some leftover buns out of the freezer, maybe make a bagged salad and drown it in salad dressing."

Olivia laughed and nodded. "I could teach you a few basic recipes that would help. You can make up batches of salad dressing beforehand so that you have something really nice rather than the bottled dressings full of sugar and preservatives. And a few ingredients can turn a bagged salad into a proper meal: sun-dried tomatoes, seeds, some nice in-season fruit or vegetable. I'll send you a copy of my first book. It contains some really nice base recipes that you can then build on. It doesn't have to take more time if you have your ingredients ready."

Erin nodded. "How about you just stay on as my personal chef?"

"I don't think you could afford me," Olivia told Erin with a chuckle.

"Can I afford *not* to have you? I think that's the real question," Erin asked playfully.

Olivia smiled, appreciating Erin's words even though she knew they were hyperbolic.

Erin looked toward the loft over the garage, wishing Vic were with her instead of looking after Willie. Vic would have handled the situation much more gracefully than Erin, she was sure. Maybe it had even been Vic on the phone, asking whether it was okay to pop by. She usually wouldn't bother to ask but, if she had seen that Erin had a visitor, she might.

"I made dessert, if you're finished with the main course," Olivia said, looking at Erin's plate. She was just toying with what remained, no longer hungry. It was good food—excellent, in fact.

But Olivia taking Erin's phone had triggered something. Erin no longer wanted to sit there, visiting and eating with the stranger. Her stomach gurgled and she felt nauseated. Her muscles were tense, even though she was doing her best to relax them. She closed her eyes and thought about doing her tai chi practice in the backyard, her toes digging into the sweet-smelling, soft grass.

"Dessert?" Olivia prodded again, her voice taking on a note of frustration.

It was rude of Erin not to have answered immediately. She didn't know why she was so distracted. She pasted a plastic smile on her face.

"Of course. That sounds delicious."

It was perhaps not the right thing to say, since Olivia hadn't even said what she had made. Olivia frowned, lines appearing between her brows.

"Dessert sounds great, I mean," Erin told her. "I would love something sweet to finish off this excellent meal."

"You didn't eat very much."

"I can't if I want to maintain my figure," Erin protested, putting her hand over her stomach. "I've put on weight since I opened the bakery. Go figure! I'm so short-waisted that every pound is obvious."

"Tell me about it," slim little Olivia agreed. "Tasting food in the kitchen is the bane of a chef's existence. For women like you and me, anyway."

She put her hand over Erin's briefly, affectionate, connecting with her. They were part of a sisterhood—short woman chefs who didn't want to end up shaped like blueberries.

"Well, you don't need to worry about this dessert," Olivia assured her. "I wanted to go with something fresh and local and, seeing as the late summer berries are in season right now, I thought fresh berries with stevia-sweetened, whipped Greek yogurt would be a fresh, sweet, low-cal treat we could both enjoy."

Erin's mouth watered at the description. She nodded. "Yeah, that sounds really good."

Olivia smiled and nodded her approval. She stood up and went to the fridge to pull out the dessert ingredients she had prepared. Erin eyed her phone, wondering if Olivia would notice or would be upset if Erin grabbed her phone back. As long as she only took a quick, covert look and put it in her pocket, Olivia shouldn't mind too much.

She waited until Olivia's back was turned while she filled parfait glasses with layers of whipped yogurt and berries, then reached across the table for her phone and casually slid it across the table toward her, and then into her lap. She exhaled slowly.

It *had* been Terry who had been trying to get her.

Olivia brought the glasses with long-handled spoons to the table.

"Those look gorgeous," she told Olivia. "Almost too good to eat!"

"Almost," Olivia agreed. "But not quite."

Erin dipped her spoon into the yogurt topping, mirroring Olivia's movements. As she brought it up to her mouth, she caught a whiff of something that wasn't quite right. She eyed the yogurt. It looked perfectly fine, of course. White and smooth and rich. What had she smelled? The stevia? Some people swore by it, but Erin had never liked the smell, even though most people said it was undetectable.

But it wasn't the sweet, faintly licorice smell of stevia. It was something else. Unless it was a form of stevia that had been highly processed with other chemicals, and Olivia had professed to use ingredients as close to their natural states as possible.

Olivia raised her brows, watching Erin. "Something wrong?"

"No, I'm just admiring it," Erin said, smiling. "You have to feed all your senses, right? Enjoy the whole *experience*."

"Of course," Olivia agreed. "Just what I was saying."

Erin glanced down at her phone again. She couldn't help it. *Where* was Terry? Was he calling to say he'd be late getting home, or was on his way? He often texted her if she didn't answer but, so far, he hadn't sent her a text to let her know what he'd been calling about.

"Would you excuse me for just a moment?" Erin put down her

spoon and rose to her feet, sliding her phone into her pocket as she did so in a movement she hoped was invisible to Olivia. "Sorry."

She headed straight for the bathroom and shut and locked the door.

Now what?

She couldn't identify what it was about Olivia's mood and actions that had suddenly put her off. Another time, she would have laughed off Olivia's actions and agreed that it was time to put her phone away. She would have eaten the dessert even though there was a faintly different scent about it.

Olivia had been so kind to come and cook for her, but she was letting her imagination run wild, keeping her from enjoying the meal and showing her gratitude for Olivia's gift to her.

She didn't want Olivia to overhear her talking, so she texted Terry rather than calling him.

Missed your call. You coming home?

She waited for his answer, moving around the bathroom, flushing the toilet, running the water, opening and closing the cabinet, trying to make everything sound normal and natural while she waited for Terry's return text.

She was expecting it to come right away, but maybe he had called her to tell her that he was going into a meeting and wouldn't be able to answer any calls or texts for a while. Maybe he had found something when he had looked into the strawberry emails she had received and needed to present it to the sheriff or other law enforcement officers before deciding on a course of action. It could be good news. He might have made some progress and wanted to tell her in person when he got home.

"Erin, is everything alright?" Olivia inquired through the door.

Erin swallowed. "Sorry, I'll be out in a minute. I just... took a turn. I think I forgot my meds." She tried to make it sound normal and believable, not like something she was just making up on the spot. "I'll be fine in a few minutes."

"Meds? Meds for what?" Olivia demanded.

It wasn't polite to ask someone what meds they were taking.

You could discuss it if someone disclosed their medical condition and what they were taking but, if not, it was pretty intrusive to ask.

"Sorry, be out in a minute," Erin repeated.

"Erin, I'm worried. Why don't you unlock this door so I can make sure you're okay? I just don't want you to faint or something while I can't get in to help you. After what happened to Montgomery..."

Erin suppressed a chill at the words: *After what happened to Montgomery.* What if it hadn't been Mavis? Once Erin had started putting all the clues together, Mavis had been the obvious suspect, but what if she had made too many assumptions?

Olivia rattled the door handle. "Erin?"

"I'm fine," Erin told her. "Don't come in."

"Was it something I said or did? Erin?" She rattled the door-knob again and bumped her shoulder into the door. Not hard, just experimentally. Erin looked around the bathroom for something she could use to defend herself. The plunger? An aerosol can?

"Oh, no. I'll be okay. I just need a few minutes."

Terry wasn't answering her text. Erin tried Vic.

Hey, are you busy?

Vic's answer was quick, filling Erin with relief. She had been afraid that no one would answer her.

Just spending some time with Willie. He says hi.

Can you come over for a minute and bring your friend?

She held her breath, waiting for Vic's reply. Her heart pounded hard and fast.

My friend? Vic texted back, *U mean Willie?*

No, your little friend.

She waited for Vic's response, but nothing came through.

CHAPTER 44

*D*espair welled up in Erin's throat.

She tried to keep herself calm. At the moment, she was in no danger. She didn't even know for sure that there *was* any danger from Olivia. She might just be the concerned friend that she appeared to be. Or a stranger who was trying to be her friend.

Even if Olivia had malice in her heart, Erin was protected for the moment by the locked door. It wouldn't withstand a full-on assault, but it was an obstacle, and maybe Olivia would decide it wasn't worth breaking down the door and showing her hand. She had acted covertly until now, being very careful to cover her tracks and not take direct action. She was not the type to rush in boldly and operate openly.

Erin hoped.

Terry was in a meeting and Vic was with Willie, clearly not understanding what Erin was trying to tell her. Maybe she thought Erin had meant to bring Nilla, her little white dog with her—Man's best friend. Nilla might be able to help. He was a brave little dog and not afraid to attack when he thought his people were in danger.

She should have been clear in her text to Vic, but she was used to referring to Vic's weapon obliquely, since she knew it was not properly licensed. Erin looked down at her phone, wondering whether to send another message, clarifying and encouraging Vic to come over quickly.

"Erin," Olivia banged the door again. "Just open the door, please. I want to make sure you are okay."

Was Olivia armed? Erin hadn't even considered that possibility. Olivia was a poisoner—someone who worked in the shadows. But Erin didn't want Vic rushing onto the scene without being properly prepared.

It had been a mistake to contact her. She should have tried the police dispatcher, even if Olivia did hear her talking to her. That could have been a deterrent in itself.

They both arrived at the same time.

Erin heard the front door open and Terry call her name. And at the same time, the back door opened and closed quickly. There was a moment, Erin imagined, when Terry and Vic both stared at each other, confirmed that Erin and Olivia were not in the kitchen, and then moved into the house, maybe with a hand signal or mouthed instruction from Terry telling Vic to fall back and let him go first.

"What are you doing?" Terry demanded. "Hands in the air!"

"I'm just checking on Erin," Olivia protested in an affronted tone. "She's not feeling well. She said something about not taking her medication, but she won't open the door so that I can confirm that she's okay. I'm afraid she might be having… some kind of episode."

The last was, Erin suspected, an attempt to deflect suspicion if Erin came out with some wild story about how Olivia was trying to kill her and had been the culprit behind Montgomery's death.

"Hands up!" Terry ordered again.

"Officer, I'm not sure what you think is happening here, but you can see I am not armed. I'm just talking to Erin. You can ask her. I haven't done anything."

Terry's voice was closer. "Put your hands up unless you want me to have my K9 secure you."

There was a thump on the wall as he probably pushed Olivia into position and frisked her for a weapon. Erin breathed slowly, thinking about her tai chi and the breath control she had practiced with that discipline. Everything was fine. She could relax.

"Erin?" Terry called. "Are you okay? Everything is secure."

"I'm good," Erin told him, her voice much smaller than she expected. There was no need for her to feel so weak. She forced herself to move to the door. She put her hand against it to begin with. Steadying herself. Reassuring herself that everything was safe and secure on the other side of the door, just like Terry had told her. As if she were Reg Rawlins, professed psychic, able to feel the atmosphere through the locked door.

With one more fortifying breath, she unlocked the door and turned the handle to open it.

Terry stood in the hallway with Olivia, who had been hand-cuffed and looked a little stunned at the turn of events.

"You see?" she told Terry, "She's just fine. Now if you would release me, I'll head back to the B&B. This is all a bit much for me."

"Shut up," Terry told her irritably. Not the way he usually talked to suspects. "Erin?" He touched her arm. "You okay?"

Erin nodded. "Did you know…?"

"Mavis didn't get here until after Montgomery died. She wasn't the one playing the loud music. And Montgomery's wallet was misplaced or stolen. Twice."

"Twice?" Erin had thought that Mavis was the most likely suspect for having switched the cards in his wallet. She had been close to him. She had probably been tasked with putting the cards in his wallet in the first place. She would have no difficulty making sure that one of them was the old card without strawberries. Or making certain that they all were and then switching them back again after making sure that he was dead. She would have had access to his room because of her position working for him.

But if the wallet had disappeared twice, then that argued against Mavis being the culprit. Someone had taken his wallet once to put the wrong cards in it, and then again to take them out and cover her tracks. Someone close at hand like Olivia.

"What are you talking about?" Olivia demanded. "What does Montgomery's misplaced wallet have to do with me?"

"Because you were close by to steal it and make sure that his allergy cards were replaced with the ones that didn't include strawberries."

"How would I even have a card like that?"

"Maybe he gave it to you when he visited your restaurant," Erin suggested, "or maybe you had your own fakes made."

Olivia shook her head. "You're crazy." She turned to Terry. "Would you please let me go now? I don't know what you think I've done, but you can see that Erin is just fine and I haven't done anything to her."

CHAPTER 45

$\mathcal{E}$rin moved down the hallway, past Terry, K9, and Olivia. Vic stood here, her gun in her hand, her mouth a grim line. She looked confused about what was happening, but she was there and ready to do whatever was necessary to protect her friend. Erin knew that Vic wouldn't hesitate to use her gun, even if it meant she was arrested for carrying an unlicensed weapon or committing manslaughter.

"Thanks," Erin told Vic sincerely. "I guess the cavalry showed up after all."

"Olivia...?"

"She's the one who killed Montgomery." Erin looked at Olivia. "I thought it was Mavis, but I didn't suspect her."

"But it was the strawberries," Vic protested. She appeared to suddenly become aware of the gun in her hand, and turned away from them briefly to secure it in her bra holster. "How can she be responsible for Montgomery's death when she wasn't the one who gave her the strawberries?"

"Exactly," Olivia said smugly. "How can you charge me with something you know someone else did? I didn't give Montgomery the food that killed him. I didn't tell anyone else to do it."

"If you're guilty of making sure that Erin couldn't know about his strawberry allergy, then you are responsible for his death," Terry said firmly. "If you swap out his allergy cards so that she doesn't have any way of knowing about the strawberry allergy, then you *are* guilty."

She smiled. "Are you sure of that, Officer Piper?"

Terry's expression didn't change. But Erin knew he must be trying to sort it out. Did they have enough to charge her? To prove that she had been the one to swap the cards? Was swapping the cards enough to convict her of murder? Or at least manslaughter?

"There's something in the dessert," Erin told him. "That's why... I think she came here because she knew I was getting too close to the truth. And then... I sort of told her what I had figured out about the emails."

"You should be more careful who you talk to. Are you okay? Did you eat any of the dessert?"

"No."

"What did you put in it?" Terry gave Olivia a little shake by her handcuffed arms. "We're going to find out anyway, so you may as well tell me."

"I don't know what you're talking about. Why would I put something in the dessert?"

"We'll have it tested. The lab will find out what you put in it."

She shrugged. "I don't know what you're talking about. If there is anything wrong with the dessert, it must be because someone else put something in there. I didn't. So maybe it was her. Or you. To set me up."

Erin and Terry exchanged glances. They both knew how things could go sideways in court. The problem was that there wasn't a lot of evidence against Olivia, only conjecture. Until it came to the poisoned dessert. And if her lawyer successfully argued that it was planted there in order to convict her because they didn't have enough evidence in the Montgomery case...

"I'll get her out of here," Terry said, his voice still flat and unemotional, not reacting to what Olivia said or the fact that she had tried to poison Erin. "And call in the others to take control of the scene and evidence collection."

It would help if someone other than Terry collected the evidence. But it wouldn't be a slam dunk. The police department was a close-knit group and Terry, Erin, and Vic had been in a position to tamper with the evidence before the rest of the department got there.

"We'd better go outside too," Erin told Vic. "Make sure we're not in the house when Sheriff Wilmot and the others arrive."

Vic nodded her agreement and they all trooped outside.

The air was still warm, though the sun was going down. It didn't take the rest of the police department long to arrive. Bald Eagle Falls was a small town and, unless someone were shopping in the city or on vacation, they were close at hand.

Stayner took custody of Olivia and put her into his squad car. Sheriff Wilmot headed for the house.

"I'll come in with you," Erin offered. "I need to lock Orange Blossom up so he doesn't get out of the house. I wouldn't want to lose him."

She was terrified at the thought of Orange Blossom someday getting out on his own and being hit by a car or attacked by a dog or wild animal.

"I'll take care of the cat," Wilmot said, barring her way.

"He doesn't like strangers. He'll scratch."

He nodded. "I'll be careful. Sorry, you need to stay out."

"You can just shut him in my bedroom at the end of the hall. Hopefully he won't howl for too long and will go to sleep on my bed."

But she knew he would yowl for a good long time. She knew her cat. And Orange Blossom had a singing voice that would keep the whole neighborhood up. Erin looked at the time on her phone. It was getting close to her bedtime, but that would be delayed now.

She retreated and let Wilmot go into the house on his own. Orange Blossom did not escape and come running out, so at least he would be safe, though Sheriff Wilmot might sustain extreme cat scratches and bites.

Vic joined Erin and put her arm through hers. "Are you okay?"

"Yeah." Erin sighed. "I'm fine… no harm done. It was just a bit scary. Only I didn't know whether to be afraid or not. I wasn't sure… whether she had really done anything to Montgomery or not, and whether the dessert was poisoned."

"But you think it was?"

"It smelled funny," Erin explained, not sure that was actually proof of anything.

"Well, knowing your super-smeller, you're probably right, then. If one person could sniff out an odor undetectable to the normal human, it would be you."

"I don't know." Erin rubbed her forehead. "I feel like I might have just made it all up. I mean, I know that I didn't, but… there's no proof of anything."

"Until they test the dessert."

"Well, yes."

"You didn't know that Terry was on his way?"

"No. I couldn't answer the phone when he called me, and I guess he couldn't answer when I texted him back. He was probably driving at the time. But I was afraid he had gone into a meeting; that's why I texted you. I didn't know what else to do."

"Well, she didn't have a gun, so you probably would have been okay. You may just be the baker, but you're pretty tough. She didn't look any bigger than you."

"I hoped that it wouldn't get physical… with her being a poisoner. That she wouldn't dare."

"You need to get one of these," Vic said, touching the spot under her bra where her gun lay.

"I'm not getting a gun," Erin said immediately.

"You would have been able to protect yourself," Vic pointed out. "What would you have done if you hadn't been able to get one of us? If you had a gun, you wouldn't even have to wait for her to break the door down. You could drill her through the door. And even if you missed, she would know you were serious."

"I'm not getting a gun," Erin repeated.

Terry was talking to the other law enforcement officers, then came over to speak to Erin and Vic when he was finished. He shook his head at Erin.

"She insists that it was for you. She did you and all of the other potential victims of Montgomery a favor by 'encouraging him to find another line of work.'"

"She doesn't admit to trying to kill him?" Erin asked. It would have been nice if Olivia just confessed her guilt. Then they wouldn't need so much hard evidence to prove what she had done.

"No such luck," Terry agreed with a rueful smile that suggested that he, too, would have preferred it if she just confessed. "She admits to doing things to harass and annoy him, but nothing with malice. Nothing intended to actually kill him."

"What about the wallet cards? Does she admit to that?"

"Of course not. She knows where to draw the line. Not the act that caused his death. Following him, playing music to bother him, sending him flowers or other things to trigger headaches. But not the big allergies. And not the act of removing the card that included strawberries."

She was smart. Too smart. Erin was worried she would get away with everything.

"What about the emails she sent me to get me to make strawberry muffins for the tasting tour? She did that, right?"

"Not that she will admit to. But the forensic guys have a good start on tracing those. They agree that they were all sent by the same person, not different newsletters. If they can trace the IP address to her home or one of her devices…"

"I sure hope they can get something solid on her."

Terry and Vic both nodded their agreement.

"How would she have known he was coming here?" Vic asked. "No one knew when he was going to be here."

"But a few people knew he was coming to Bald Eagle Falls, even if they didn't know the date. I talked to more than one person about it. His tour route was leaked."

"Well, we've got the dessert," Terry reminded her. "I don't know what she put in there, but the lab will identify it."

"I hope so. And I hope it's something really awful," Vic said emphatically. Then she realized how it might sound. "Not so that it would kill you," she told Erin quickly. "I mean so that they can nail her for trying to poison you, not just a prank or a mistake."

Erin eyed her, laughing. "Uh-huh."

CHAPTER 46

$\mathcal{E}$rin was back at the bakery with Vic. It felt strange, as if she had been on an extended vacation instead of just taking a couple of days off to recover from her encounter with Olivia.

As Erin had expected, the police investigation had meant that she was not able to get into her house and get to bed until much later than she normally would have. And even when she was allowed back in the house, she was too wound up to think of going to bed. Every creak and groan of the old house made her jump, and her guts were tied up with anxiety. She hadn't eaten much for supper but, even when she got hungry, she couldn't look at food. The smell of the whipped dessert was still in her nostrils and, apparently, her primitive brain had decided she needed to be on the alert for any other murder attempt, and she wasn't able to settle down for a long time. Even watching a long and boring movie, cuddled up with Officer Piper on the couch, safe and protected, was not enough to convince her body that she was safe and could go to sleep.

It was her usual wake-up time before she was able to crawl into bed, and longer before she was able to get a few restless hours of sleep. Then, her body was awake again, wanting to know why she was off her schedule and when she was going to work. It was one of those days where time was all mixed up, dragging behind and jumping ahead, and she never had any idea what time it would be when she looked at her phone.

But the next day, she forced herself to follow her regular schedule, even though she was tired when she got up. She would get back on a normal sleep and work cycle if she made herself follow her usual schedule. Vic had decided that Willie was out of the woods and that she could leave him alone while she helped out at Auntie Clem's, provided he answered the phone whenever she called. Willie promised to do so to get her out of the house and regain some of his independence and personal space.

"That man just hates conventional structure and roles," Vic said, shaking her head, but there was a big smile on her face. She loved Willie and his ways and was glad to see him acting his old self again, smothered by too much attention. It told her he was healing and getting back to normal. "I swear if he had to work a nine-to-five job, he would explode into a ball of fire. Spontaneous combustion. He just couldn't do it."

"Well, it's a good thing he doesn't have to, then," Erin agreed. She was glad that Willie was feeling better. He had been in pretty bad shape the night they had taken him to the hospital. It was good to see him bouncing back and being feisty about what he would or wouldn't do. "I'm sure glad he's feeling better."

"Yeah, me too. The doctor in charge of his chelation says that, hopefully, this was just because of how quickly his heavy metal levels have been changing and is actually a good sign that his body is bouncing back and able to fight off what it sees as toxins or invaders. And hopefully… we'll see a big improvement in his health and mental state soon. She's adjusted some of his treatments and hopes it will ease the process." She shrugged. "I don't know. Most of it is over my head, so I don't know if I'm saying it right. But here's hoping he gets back to normal soon."

Erin showed her crossed fingers. "Hope so."

Vic went to the front door of the bakery to unlock it and let the morning crowd in. Everyone was concerned about Erin's absence and wanted to hear all about Olivia and what would happen to her.

Erin looked at Vic before launching into an explanation.

"She has been arrested for some charges of harassment of Montgomery and attempted murder of me. They don't know if the attempted murder will hold, but want to start with something high to bargain down from."

Teenage Joshua Cox had come to pick up baking for Mary Lou while she took care of Roger, but Erin knew he was really there as an investigative reporter to get the scoop on Olivia for a story he was writing for the Bald Eagle Falls weekly paper. He had his notepad out and was writing busily away even before digging deeper.

"Why hasn't she been charged with Montgomery's murder? If the stuff that she was doing led to his death, and that was what she had intended, why hasn't she been charged?"

Erin took a breath, inhaling the yeasty smell of freshly baked bread, a soothing balm to her anxious mind.

"Because they need to be able to prove it and, so far, they don't have enough. She admits she was harassing him, trying to drive him away from being a food critic. But she won't admit that she was trying to get him killed by influencing me to make the Morning Sunshine Muffins and changing his allergy card so that no one here would know that he was allergic to them. And I'm sure they'll argue in court that she never thought that her interference would lead to his death and was horrified by what happened."

"Do they know what was in the dessert? The one that you didn't eat?"

"They've done some preliminary testing, and I guess it was eyedrops. Tetra..." Erin tried to get the syllables straight in her mind. "Tetrahydrozoline."

Joshua's pencil paused. "Can you spell that?"

Erin laughed. "I can barely say it."

"Okay, just a second. Say it again, and I'll give it my best attempt. Then I can Google it later."

Erin repeated it for him but had difficulty doing so without mangling it. It never sounded the same when she said it out loud as it did in her head, and she was sure she probably got it wrong. But Joshua would sort it out.

"I've heard of it," Joshua said. "I thought you said that you smelled it. I thought tetra—that stuff—was odorless."

"I guess the scientists never met Erin or another super-smeller like her," Vic contributed. "She can smell a lot of things that I would have said were impossible."

"Maybe something else in the eye drops has a smell," Erin said. "A preservative or other chemical. But I could smell something weird."

"Good thing you did," Vic assured her.

"Does she admit to putting the eyedrops in your dessert?" Joshua asked.

"Initially, she said she would accuse me or the police of setting her up. But after talking to her lawyer, she switched to, 'I didn't know it was that bad. I just thought it would make her sick.'"

"Doesn't everyone know it's fatal?"

Erin shrugged as she assembled the items on Mary Lou's shopping list for him. "I guess it's believable that she might think it would just cause an upset stomach. If you look online, people use it for a prank sometimes. It isn't always fatal. It depends on the dose."

"Well, you can bet that Olivia Morgan didn't just intend to make you sick," Vic declared. "Why would she want to do that?"

"To get me off the case until she could disappear. But I don't think she ever intended to run away and change her name. She wanted me out of the picture permanently so I couldn't cause any trouble for her. Especially once she knew I had figured out the part about the emails. I didn't tell her I had already sent them to the police. I think she was hoping to keep me from pursuing it."

"I don't understand how she could make you make something with strawberries in it and keep you from finding out that he was allergic," Mrs. Peach said, leaning on her walker as she waited for Joshua to be served. He really should have let her go first, but Erin suspected he had been too eager to get his questions answered and had tunnel vision, not even noticing Mrs. Peach with her walker.

"She couldn't *make* me," Erin explained, "but she sent a bunch of emails to try to put the idea of using strawberries into my head. And there were people I talked to in cooking forums online about strawberries, too… they're trying to track down if any of them were Olivia. Or if *all* of them were Olivia."

"But how could she keep you from discovering he was allergic to strawberries?"

"Well, she couldn't be sure, not directly. But the big thing was swapping the wallet cards with his allergies listed. Then, he could have been served strawberries by anyone. But he wouldn't eat them if he could see them. He got so much in just one bite of my muffins because he didn't know they were there, and they were hidden in the middle of the muffin in a kind of sauce. So he didn't know until he got a pretty big dose that they were strawberries, and then because of all of the other factors, even grabbing the epinephrine auto-injector as soon as he could, he wasn't fast enough to stop the allergic reaction."

"It was such a severe reaction that it probably didn't matter how much epinephrine he got," Vic said with a sympathetic glance in Erin's direction. "I don't know all the technical terms, but the reaction was already activated and stopped his heart before the epinephrine could work."

Erin blinked and turned away for a moment. She put the rest of Mary Lou's order into a bag and handed the list to Vic to ring it up.

"I didn't like the guy, and I've heard a lot about the number of people he was horrible to, the careers he ruined… but it still bothers me that I had anything to do with it."

"Well, it's just like with Trenton Plaint's death," Mrs. Peach told him. "You can't help what other people decide to do with your muffins."

There was silence for a few minutes while everyone considered this. Joshua had to put away his pencil and pad to pay for the baking for his mother. He probably had other questions to ask, but he knew better than to hold up the line at Auntie Clem's.

"I'll call you," he told Erin, "If there is anything else I need to follow up on."

Erin nodded. "Okay. I'll talk to you later."

She watched him head for the door and walk out. The bells tinkled, marking his departure.

Mrs. Peach looked around as she pushed her walker forward.

"And where are all of those young people who were throwing around accusations after Montgomery's death?" she asked. "It seems like they've all disappeared into the woodwork now."

"I haven't seen anyone," Vic agreed, "it's been as quiet as a church."

"Maybe they're all over at the jail now," Erin contributed. "Shouting their slogans and waving their signs. I'm glad not to have them here. I'm looking forward to everything going back to normal again."

CHAPTER 47

*H*ow is the sale going?" Erin asked Charley after finishing speaking to the last school class.

Charley was manning their booth in the school gym. They were raising money for the food bank in the city.

"Money is still trickling in," Charley confirmed. "We've had a few good runs, but I think that most of the money is in now. It will be a good chunk for the food bank."

"Good," Erin approved. She looked at the time. "School will be out in another hour or so, and then we can knock this down and see how much we made."

Erin turned at the tugging on her sleeve. It was Peter Foster, her favorite customer.

"Hi, Peter. Here to buy a muffin?" Erin suggested.

"No, I already got one."

"Oh, good. What do you think of our little fundraiser and education day?"

"It's been really good!" Peter told her. "I like the talk that you gave. About your sister and how hard it is for people who are celiac or allergic to wheat or other grains."

"Well, I hope it helps people to understand why I do what I do," Erin told him, giving his shoulder a squeeze. "And why I think it is so important to make sure that you and anyone else who is gluten-intolerant or allergic have lots of choices. I think everyone needs to have access to good, tasty baking."

"I'm glad you opened Auntie Clem's here," Peter told her. "It is my favorite, favorite store."

His eyes shone and his cheeks were pink. Erin thought about pictures of the children she had seen in medical journals who had been afflicted with celiac disease in previous centuries. How they had starved to death. Just like she had watched Carolyn starve to death when her system had become so damaged that she wasn't able to absorb the nutrients she needed anymore. Peter looked so healthy and strong.

He was so bright and friendly and would be able to grow up instead of being doomed to fade away to nothing. There was no way she would ever give up her mission to provide him and others like him delicious baking in all of its forms, so that he could have fun and be like his peers and grow up to become a great man.

That was why Erin did what she did.

Did you enjoy this book? Reviews and recommendations are vital to making a book successful.

Please leave a review at your favorite book store or review site and share it with your friends.

Don't miss the following bonus material:
Sign up for mailing list to get a free ebook
Read a sneak preview chapter
Other books by P.D. Workman
Learn more about the author

DON'T MISS A THING! GET THE LATEST NEWS AND A FREE EBOOK

Your First Taste

PREVIEW OF CUSTARD
CREAM CONSPIRACY

PREVIEW CHAPTER 1

*I*t was a perfectly normal day until Erin was bowled right off her feet.

She had finished her shift at Auntie Clem's Bakery and was on her way over to The General Store to see Mary Lou about some more jam. The Jam Lady jams were always a good upsell to go with her handcrafted gluten-free breads, and she felt good about supporting a friend in the community as well. It was a win-win-win. Good for her and her business, good for Mary Lou and her family, and good for the customers, who went home with a yeasty, delicious loaf of bakery-fresh bread and a jewel-toned jar of blueberry jam.

Erin had been hoping that The Jam Lady, whose identity was known to only a very select group of people in Bald Eagle Falls, would be able to start making jam again. She had been excited to receive part of the first batch produced after the Jam Lady's lengthy convalescence.

Maybe Erin's head was in the clouds as she dreamed of a taste of the sweet blueberry preserve and wasn't watching where she was going. But Bald Eagle Falls was a sleepy little town, and she didn't usually have to worry about being run over. It wasn't the big city.

And it wasn't like she was walking on the road. She should have been safe from harm on the sidewalk.

And it wasn't a car. *They* all stayed on the street where they were supposed to, and when Erin was blasted from behind, she had no idea, to begin with, what had happened.

One minute, she was on her feet, and the next, she was slammed into the very solid wall of the building next to her. It felt like being hit by a truck. She was hit in the back, and then her face and head hit the wall, followed by the rest of her body.

She was too startled to even shout out in surprise; she just went down in a heap.

Someone else was there, swearing and tangled up with her, their legs flailing to separate and get a purchase on solid ground again. Erin's head hit a solid surface again, this time the back of her head on the pavement. Not really hard, but hard enough that it hurt.

A hoarse voice swore at her, or maybe the other party was just upset by the collision and was hurt himself. Or herself. Erin couldn't really determine the gender to assign to the low growl. She saw a flash of black cloth as the other person involved in the accident extricated himself, and then heard an electric whir.

Then she was by herself on the sidewalk. She was sweating, though it wasn't as hot as it had been lately. Her clothes were sticking to her in the warm Tennessee air. Her purse had been upset, items scattered across the pavement. Erin gathered the bits and pieces together in a daze, jamming them back into the cavernous safety of her shoulder bag. Her planner. Her sunglasses, a compact, feminine items, several pens, her keychain...

"Erin, are you okay?"

Mary Lou hurried up to Erin. Erin had never seen Mary Lou in a hurry or disarray before. Mary Lou was always perfectly groomed and manicured, every line of her shirt and pants lying exactly as it should without a wrinkle, her short blond-turned-gray hair coiffed and styled to perfection. She didn't rush or get upset, even when her personal and family life had been in shambles.

"I saw it all through the window," Mary Lou told Erin, reaching down to her and helping her to her feet. She peered into Erin's face worriedly. "Those contraptions should be banned! I can't believe they are allowed on our sidewalks."

Mary Lou handed Erin her planner, which she jammed into her shoulder bag.

"What contraptions?" Erin asked vaguely, looking around. Everything seemed slowed down and weirdly out of place. Like she was out of step with the rest of the world.

"Electric scooters. They are all over the city now. Part of the whole trend to make the city walkable. How is it walkable when you could be mown down by one of those things at any moment? Are you okay, Erin?"

"Yes, yes, fine," Erin murmured. She looked around herself. "Is that what it was? A scooter?"

"I don't know why anyone would go down the sidewalk that fast. Even if they are allowed, there should be some kind of regulation of the things! Speed limits. Yielding to pedestrians." Mary Lou shook her head. "It's all this tourist traffic. People just don't know how to behave in a small town. How to *slow down*."

Erin supposed that she was partly responsible for the increase in tourist traffic. Ever since Gerald Montgomery had died of an allergic reaction to one of Erin's muffins, his fans and followers had been traipsing to Bald Eagle Falls to try the breakfast muffin out for themselves. The steady stream of visitors had slowed, but there were still a lot of people in Bald Eagle Falls who Erin didn't know, and who didn't know the town or its unwritten rules.

"Sorry," she apologized to Mary Lou. She straightened her shirt and ran her fingers through her short, dark hair to smooth it back neatly into place. She probably looked like a mess. She looked at her wet fingers, sticky with blood.

"You're hurt," Mary Lou observed. "Here, sit back down." She helped Erin to sit on the curb, ignoring her protestations that she was fine. "Where's Vic? Where's Terry?"

Erin shook her head. She usually drove with Vic the few blocks from the bakery to the house she had inherited from Clementine, but Vic had only put in half a day and had gone into the city with Willie for a doctor's appointment.

Terry, her handsome cop boyfriend, was probably out walking a beat as usual, with K9, his German shepherd, at his side.

"I'm fine," Erin told Mary Lou. "I don't think it is anything. I'll just wash up when I get home."

"You hit your face too, I saw when he ran you down. Why would anyone be going so fast on the sidewalk?"

A police car gave a short whir of its siren and pulled up next to where Erin was sitting on the curb.

"Did you see what direction he went?" Stayner demanded, rolling down the passenger side window to talk to them.

"That way," Mary Lou motioned in the direction the scooter rider had taken off in, "I think he turned right onto First—"

Stayner pulled away again with a screech of tires. Erin stared after him, still feeling stunned from the collision. She had expected him to stop to help, to see how she was, sitting there bleeding on the curb. Erin supposed that as a cop, it was important for Stayner to see if he could catch the perpetrator, but it seemed like he should at least make sure Erin was okay first. Maybe he had assumed that since Mary Lou was there, she could take care of anything Erin needed and he didn't have to stop.

Mary Lou muttered something under her breath that Erin suspected was not too complimentary.

"He's not the best with people," Erin commented, putting her face in her hands and her elbows on her knees to steady herself. In that position, she felt stable and wouldn't just fall over at the slightest breeze.

"Officer Piper?"

From Mary Lou's tone of voice, Erin knew that she was calling Terry on the phone, not seeing him approach, so she didn't take her face out of her hands to look.

"Erin was knocked down. She's hurt. I think you should come and see to her."

"I'm not hurt," Erin mumbled. "Just a little bruised. You'll scare him."

"She's scraped up," Mary Lou amended. "It isn't an emergency.

Though with how hard that guy hit her, she should probably see a doctor. Make sure there isn't anything serious."

Erin couldn't hear Terry's reply, but by Mary Lou's quick goodbye and no further conversation, Erin assumed Terry had told her he was on his way.

He could drive Erin home, and then she could lie down until she felt less shaky.

PREVIEW CHAPTER 2

"What exactly happened?" Terry demanded as he walked up to Erin. "Erin, are you okay?"

"I'm fine," Erin mumbled through her hands. She knew that she should pull her hands down and let him look at her face, but she felt comfortable in the position she was in and didn't want to move.

"There was a scooter," Mary Lou explained. "One of those electric ones. And the... what do you call someone who rides a scooter...?"

"I don't know," Terry's tone was clipped. "A scooterist?"

"Scooterist?" Mary Lou repeated dubiously. "Okay, the scooterist was going down the sidewalk way too fast. If he's going to go that fast, then he should be on the street, not on the sidewalk. And he ran Erin down. Just came out of nowhere and crashed into her. Knocked her into the wall, and fell and got tangled up with her, and then he took off without even helping her out. I don't think he even said anything to her, did he, Erin? Did he even say he was sorry?"

"He was swearing."

"Oh, lovely," Mary Lou cleared her throat. "This is the generation we are raising now. Kids who swear at someone they knock down instead of apologizing. Zipping around here on those contraptions. It's dangerous!"

"Male?" Terry questioned. "Teenager?"

"I don't know," Mary Lou said. "I assumed so when I saw him, but I didn't get a good look. Officer Stayner went after him; maybe he'll have better luck. I just thought… well, it wouldn't be a woman, would it? Or an older person?"

"Lots of people ride electric scooters," Terry said with a shrug. "Helps people get from one place to another more easily. Especially those who aren't up to walking long distances."

"Hmm."

Erin could feel Terry sit down on the curb next to her. He rested his hand on her back to begin with. A light touch. Warm. Reassuring.

"Erin. Can you let me look at you? See if you're hurt?"

"I'm okay," she assured him. "Just bumps and bruises."

"Let's see. I've got a first aid kit in the car. I can clean you up, get you bandaged up and on your way."

"I'll just go home," Erin told him, finding it more difficult than she expected to pull her face away from her hands and let him look at her. "Have a hot shower and lie down for a while."

"Yeah," he agreed. "That sounds good. Once I've had a chance to look at you. I'm sure you're right and it isn't anything to worry about."

He gently pulled her shoulder back, coaxing her hands away from her face. Erin blinked in the bright light. The sun was getting lower in the sky, but it was still too hot and too bright for Erin's eyes and the headache starting to form behind them. She blinked back tears and rubbed at the corners of her eyes.

"Just hold still a second," Terry advised, holding her chin gently with one big hand. His handsome face took on a look of concern. K9 whined, his head almost at a level with Erin's.

"I'm fine," Erin told K9. "Just a little bump."

Terry prodded the sore spot on the front right corner of Erin's head. "That's not such a little bump. It's swelling up pretty good, and you might need a couple of stitches across there. Where did he hit you? How did you fall?"

"He hit me… in the back and side. Knocked me into the wall. I hit there, and then fell down, and he fell down, and I hit my head—"

"You hit it a second time?"

"In the back," Erin explained. She felt for the sore spot in the back of her head. There wasn't as much of a goose egg there. Not as serious. It was bleeding, but scalp wounds always did.

Terry poked around some more, moving her hair around to get a good look at her scalp. He leaned back away from her again. "I think I should take you to the hospital."

There was no hospital in Bald Eagle Falls, so that meant a trip to the city. Erin didn't feel like going all that way for nothing. She'd had a collision on the sidewalk. It wasn't the end of the world. People had minor accidents all the time. She would go home with a few cuts and bruises and be back at work like she was supposed to be tomorrow.

"Terry… it's nothing."

"You can't see it. I think it is severe enough to warrant looking at it."

"It's just a bruise."

"Exactly how hard did you hit the pavement?"

"I was just walking. So I wasn't moving fast. And I hit the building first, so that absorbed most of the shock. I just hit my head when I landed because it happened so fast and I wasn't braced for it." She cleared her throat. "It wasn't that hard," she asserted. "I didn't lose consciousness. Mary Lou was right here. She can tell you that. I've been coherent."

Terry looked at Mary Lou, who agreed. There was a murmur of voices closing in around them. Erin had a knot in her stomach as she realized people were gathering to watch her, whispering to each other, speculating as to what had happened and how badly hurt she was. She raised her hand as if shielding her eyes from them would prevent them from seeing her.

"Any dizziness?" Terry drilled.

"No. Maybe just a little."

"Double vision?"

"No."

"Nausea?"

"No."

Not really. She wasn't feeling great, but that was because of all the attention, not because of the head injury.

"Tiredness?"

Erin laughed weakly. "Well, yes. I'm tired. I've been up since the wee hours of the morning working. What do you expect? I'm tired and I don't want to have to drive to the city and then sit around in the hospital for hours until a doctor has a chance to look at me, wave his finger around in front of my face, and then tell you that I'm perfectly normal and should go home to bed."

"It would make me feel a lot better."

"Well, not me. I want to go home and have a shower and a bite to eat and then veg in front of the TV until bedtime. How about I do that instead?"

"Someone should be watching you."

"Then why don't you come over and watch me?"

Terry gave her a slow grin, the dimple appearing in one cheek smudged with five o'clock shadow.

"I'm not supposed to be off for a couple more hours."

"And if you had to take me to the hospital in the city, wouldn't you call Sheriff Wilmott and tell him that you needed the time off? And wouldn't Stayner or one of the others cover for you?"

"Of course," he admitted.

"Then tell them that you need to take time off to watch me and make sure that I didn't suffer any ill effects from the accident. It isn't like they won't know what you're talking about. You're not skipping out of work. I *was* in an accident."

Terry had a strong sense of duty that Erin had to work against. He put in more than his share of time with the Bald Eagle Falls police department, and taking a couple of hours off early one evening was not a problem. No one would object.

"You really should take the time off and keep an eye on her," Mary Lou advised, her expression serious.

"Yes," Terry agreed, drawing the word out, still unsure whether he would tell the sheriff he needed to take the rest of the day off.

"Brain injury is nothing to fool with," Mary Lou told them.

And Mary Lou was someone who knew that better than most. She spoke with authority.

"Okay," Terry agreed finally. "I'll let the sheriff know that I'm clocking out early. I'm still around if there is an emergency and they send out a call."

Erin relaxed. It would be nice for both of them to be home for the evening. With nothing to do but cuddle in front of the TV and enjoy each other's company.

~

Muffin to Hide, Book #23 of the *Auntie Clem's Bakery cozy mystery* series by P.D. Workman
can be purchased at pdworkman.com

~

ABOUT THE AUTHOR

P.D. Workman is a USA Today Bestselling author, winner of several awards from Library Services for Youth in Custody and the InD'tale Magazine's Crowned Heart award, and has published over 100 mystery/suspense/thriller and young adult books, including stand alones and these series: Auntie Clem's Bakery cozy mysteries, Reg Rawlins Psychic Investigator paranormal mysteries, Zachary Goldman Mysteries (PI), Kenzie Kirsch Medical Thrillers, Parks Pat Mysteries (police procedural), and YA series: Tamara's Teardrops, Between the Cracks, and Breaking the Pattern.

Workman loves writing about the underdog, who the reader may love or hate. She has been praised for her realistic details, deep characterization, and sensitive handling of the serious social issues that appear in all of her stories, from light cozy mysteries through to darker, grittier young adult and mystery/suspense books.

> P. D. Workman, does not shy from probing the deep psychological scars of childhood trauma, mental illness, and addiction. Also characteristic of this author, these extremely sensitive issues are explored with extensive empathy, described with incredible clarity, and portrayed with profound insight.
>
> — —KIM, GOODREADS REVIEWER

Some of Workman's titles have been translated into Spanish, French, Portuguese, German, and Italian.

Workman began writing at an early age and is a prolific reader as well as writer. She is also passionate about teaching and learning, expresses her creativity through art and cooking, and loves exploring the Calgary parks and green spaces where the Parks Pat Mysteries are set. She was a legal assistant for many years and has done extensive charitable work.

Workman was born and raised in Alberta, Canada, and is married with one adult son.

Please visit P.D. Workman at pdworkman.com to see what else she is working on, to join her mailing list, and to link to her social networks.

If you enjoyed this book, please take the time to recommend it to other purchasers with a review or star rating and share it with your friends!

tiktok.com/@pdworkmanauthor

facebook.com/pdworkmanauthor

x.com/pdworkmanauthor

instagram.com/pdworkmanauthor

amazon.com/author/pdworkman

bookbub.com/authors/p-d-workman

goodreads.com/pdworkman

linkedin.com/in/pdworkman

pinterest.com/pdworkmanauthor

youtube.com/pdworkman

patreon.com/pdworkmanauthor

reamstories.com/pdworkmanauthor